The Way It Seems

Selected Short Stories
Knud Sørensen

translated from Danish by
Michael Goldman

SPUYTEN DUYVIL

NEW YORK CITY

Acknowledgements

Many thanks to the following journals in which these translations
first appeared.

Apple Valley Review: "Just one load of gravel"
Columbia Journal: "A dress for Astrid's confirmation"
Harvard Review: "Evening Milking"
The Missing Slate: "The Congratulant"

Sincere appreciation to The Danish Arts Foundation for their
financial support towards the translation and publication of
this book. Sincere appreciation as well to Knud Sørensen for his
cooperation in the translation and publication of this book.

THE DANISH ARTS FOUNDATION

Library of Congress Cataloging-in-Publication Data

Names: Sørensen, Knud, 1928- author. | Goldman, Michael (Michael Favala) translator.
Title: The way it seems : selected short stories / Knud Sørensen ; translated
  from Danish by Michael Goldman.
Description: New York City : Spuyten Duyvil, 2018.
Identifiers: LCCN 2017057770| ISBN 9781947980280 (pbk.) | ISBN 9781947980297
  (hardcover)
Classification: LCC PT8176.29.O239 A2 2018 | DDC 839.813/74--dc23
LC record available at https://lccn.loc.gov/2017057770

About Sørensen's writing

"Knud Sørensen's formidable literary output bears a vulnerability, an embracing, gentle warmth, and a penetrating apprehension of emotional depth in commonplace events. May his work take flight and find readers around the globe."
Dorthe Nors, Danish author of Karate Chop

"...relates sensation and realization to the reader, regardless of age, on the words' and language's own terms."
Gerda Buhl Andersen, Morsø Folkeblad

"No one has, for so many years and in so varied and detailed ways, written about rural life and the radical changes it has undergone, as Knud Sørensen."
Erik Svendsen, Jyllands-Posten

"Knud Sørensen has acquired a unique, compassionate and deep insight into the mentality and the psychological shifts among farmers and rural people as a result of the total change in their circumstances over the past 60 - 70 years."
Johannes H. Christensen, Jyllands-Posten

"...builds on dialogue, but a special Knud Sørensen-ish dialogue, where what people say points to what they don't say, and therefore that is told too, and all the more so."
Jens Smærup Sørensen, Awards speech at Knud Sørensen's receiving the Grand Prize of the Danish Academy, Nov. 2014

"... through a half century in poetry and prose Knud Sørensen has created a great and original body of work about life in Denmark ... his matter-of-fact descriptions of daily life point to both the period's economic-political ups and downs and the larger and fertile connection to nature and thereby the basis for existence."
Lars Ole Knippel, Jyllands-Posten

The Way It Seems

CONTENTS

Just north of the church is a road going east. It's a good, broad paved road, but it hasn't always been that way. Until a few decades ago it was a narrow, winding dirt road that went by the charter school and two or three low cottages, where some working people lived. If you kept going down that road, you came to the property of Morten Andersen.

The school isn't there any more. First it closed, then the building was torn down to make way for a new road to the county development behind it. But the school was memorialized by naming the road "Charter School Road." Today the old workers' houses are owned by people outside the parish. You wouldn't recognize them—the houses. Two of them are distinguished by their owners' enthusiasm for passive solar, and the third one just about disappeared entirely during a so-called renovation, which more or less evolved into a new construction. It's especially noticeable by the height of the roof, but no sensible person would complain about it, even though the style is a bit foreign to the area and the swimming pool a bit ostentatious. It was in that vanished, nostalgic house that at least three generations acquired their tuberculoses.

Farther out lies the property that was Morten Andersen's. There you see large new buildings, and most prominently, a silo, whose company name can be seen for hundreds of yards. For years it has stood there, circumventing the conservation laws prohibiting signage in open land. It's not Morten Andersen's property any more, but Kristian Iversen's. His name is pretty meaningless; he doesn't even belong in this story, which plays out back then, at the end of the thirties.

Morten Andersen is still alive, and he's not too hard to recognize when he's in town. He rides his wife's old bicycle, which he adopted, back when arthritis made it difficult for him to mount a bicycle in the traditional male fashion. If it's a weekday when you're in town, there's a good chance you might see him. He likes to run errands, mostly to pass the time, now that there's not so much activity at home. After he sold the property, he bought a little 900 sq. ft. house—a love shack, as his as his new neighbor Marius Beck calls it, whenever he gets the opportunity. It sits way back in the development. There's a yard, where everything is under control. Morten has never had it as good as he does now; at least that's what people say.

But as I was saying—back in the thirties.

When Morten first bought the property, it was the end of the twenties, and it was no more than a sagging house out on the outskirts, with seven or eight acres. A little farther out than what people called "Siberia." No one could live off of such a small—and lousy—piece of land, so Morten had his milk route, and he went and helped with the field beets, when it was that time of year, and with threshing, when it was that time of year. Besides three cows, a couple of pigs, and the two Russian horses, he had bees which gave honey, and chickens, which gave eggs and poultry. All told, it brought in a bit of money, and people said that in his savings book he was accumulating more than just the bare minimum.

I wrote earlier that the story I am about to tell played out at the end of the thirties. It does, but there's also an episode in the middle of the thirties that ought to be like a kind of prelude.

They were hard years. Unrest, unemployment, foreclosure auctions—it was impossible to predict who would get hit. Often, people felt it was completely unfair. Interest was way up around five.

One of them who got into difficulties was Marius Beck, despite his youth. People said the father, one of the region's most prominent men, had retired much too early. He was one of the two only real proprietors there for miles around. The auction block threatened, but Marius was saved by an arrangement.

It was a hardship for the grocer and the feed supplier, and it got relatively even more so for the carpenter, the mason and the blacksmith. They didn't get paid for much of the new barn they had built for Marius. People talked about it quite a bit, but in all fairness it must be said that the mason, the carpenter and the blacksmith probably would have lost even more if the lawyer hadn't been so lucky in his negotiations leading up to that agreement.

It would be wrong to say that Morten Andersen wasn't affected by the crisis. But he had what he needed to take care of his own, and people even said that his savings book kept growing.

Then came the day when Morten was in the grocery to pay his quarterly bill. It had been a good quarter—the hens were laying well—almost every other day he transported a basketful of eggs to the grocery. So it was one of those quarters when it was Morten, and not the grocer, who was getting paid. They lived sparingly, Morten and his wife—almost no coffee in the chicory, rarely butter in the house. It was only with respect to sugar that the wife couldn't resist.

The grocer wasn't too happy about paying out money. He counted it up and slid it across the counter to Morten, but he didn't give him a paper cone of candies, and a cigar, like he always did when it was the customers that had to shell out money. Morten stood there a second, waiting. The grocer didn't react. So Morten tossed a nickel on the counter and asked for a cigar. They agreed on one of the good three-penny ones. Morten asked for a light.

Then he went outside leaving the grocer stewing in his own juices. Morten stood there on the step feeling satisfied. The sun was about to break through after a couple of days of rain; the air was light, and the cigar smoke had about the same hue as the sky.

Then up walked Marius Beck. Even though the more mature

people in the parish still considered him an overgrown lad, he had followed in his father's footsteps as chairman of the cooperative and he probably had to go inside to talk with the grocer. Marius looked at Morten and, with more than a little virtuous indignation in his voice, said, "Look who's standing here smoking a cigar."

Morten took a deep drag. Then he exhaled. He nodded. "And I bought it myself," he said. "Cash."

He couldn't quite keep a serious face as he stepped down from the stone step and passed Marius with a slight nod in parting.

That was back then in the depression year 1936.

The actual story is from '39. That was the year Morten Andersen bought Lars Pedersen's widow's property out there at the end of Charter School Road. It was a run-down property, probably was really in need of a hard-working man like Morten, but it had just enough size that you could defend calling it a farm.

Rumor has it that Morten started calling himself a farmer. Where the rumor started isn't certain, but it could easily have been the operator. Olina had probably seen some papers when Morten got a telephone.

He gave up his milk route, which was taken over by a hemmed-in small landholder who really needed it. Morten set about putting the property in order. For quite a while we barely saw him.

Then one evening in October there was a lecture in the meeting house. It was a lecture with slides—a travelogue—so the turnout wasn't too bad. By the time it was set to begin, the room was almost full.

Now we've never really had anything like station or class differences here. That kind of thing was only in bigger cities. But still there was a bit of order to things, and people who felt like they belonged together, sought each other out.

So it had become kind of a tradition, that at the three or four tables at the front, by the piano, the "big boys" sat, as some people called them. They were the proprietors—if they both were there—and the farm families. At the table behind them sat mostly head farmhands, farmhands, and farm maids; and farthest back, just inside the door, sat the ones who some of the others a bit good-naturedly called "the rabble." They were the area's small landholders and working people, enjoying one another's company.

That evening, as I mentioned, it was pretty full by eight o'clock. One of them who arrived a bit late was Morten Andersen—his wife wasn't there, but she rarely was—and Morten started to walk up the middle aisle. He walked past his usual table, past the maids and hands and foremen and situated himself at one of the front tables. And not only that, at the one where the biggest boys usually sat.

It aroused attention, but naturally no one said anything. As I said, there has never really been anything like station or class differences here in town.

After the lecture there was coffee, and lots of lively conversation in the room. Morten Andersen directed a few words towards the people sitting closest to him as well, and one of them asked him how things were going with the farm.

Then came the moment when Marius Beck started offering cigars to everyone. He took one first, then he offered one to Lars Kristensen, then to Børge Riis, who was sitting next to Morten. Marius hesitated a second, which no one in the room failed to notice. Then he offered the box to Søren Olesen, who was sitting on the other side of Morten. Søren happily took a cigar and bit off the tip. And Marius gave him a light.

Morten started fishing out his pipe and tobacco. He sat for a long while, tamping it, while eighty-six pairs of eyes carefully looked the other way. Eventually, with difficulty, he found an unused match in his box. It broke when he struck it. He took out another and that one took.

A thick smoke settled around him.

At the next oppressive quiet that spread in the room, the schoolteacher suggested everyone sing a song, and the crowd was quite eager. In fact there were so many suggestions that they had to sing two. Afterwards the lecturer answered questions.

Morten Andersen remained seated. He didn't ask any questions—usually it was only the teacher and the priest who asked any—but he sat there, just as interested in what was being said as all the rest.

When the evening was over, Morten nodded briefly to his table companions and hurried off. He had a short night and a long workday ahead of him, and no farmhand to set to the grunt work, as Marius Beck called it, when he stood chatting in a little group afterwards—they and him, who were nearly his equals in property value.

"But he does have a very capable wife," said one of them. Everyone nodded in agreement. She was all right; there was nothing snobbish about her.

People split up. Back then there wasn't any streetlight here, so people on foot were quickly swallowed up by the dark. The bicycle riders weren't visible very long either. But the few people, like Marius Beck, who had cars, them you could follow far out into the night.

But Morten Andersen had been home for quite a while already. By the time Marius Beck, after three of four tries, had gotten the Chrysler going, Morten was already lying on his side of the double bed. He had been very careful not to wake Margrethe. There was no reason to give her a report just then.

And in the morning there would surely be other things to talk about.

The Cow

"You'll never learn how to sow seeds," said his grandfather.

Martin smiled, and took yet another handful of sand. He tossed it diagonally in front, and most of it landed over in the manure trench.

His grandfather shook his head. "Now, pay attention," he said. He took a handful of sand, spreading it between his fingers while, almost without moving his arm, he strewed it in a fan design across the barn aisle. "Like that," he said. "That's how you do it."

The sand dampened the sound of their clogs. It was almost like walking on carpet.

Martin tried again. "No," said his grandfather, "not in clumps. Now watch."

They finished up. His grandfather took the sand pail with him to the section of barn with the horse stalls, and Martin walked backwards down the barn aisle, trying to walk in exactly the same footprints as before.

"I wish my grandpa was an Indian," he thought. "Then he wouldn't be able to find me." Martin took a very wide jump sideways over the manure trench and into one of the empty stalls. He ducked down.

The sow was sleeping in her pen on the other side of the aisle. In the stall next to Martin was the big black cow. It's stomach was constantly working.

"Grandpa," yelled Martin, "Why isn't the black cow out with the others?"

"It's best it stays inside."

"Why?"

"It's best."

A couple of flies were stuck to the fly paper, but not dead yet. They buzzed, almost like bees.

His grandfather walked back in and stopped. Rather surprised, he said, "Where is that boy gone now? He's never where he's supposed to be." Martin grinned and pressed himself tightly against the partition between the stalls.

His grandfather started walking through the barn, looking to the right and to the left, still wondering where the boy had gotten to. Martin was still grinning.

His grandfather stopped briefly at the end of the stall where Martin was hiding, but luckily he looked the opposite way—down at the pig. "No," he said. "He's not here either."

He kept walking.

"Look at the tracks," whispered Martin. "Look at the tracks."

But his grandfather didn't hear him. He said, "I'm going in to have my coffee. I'll find that kid later."

At that moment the dog outside started to bark. Someone said, "Okay, okay," and you could hear a bicycle being placed against the gable. Then there were footsteps in the gravel.

Martin peeked out from his stall, and his grandfather took the broom, which he had just put aside, and started banging the end of the shaft down against the floor, as if the broom head weren't on tight enough.

A man appeared in the doorway. "Hello," he said. He opened the bottom part of the door and stepped inside the barn.

"Hello," said his grandfather.

The man had on dark clothes and a white shirt with no collar. He wiped his forehead with a handkerchief and said, "It's going to be hot today."

"Good for the hay," answered his grandfather.

The man wasn't wearing clogs; he had on black boots, like the ones his grandfather used when he went to church.

The man bent down to take off his bicycle pant clips and his eyes met Martin's. "This must be your head farmhand," he said.

His grandfather smiled. "That's Martin." Martin took a step back and grabbed the broom, which his grandfather had put aside again, and started vigorously sweeping the otherwise newly-swept manure trench.

"Alright, alright," said his grandfather, "take it easy."

The stranger walked forward into the stall next to the black cow. "Is this her?" he said. His grandfather nodded.

The stranger let his hand glide over the cow. He patted her a little.

"She's not all that young," he said.

His grandfather didn't say anything. The man felt underneath the cow.

"Yes, yes," he said.

"We're about to go in and have coffee," said his grandfather.

"Much obliged."

They walked across the farmyard and in the scullery door. Martin and his grandfather placed their clogs on the sack just inside the door and put on their slippers.

They all went into the kitchen.

"Make yourself at home," said his grandfather to the stranger.

"Thanks," said the man. He shook the grandmother's hand and sat down at the table. Martin stayed standing and watched.

The stranger looked around. "It's been some time since we've done business together," he said.

The grandfather nodded and said, "A couple of decades or so."

"You're doing a nice job here," said the stranger. "This is no easy property, this one."

"It's good enough," said the grandmother. She put cups and saucers on the table, margarine and cheese, sugar and cream. "There's nothing wrong with the property. It's the times."

The stranger said, "Right. The times. We've got to do something about these times."

His grandmother poured coffee. Martin slid into his place at the bench next to his grandfather. "Oh, my goodness," said his grandmother. "I forgot to get one for you, Martin." And she took a cup and went out into the pantry and came back and handed Martin the cup. She said he could go out himself and fill it with water. And Martin walked out to the pump just outside the scullery door and pumped very carefully, because he knew that if the stream came out too strong it would wash away the rhubarb juice in the bottom of the cup. He was successful this time, and he returned to the table, carefully balancing the full cup.

His grandmother had spread butter and sugar on a piece of bread for him.

The stranger said, "The head farmhand is hungry too." And Martin took a couple big bites of his bread. Then he drained his glass, almost in one gulp.

"My goodness!" said his grandmother. The stranger laughed. "He'll amount to something someday. He's got some appetite."

Then they talked about the neighbor. And wages. And the times. And about Stauning. And the times, again. And the stranger mentioned, albeit hesitatingly, someone named Knud Bach, and the grandfather's mouth tightened to a thin line. The stranger quickly asked, "What do you want for her?" and the grandfather looked at the grandmother and said, "Twenty-two."

The stranger shook his head and said, "If you had said twenty I would have said yes."

"That's a good cow," said the grandmother.

"There's no shortage of good cows," said the stranger. "Only of money."

He said thanks for the coffee and he and the grandfather stood up. "We'd better go look at her again."

They went out through the scullery, and Martin was going to join them.

His grandmother caught him. "You stay here with me," she said. "We're going to the store."

So they left, with two baskets full of eggs, which the

grandmother carried, while Martin was a knight, galloping back and forth on the road. Sometimes he hid himself behind telephone poles, and his grandmother could never find him.

"It's so easy to fool you," he grinned.

"You're a rascal," said the grandmother, switching the two baskets, even though they seemed to be about the same weight.

Martin's horse was getting tired too. He slowed to a trot.

When they came home from the store, his grandfather and the stranger were still in the barn.

"You have to admit," said the stranger, "that twenty-one is too much for that cow."

"Not any more so than twenty isn't enough," said the grandfather.

They smiled at one another. Martin stood there looking at them. First at the one and then the other.

Then Martin said, "You know, that cow is really mine."

The stranger looked at him, surprised. His grandfather chuckled. "We have always said that one of the cows and one of the lambs is his," said his grandfather. "And for now, she's the one." He gave the black cow a pat. "Just wait," he said to Martin, "and you can choose whatever one you want from any of the others, plus you get fifty *øre*."

The stranger shook his head. "It's always the middlemen who steal the profits."

Martin started jumping, with his legs together, back and forth over the manure trench. If you stepped in it twice you were dead.

His grandfather grabbed him by the arm. "Stop that," he said. "We don't want all that jumping around in here."

The stranger laughed.

"I'm leaving, anyway," said Martin, walking out. The white-washed buildings blinded him. "Grandpa," he yelled, "aren't we bringing in hay today?"

Underneath the willow, Martin sat down on the wheelbarrow that was standing in the shade.

"It's not called a wheelbarrow," he thought. "It's called a wheelborrow." He said it out loud: "wheelborrow." It sounded strange. He couldn't say it in a high voice. He made his voice as deep as he could: "wheelborrow." It made him cough.

Finally it was noon.

There wasn't much conversation over lunch. They had pancakes with rhubarb compote, and afterwards the stranger said he wouldn't mind sneaking over to the barn and getting a little shut-eye while the others went in to take their afternoon naps. The grandmother said they would call him when it was time for coffee, and the stranger walked out to the barn. His grandparents were also going to rest, but first Martin had to go out with his grandfather to move the six cows, who had been neglected because of the all the bartering. Martin and his grandfather walked across the field, and some of the way, Martin got to carry the mallet.

"Yeah," said the grandfather when they were finished. "this field really is best suited for seven."

Then they walked back, and Martin thought about the cow with the crooked horns. He said, "I think I'll trade the black one for the crooked-horned one." His grandfather clapped him on the head and said that the crooked-horned one was a good cow too, but he wondered if maybe Martin would rather have the Holstein, since she was a calf of the black one. But Martin didn't change his mind. The crooked-horned one and fifty *øre*.

His grandfather and grandmother went in for their afternoon naps, and Martin was told to keep quiet. Which he usually did.

And then there it was again. The horribly quiet noontime, when only the flies were moving. Martin walked out to the barn and the black cow, and then he tried to get the dog to go with him for a walk out towards the hills, but the dog just wagged its rear a little and went back to sleep.

Martin snuck over to the hay barn door and carefully opened it a little. He looked inside. Over on a pile of hay the stranger was lying on his back. He had taken off his jacket and unbuttoned his vest. His boots were off too, and Martin could see there were holes in his socks. Probably no one was supposed to see that. Martin felt embarrassed, and quickly he shut the door.

Then Martin walked over to the garden to look at the red currants. They were just about ripe, and there were so many that no one could tell if he picked a few.

It was different with the black currants. But they were black and he wasn't supposed to eat them.

Martin stayed in the red ones.

When he came inside, his grandparents were up, and his grandmother was putting out things for coffee. "Would you hop over to the barn and tell him coffee is ready?" she said.

"Can't we just yell?" asked Martin.

"No," said his grandmother. "You walk over politely and wake him up and ask if he would please come over for coffee."

"If you say so." Martin walked out slowly, across the farmyard, singing loud and shrilly, "It's time for coffee, I say, it's time for coffee," and he fumbled much more than usual with the barn door latch before opening it, and the man was sitting there—luckily—with his boots on and his vest buttoned. Martin smiled to him and said that he should please come over and join them for coffee. The man smiled back, thanked Martin very much for the invitation, and they walked together across the farmyard, in through the scullery and into the kitchen where his grandmother was pouring coffee. The afternoon could now begin.

Afterwards, the bartering continued in the barn. "Twenty-one," said his grandfather. "Twenty," said the stranger, and there was a kind of pleasure about the whole thing, like when you suck very slowly on a cube of sugar to get it to last as long as possible. And they kept talking about unrelated things, about "back then" and about "the expert hunter," about Martin's parents, and sometimes they had to move back a bit from the cow, so it wouldn't splash on them, but then later they would move closer again, and his grandfather would give the cow a couple of pats and say "Twenty-one."

"Twenty," said the stranger, and they smiled at one another.

Then the stranger said, "That's not that much for such a good cow, but it's just the times. And it's not going to get any better until we get it under control." And his grandfather shook his head and said, "I know. Where's it gonna end?"

The stranger said, "That's up to us."

"We can't do anything about it," said his grandfather. The stranger was silent. He looked at the grandfather, attempted a smile and remained silent.

The sow woke up, grunted, turned over and fell noisily back to sleep.

Then the stranger said, "We can if we stand together. Like the workers did. If we do like Knud Bach says."

The grandfather shook his head and the stranger quickly added, " If we say no to auctions; if we don't let the sheriff come in. If we stop sending milk to the cities and stop putting English pounds in the national bank, then they'll sing a different tune."

His grandfather shook his head. "I don't think so. Then things would really get bad."

"That's just it," said the stranger. That's what's wrong with most of you. You don't have the guts to do what needs to be done. We're the ones," he said, almost like a preacher, "who have the keys to the cupboard and the cashbox."

His grandfather stood there controlling himself. Then he said, "If we don't sell milk to the cities, and if we don't bring in the English pounds, how are we going to eat?"

"Don't you get it?" said the stranger earnestly. "If we stand together in the Farmers Cooperative it'll be over fast. Everything will get better in no time. We just have to stand together, like the workers. They know how this works."

"There's a lot of people unemployed," said his grandfather.

"They understand," said the stranger. "And the king will understand too, if we stand together. The king has always been a friend to the farmers."

His grandfather didn't respond. Martin imagined the king, relaxing in their sitting room. He thought *The king is grandfather's friend.*

The stranger said, "New times are coming. The greatest experience I ever had was the farmer's march to the castle last year. All evening and all night extra trains rolled into Copenhagen, filled with farmers. Others came on bicycles or on foot, and Copenhageners went out into the streets and invited us in. I was invited in to a workingman's family, and we understood one another, I tell you; we understood one another. Workers and farmers understood one another. It might be hard to believe, but that's how it was."

His grandfather pulled back a little. He took out his watch, looked at it and slipped it back into his vest pocket.

The stranger continued, "And the next day—50,000 farmers in the castle courtyard. And we sang and sang, and there was this solidarity and it was just beautiful—all of it."

His grandfather cleared his throat. He looked out the window. Then he cleared his throat again.

"That's what we have to do," said the stranger. "We have to realize that we're the ones that have the power. We just have to take it." He laughed. "We'll win you over some day."

"It's getting late," said the grandfather.

"Right, right," the stranger said quickly. "We'd better finish up. Let's say twenty-fifty then." He lifted his hand slightly.

"Twenty-one," said his grandfather.

The stranger stopped short, surprised. "But I thought," he said, "that we were in agreement about twenty-fifty."

Martin could feel a strange tension in the barn, and he didn't like it. He took his grandfather's hand. "Grandpa," he said, "I don't need the fifty *øre*."

His grandfather waved him away, irritatedly. "Hush, boy."

Martin could feel himself blushing, but he tried to pretend like nothing happened. He walked through the barn and outside. It was still oppressively hot.

Martin walked over to the kitchen. "Could I please have a glass of juice?" he said.

Martin and his grandmother were sitting at the kitchen table when they saw the stranger come out of the barn. He took off his jacket and tied it around his handlebars. Then he put on his pant clips, pulled the bicycle over to the driveway, and rode off.

After a bit his grandfather came walking out. He stood there watching the stranger go. Then he came inside the house.

"Well?" asked the grandmother.

"He didn't buy it," said the grandfather. "I didn't want to sell it to him."

"What was the problem?"

"Nothing. I just didn't want to."

The grandmother looked confused. "He didn't offer enough?"

"It wasn't that," said the grandfather. "He would have paid fair enough. Now the butcher can have her. We'll get by."

The grandfather took out his purse and gave Martin a fifty *øre* coin. "That's for you," he said.

Then the grandfather walked back out, put on his clogs, and headed out to the pasture to bring in the six cows.

Martin ran out after him. "Grandpa," he said, "is the crooked-horned one mine now?"

"That's right," said his grandfather. "A deal is a deal."

Evening Milking

After they had sopped up the last of the gravy with a clump of bread, and as his mother was just starting to clear the table, Kristian said, "Mr. Ibsen said to say hello and that he was going to come over this afternoon to talk with you."

Kristian's mother stopped in the middle of her movement over the table with the father's plate in her hand. "Ibsen, the new teacher, what does he want?" She looked uneasily at Kristian. "Are you behaving?"

Kristian's father sat there looking a little withdrawn. "It's probably not that," he said.

The mother continued, "Didn't he say what he wanted?"

"No," said Kristian, "He just said that I should say he was going to try and stop by after he let out the little kids."

His mother still was looking at him dubiously. "Did you do something?" she asked again.

"Not that I know of," he said.

The father grumbled. "It's probably not that," he said again. And to Kristian he said,"You had better keep going in the sugar beets."

Kristian excused himself and disappeared. His mother was still standing at the table with his father's plate in her hand. "I wonder what it could be?" she repeated. The father said nothing. He got up and went in for his nap.

The mother cleared the table and wiped the tabletop. Now she was busy. She checked the pantry to see how much bread was left.

She washed the dishes. No nap for her. She had to dust the living room, and clean up all over.

It was almost three-thirty when Kristian saw his teacher come walking down the county road. He himself was working in the opposite end of the field, but his father was almost out by the road. Kristian could see how his father also saw the teacher coming and adjusted his speed so he would make it to the end of the row, by the roadside ditch, when the teacher arrived. Kristian could feel how his own movements got clumsier. He figured it must be a kind of nervousness. The teacher had said: "I'm going to have to talk to your parents." He didn't look up when his father and teacher greeted one another, but he kept working, as if he didn't even notice. He reached the end of the row by the hillock, and when he moved to the next row, he looked out at the road. His father and his teacher were standing there talking.

After a little while he noticed they were gone They were on their way across the pasture towards the house, which, from where Kristian stood, looked almost like it had blended together with the willow trees that were planted as a windbreak to the west. It was a rather long, low house. "We'll build a new one one day," the father had said now and again. "New barn, new farmhouse. Then it will have three wings," he said, "and when we get a bit more land, it'll be perfect."

Now his father and his teacher disappeared around the eastern corner. Kristian stood watching them. He felt some restlessness in his body. So he kept hoeing. For what seemed like to him like forever.

It was his mother who came and called him in. "Kristian!" she yelled, "Come!" And Kristian came. He threw down the beet hoe and skipped towards home across the rows. "Come!" she yelled again, "We're going to have our coffee!"

They had coffee in the living room, where a vague smell of winter's cold and dampness still hung in the corners. The teacher sat on the sofa with the horsehair cover. The others sat on chairs. A tablecloth had been laid and his mother had on one of her nice aprons.

There was the remainder of a coffee cake from Whitsunday,

and there was a whole new round two-layer cake with icing that his mother had managed to make, and there were cookies and sugar cubes, in case the teacher was one of those people who liked to dip a sugar cube in his coffee and then eat it. They used the little cups with flowers on them.

"Please, have some," said his mother, offering cake to everyone.

They didn't talk very much over their coffee. At one point the father asked the teacher how he liked the area, and the teacher said he liked it. He said a bit more about how he happened to end up here when he otherwise was used to living further east. The father and mother said that it must be quite different.

The layer cake was good. It had none of the staleness of the coffee cake. And the mother had spread strawberry preserves in the middle.

They talked a bit about the war and about commodities that were running low, and the teacher talked about the poor southern Danes who were forced to put on German uniforms. "Thank goodness we're neutral," said the mother.

The teacher looked at Kristian. "Did you get some work done?," he asked, "and did you do your homework?"

Kristian cleared his throat and nodded. Yes, he had. And he felt tension in his body. Now it was going to come out.

But nothing came out. Not other than his mother indirectly attempting to approach the question of the teacher feeling lonely in the large teacher's quarters. And she advanced far enough in her questioning that if the teacher had been engaged or was considering marriage, he would have said so.

But he didn't say anything. Kristian's mother said, almost to herself, that he was still young.

The teacher hadn't said anything yet about it, as far as Kristian could tell. His mother was grasping at straws, and it was evident she was sitting there speculating what the reason for the teacher's visit could be.

Finally the teacher said, "Well there was actually something I wanted to discuss with you. But maybe it would be best…" and he glanced over at Kristian, "maybe it would be best if…"

"Kristian," said his father, "you can go back out to the sugar beets." Kristian left, relieved and nervous. They sat there watching him go.

"That's a smart boy you have there," said the teacher. The mother said, "He's a good boy."

"It's him I came to talk about," continued the teacher. "Kristian is the smartest student I've ever had, both here and there where I'm from."

The father cleared his throat. A bit proud and a bit unsure. There was a short pause.

"I can't teach him anything else. He's finished all the math books, even some I had from college, which he shouldn't be able to do at all. I don't know what else to set him to when the others have math."

The father sat there. Then he said, "Good thing it's his last year." And the mother said, "He's been confirmed of course, and he's going to go work at Lars Peter's farm."

"We have to do some building so there will be more here for him to take over, when the time comes. That's what we're thinking." The father looked out the window. "There's also a pond I can probably buy."

The mother got up and walked out to the kitchen and returned with more hot coffee. She poured for everyone and for a little while the only sounds were the tinkling of teaspoons in their cups.

"Please have another cookie," said the mother.

"Kristian could also have a different kind of future," said the teacher carefully.

The father and mother looked at him, but said nothing. The

father cleared his throat.

"I mean," said the teacher, "with the ability that boy has, there's a lot of possibilities."

"He's a good boy," said the mother. "and he's no worse off than most of the others."

"He's a strong boy," said the father. "And he likes to work. He'll be alright. And he's our only one."

The teacher was far away in his own contemplations. He took a cookie without being asked and sat breaking it into small pieces before inserting them one by one into his mouth. Then he launched into it.

"I came to tell you that I think you should let him go to the preparatory school."

"Preparatory school?" The mother looked shocked. "But no one around here sends their kids to prep school."

The teacher replied, "That's because there's no one around here who has a boy as smart as yours."

The mother said, "But what will people think if we send our son to prep school?"

The father muttered. The teacher said, "This is about Kristian, not about what people say." And he continued, to the father, "I have spoken with the headmaster about Kristian. There could be talk about a half-price tuition, and, most likely, he could skip a grade, too."

"We have always paid our own way," said the father, "and we could also pay for Kristian, if... I mean, if we needed to." He looked annoyed. "What's the point in going to that prep school, anyway?" he asked. "What good is it for Kristian to stay in school?"

A fly that had woken from its extended winter hibernation landed on the tablecloth and began wandering clumsily around the table. The mother waved it away.

The teacher said, "He could do lots of things. There would be so many possibilities for him with a diploma. He could even study further. He could become a teacher or a priest or a doctor or even a professor." He smiled, but when he saw the father's suddenly completely closed-off facial expression, he hurried to say, "Seriously. With a diploma Kristian could join the railroad or the postal service or the customs office—what they call civil service."

"You need a diploma to deliver mail?" asked the mother sharply.

The teacher explained that it wasn't a postman he had meant. With a diploma Kristian could become a clerk or a manager, perhaps. Maybe eventually he could become a postmaster or a railroad superintendent. In any case he could be a public servant with a steady job and a pension. A diploma would open all this to him. And Kristian has the talent," he added.

"He also has a talent for farming," said the father.

"Kristian has unusual talent for a lot of other things, too," said the teacher.

"Hm."

"Think about it."

"Hm."

No one had anything else to say, really. The mother looked at the father. The father looked at the clock. The teacher said, "I'm keeping you. I'm sorry I've taken so much of your time. I didn't realize it had gotten to be so late."

The father said apologetically, "It's the cows. We have to bring them in now."

The teacher rose and thanked them for the coffee. He shook hands goodbye with the mother. Then he followed the father outside.

The teacher said, "Let me go out with you and get the cows," and they walked north out to the pasture, where four cows stood in their tethers. The father lifted out the tether pole, coiled up the ropes and tied the cows into pairs. When the farmer led them home, the teacher walked beside them, and noticed how the cows found their own stalls when they were released.

The teacher said, "I made you late today. So let me help with the milking, too." And without waiting for an answer, he took off his jacket and hung it over the dutch door, took a milking stool and a bucket, and walked over to the first stall. He sat down, reversed his cap, so the brim faced behind, and set his forehead against the side of the cow. The first thin streams of milk resounded against the bottom of the bucket.

The father had stood there looking a bit surprised. He was just about to say something, but he caught himself. He sat down to milk in the second stall.

When they were done, they walked outside. "You had better come in and have your supper," said the father.

The teacher excused himself, but the father said, "It's better if you join us. We have to talk to Kristian."

He yelled in through the utility room, "Ibsen is staying for dinner. I'll get the boy."

The Contract
A STORY ABOUT SURVIVAL

The lord was a woman; the year was 1771. And here the world was, despite everything, the way it was and ought to be. It was far removed from Copenhagen and its Age of Struensee.

The lord was a woman—a widow– and she was a few years shy of the age when one could have spoken about her being in her prime, if she had been a man. The region's other lords nodded in acknowledgment when conversation turned to her. *Blasted females. The way she whipped that farm into shape. It was probably lucky her weakling of a husband died before it was too late. He wasn't worth much the past twenty or so years. Couldn't even breed a baby with her.*

The serfs nodded, hardly in acknowledgment, but giving no sign of opposition either. They didn't have regular contact with the lord; mostly it was just with her estate manager and her bailiff. And they were men; like the kind those men usually are.

This was no inferior estate. It had precisely the size and possessed just enough assets necessary to be afforded sought-after privileges, like tax exemption. The buildings were adequately maintained and the main structure almost regal. A large part of the topmost floor was taken up by a room that by an earlier and more romantic period would have been called a great hall. But during the couple of centuries of its existence it had been used almost solely in connection with funeral receptions. The daily chambers were more comfortable and more appropriately sized.

But naturally the land was of greatest importance. It was fertile land, and the serfs who worked it were generally good-natured. It was almost two hundred and fifty years since the buildings were last burned down by a revolt. The moat was overgrown now, and it didn't smell because of corpses.

That morning in May the lord was sitting at her writing desk. She had just concluded her daily chat with her estate manager and it appeared she was again engrossed in some paperwork. Through the window, sounds of spring forced their way into the room.

The manager, who was on his way to the door, stopped; he stood still a moment. Then, hesitantly, he neared his lord again.

The lord looked up. "Yes?" she asked, slightly irritated.

"I don't know if I told you before about my brother-in-law?"

"Your brother-in-law?" It was apparent that nothing was further removed from the lord than the manager's brother-in-law.

"Yes, my brother-in-law, Morten Andersen. He is a farmer in Nørby. Or rather, he was."

"Was?"

"He had to leave his farm." The manager shook his head. "Without a shilling in his pocket. They are living with us at the moment, which is all right for the time being, but…."

"I see." Now the lord knew about him.

After a brief pause, the manager continued. "I was thinking about the farm that Rasmus Nielsen worked. It's vacant, waiting for a new serf. And there's no widow or daughter who needs supporting."

"Without a shilling in his pocket?" There was a sardonic glint in the lord's eyes. "Can *you* loan him what he needs?"

The manager shook his head and attempted a regretful smile. The lord went back to studying her papers. When she got up a short while later, the manager had already left.

She walked over and stood by the window. Out by the manor farm the blacksmith was shoeing one of the carriage horses. She liked standing there, watching people working. The sound of the hammer blows reached her with a time delay, and she thought that if only he worked a bit faster it would still look right.

Then she looked out across the fields. Everything had been planted and was progressing. The morning mist which had been lying over the land an hour or so ago was only visible as a weak, blueish tint over the hills to the east. She ought to have felt relaxed, now that everything was off to a good start, and only the Lord's weather could stand in the way of results. She ought to be satisfied. Today seemed like it too was going to proceed the way it should.

She sighed. Her gaze fell on the smithy again. Now they were just standing there talking, those idlers.

"Yesterday I saw a farmhand who I don't think I've seen before. He was helping the boy hold a nervous horse while it was being shod."

The estate manager looked pensive.

"Could it have been your brother-in-law?" she asked.

The manager thought about it. He nodded. "That probably was my brother-in-law," he said. "It couldn't have been anyone else yesterday."

The lord appeared to not have heard his answer. The estate manager hadn't even finished his sentence before she started asking about the butter and the new dairy worker. "Is she meticulous?" she asked. The manager thought so. Then the lord said, "I've thought over what you said about your brother-in-law. I guess we had better find a solution. Bring him here tomorrow and I'll be finished looking through the papers." She added, "The down-payment isn't always the most important thing."

The estate manager nodded—thankfully and in agreement. He also started to say something about the importance of the farm being kept in good working order, and that the other serfs easily got disquieted when serfs were lacking from some of the farms.

She made a show of listening to him patiently, indicating

that he could leave now. The following morning the lord was more terse than usual. What normally was regarded as a conversation about the day's work and problems became more like a short interrogation and precise orders.

When they were finished with the regular questions, she said, "And your brother-in-law?"

"He's waiting outside."

"Bring him in."

The estate manager walked out and returned shortly with a slightly older man.

"Have a seat," said the lord to the manager, who, somewhat unsure and confused, sat on the edge of the chair next to the desk. Morten Andersen had to remain standing, naturally. One might as well delineate the future relationship between the two brothers-in-law right from the start.

Morten Andersen was sturdy and undoubtedly an able worker, and the previously independent farmer was still evident in his bearing. Once in a while he looked directly at the lord and she at him.

"It's a good farm," she said. Morten Andersen nodded. "It made the previous serf a prosperous man."

The estate manager agreed. Rasmus Nielsen had been well off, and his widow had married well, so there were no obligations.

The lord allowed herself a little smile. It was because of her that the widow had gotten married to Ole Christiansen, when his wife conveniently died. He had been behind in his land payments for several years.

She sat turning the pages of farm inventory. She read small bits and pieces from different sections. She made calculations. It was too quiet in the room. Then she said, "The way I understand it, a downpayment is impossible?"

Morten Andersen's face did not disclose the tension he felt. He looked straight ahead and let the estate manager answer.

"Yes," said the manager. "As I explained before, Morten was unfortunate, but he was able to pay off what he had to."

"And there are taxes," she said, "plus royal levies."

It was quiet a short while. The rattling of the papers was audible when she turned to a new page.

"And seed," she said. "I have provided seed grain. That must also be paid for. And he needs good draft animals as well…."

Morten Andersen interrupted. "If I may, there was a mare and a colt out there when we went out to look."

"I'm taking those," she said. "You can expect to spend ten sovereigns to purchase draft animals."

A touch of uncertainty was noticeable on Morten Andersen's expression. The estate manager looked a bit disoriented.

"Nothing to sneeze at," said the lord. She looked directly at Morten Andersen. This time his gaze wandered.

"If I may," said the manager. "You did say yesterday, that we ought to be able to find a solution."

She smiled briefly. "I'm sure we can." She took out a piece of paper and started taking notes:

No down-payment.

No taxes or royal levies the first year.

Sharecropper received seed grain: 4 acres oats and 3 acres barley.

Sharecropper receives 10 sovereigns to purchase draft animals.

She read what she had written. "This is what I will contribute," she said sharply.

The manager cleared his throat once. He glanced at his brother-in-law. "I am sure," he said, "that if we can agree on a reasonable period of years, Morten can handle this." He looked at her and her expression demanded more. "I am willing to stand as surety," he said. "Can we also agree to a bit more demesne work than the usual?" He added: "My brother-in-law is a responsible and diligent man."

She shook her head. "No," she said. "And we take care of this today or not at all." A little smile emerged. "And your security—what is that worth?" she added, almost friendly.

"Yes, well, but you said before –" began the manager. She didn't hear him. Her attention was on Morten Andersen.

"You must give me your son."

He looked at her, horrified. "My son?" And then again, "My son?" Then he collected himself. "He is all I have," said Morten Andersen. "And then the girls—two older ones and the little three-year-old. The others died young. I can't do without his work, now that –" He stopped abruptly.

The lord repeated, "You give me your son, or there is no deal."

Morten Andersen's gaze wandered before coming to rest at the desktop.

The lord stood up. "Well?" she said.

It got very quiet. Morten Andersen looked at the estate manager. The manager looked away, as if he weren't following the discussion.

Morten Andersen cleared his throat. Then the estate manager came to his aid after all. "Perhaps Morten could be allowed to think this over a bit?"

An almost compassionate smile formed on the lord's face. "It does not appear that he is in a position where he may think about it," she said. The manager bowed his head.

Then the remains of independent farmer Morten Andersen drained away.

"Then that's the way it must be," he said, bowing. And in a mumble he added, "And thank you, of course."

But Morten Andersen did receive a few concessions in the end. The contract that the estate manager drew up, at the lord's dictation, came to read: "Serf Morten Andersen has given me custody of his son of 19 years, Jens Kristian, in lieu of payment of thirty sovereigns which is now waived in exchange for the above-named son, who will be exempt from military conscription, since he is a free child of an independent farmer, given to me in good faith."

Morten Andersen made his mark below. A touch of haughtiness could be associated with the expression: 'a free child of an independent farmer.'

The farm where Morten Andersen would work out his contract was in the most remote village of the lord's authority. And the distance was the reason several days passed before the usual talk between people of the village formed any real direction.

But by then enough had accumulated so that small remarks could be exchanged. A former independent farmer—and then the general circumstances, as the others eventually found them out.

It wasn't that anyone was shocked or thought there was anything wrong with the way the arrangement had been made. It was unusual, certainly, but also quite logical. If you didn't have money, you had to make do the best you could. And when you had a well-placed brother-in-law and when your son demonstrated that he was as good as cash, then you were lucky; and what more could be said? When talk continued, it was due to the fact that such a handsome farmhand—Jens Kristian— was pretty hard not to notice. That's what people said in the village—the ones who had gotten a glimpse of him, or just heard about him from others.

One day when they were out repairing one of the hedges that the storm had torn up, one of the townspeople said to Morten Andersen, "I hear you have sort of joined the lord's family, well, well." And he stood there chuckling, looking at Morten, who, with a mallet—a post driver—was hammering a post into the ground and therefore didn't necessarily hear anything. Someone else said, "I wonder who that young man is—the new coachman up there on the farm?"

Morten Andersen worked hard, did nearly the work of two. He hadn't just lost a son, but also a farmhand. He hired a boy, him—and then the daughters—he'd have to make due with them for the time being. On demesne days he had to meet up himself with his horses. Other serfs could just send a hired hand.

The hired hands couldn't resist teasing him a bit. "Not quite the same as being a farmer, is it?" Even the dullest of them could make that observation, and the village genius said, one day, as they were driving manure out from the lord's manure pit, "The father is walking in crap while the son is sitting in the driver's seat."

The farm in Morten Andersen's contract was actually quite good—truth be told, even better than the one he had when he was independent. It was situated farthest out in the village a bit by itself; it had been moved out there many years previous on account of a fire. There were probably a few of the other serfs who wouldn't have minded moving out there. There were a couple of remarks about that too: "If only I had the devil for a brother-in-law and a pretty boy to give as a deposit."

It took a little while for Morten Andersen and his wife to settle in. Of course they took part in the festivals, but they never really got used to them, people later said. But when they spoke to one another, they never complained. All things considered, they had been lucky and they knew they ought to be thankful.

Also, once in a while, Jens Kristian came to visit them and helped out. He reported that he ate well and that the work was easy. Only people from other and higher strata of society, or from a later and better time, might think that he went around feeling resentment towards his parents.

Spring passed and turned to early summer. Early summer turned to mid-summer and mid-summer turned to harvest. Even though Morten Andersen and his family were still considered "the new ones" in the village, eventually they became part of the landscape to which people didn't pay any special attention. It was easiest for the daughters. Even by May Day the eldest had been at the celebration with the farmhands and maids and she had been paired up like all the others, keeping with tradition. So now she had a farmhand for whom she would be his lady in the coming year, and she would prepare food for him at the harvest festival, the Christmas celebration and at youth socials.

But Jens Kristian was outside those circles, and up at the manor he lived in a strange void. He was a servant—and not really one at the same time; he was a coachman, but the previous coachman had kept his job and responsibility in the horse stable; he was the estate manager's nephew, but the manager kept him at arm's length and was effectively strict and aloof to him, as if he really would have preferred to have had him out of his sight; so Jens Kristian was set to work mostly in the gardens, with the herbs and hops, when he wasn't needed as driver.

The girls in the kitchen were preoccupied with him, and they teased him whenever they had the chance.

"He looks like he's sleepwalking again," said one of the cook's maids, beckoning the dairy maid over to the window. They knocked on the windowpane. He probably didn't hear it. "Well, they didn't come home until I was lighting the stove." Now he turned his head after all, and waved to them.

"She sure is dashing around," said the dairy maid.

"And all the sewing," said one of the other girls. "You wouldn't recognize her they way she's all decked out."

It was the lord they were talking about. That's how it often went, when they started talking about Jens Kristian. She certainly had changed; and not just in her new interest in clothes—she had become almost flighty. It was noticeable to almost everyone. *Blasted females*, the region's other lords said to one another. Now they were running into her more often at the dinners and parties in the area. And her carriage was seen constantly out on the roads, as she was driven around inspecting her properties. Sometimes she was away for days at a time, suddenly having an errand in Aalborg of the kind that she previously had relegated to her estate manager. Now she negotiated with the merchants there herself, down to the smallest details—and she had started shopping!

The girls sighed—dreamily or indignantly, it was hard to tell which.

Jens Kristian learned his way around the roads, and he also learned how slowly time can pass.

When weather allowed, she ordered the open carriage for shorter trips. Sitting on the coach box, he could feel her eyes on his back. Rarely were any words spoken other than short necessary orders. She sat erect on the rearmost seat looking straight ahead. Sometimes when they arrived she seemed to have forgotten why she had wanted to visit the place.

When she was attending a social gathering, she rode in the closed carriage, of course. Jens Kristian preferred this. He felt freer, and these social trips were a welcome diversion from the daily routine. He would be accommodated in the kitchen with the other servants—and sometimes there were leftovers from the party upstairs that they got to share. It was wonderfully warm in the kitchen on such an evening. The conversation was light, the teasing good-natured, and there was always news to be gained.

Afterwards, he had to resign himself to the drive home through a crystal-clear starry autumn night. Freezing and drowsy he sat on the coach box, resisting his fear of the dark, and what it was hiding. He needed a couple draughts of the schnapps he had stowed under the coach box, and that helped to light a short-lived glow both in his body and in his courage. Periodically he set the horses to trotting, but he was too tired to keep them there very long. Also the noise was too oppressive. The proper night sound was the slow plodding of the horses' steps and the lazy creaking of the carriage wheels, disappearing into their own eternity.

Wrapped in furs and her driving cape, the lord was sitting inside the carriage. In there the emptiness was, if possible, even more intrusive and jarring than in the void outside, directly under the starry sky. She tried to sleep, but this new restlessness—or an old and forgotten restlessness that had come back to life—rattled around inside her.

She didn't so much as even glance at him, when on arrival he helped her down from the carriage.

"Where was she yesterday? Who was she with?" inquired the cook's maid in the morning.

"Me," smiled Jens Kristian.

"Ridiculous!" The cook's maid threw a damp rag at his head. "Where did you go?"

She and the other maids came closer.

"Asdal," he said. "Too far to ride home the same night." He stretched. "And now I have to do it again." The lord had ordered her carriage ready for when she had finished breakfast with the estate manager.

Months passed, but the lord's restlessness continued unabated. The carriage was traded for a sleigh in the white winter months, and the cold and wind left their traces on the skin of her face. Now and then she overnighted at various manors instead of being conveyed home at night. But the daytime hours were not much better for travel, and she was increasingly restive, often ordering that she be taken home before affairs were over.

During this period, she vacillated between being silent and

pensive to being cheerful and animated.

"What's come over the woman?" the other lords chuckled to one another. Their wives whispered to each other when she wasn't nearby, and spoke zealously and indignantly when she had left and the men were out of earshot. Otherwise they just looked knowingly at one another, and that was sufficient.

She even went home early from the county prefect's birthday celebration, where almost all of the county's leading individuals were in attendance. Thomas Olufsen was there also that night. He was the only relatively young widower among the region's lesser lords, and he had sat with her and done his best, as he also had done previously, but still she left before midnight. Or perhaps that's why. The wives whispered about it. Of course, Thomas Olufsen wasn't one of those that one's eyes would dwell on for very long; and there was something plump about his bearing, something farmer-like—but he was still a man of standing. Who did she think she was, anyway, going around dismissing him all these years.

She should be ashamed of herself.

Then it was a day towards the end of February—the twenty-seventh, to be exact. The weather had been heavy and gray from early morning, and later in the afternoon the wind started picking up. It wasn't long before snow was drifting sideways across fields and roads, filling up the abandoned wheel tracks and obliterating all traces of the previous day's activities. It wasn't just the old snow that was getting blown around, it was mostly new snow that was making the world opaque.

Inside the manor courtyard it wasn't so bad. It was sheltered, partly by the buildings and partly by the stunted tree plantings to the west and north, which weren't so decrepit that they couldn't parry even the worst storms. Jens Kristian was stopped with the sleigh in front of the steps, waiting for the lord to decide that she wasn't going to ride to Baggesvogn after all, like she had ordered. But then she appeared, wrapped in furs and kerchiefs and large boots on her feet.

"Get my baggage," she said.

Jens Kristian retrieved the large leather chest that contained her society clothes, her shoes and jewelry, and placed it on the front seat of the sleigh.

"There's a snowstorm," he said.

"Right," said the lord.

Jens Kristian closed the door and situated himself on the coach box. *Okay. If she wants to.* He shook the reins and the horses started off.

The first section wasn't so bad, while they were in the allée. But out on the highway it got more difficult, impossible even, one could say. All landmarks were covered over, and visibility was no more than a couple of yards. The horses stopped. Jens Kristian tried half-heartedly to get them to keep going.

Then he crawled down, waded over and opened the door. "The horses can't find their way."

She allowed herself a little smile. "Does that matter, when you can?"

"I can't either," he said. "It's impossible to see."

He couldn't tell if she were really as displeased as she looked.

She said, "Then I guess we have to turn back."

Relieved, Jens Kristian got the sleigh turned around and was miraculously able to avoid the one horse getting stuck in the ditch when it stepped through the snow cover. Now they were walking into the wind, and the snow was right in his eyes so he was even more blinded than before. Their tracks were already covered, and he was starting to regret that he hadn't made the horses keep going in the other direction. They would have made it to someplace. But this was like driving blindfolded, and it was hard to keep the horses moving forward.

But the Lord was with them. Ahead, like a denseness in the snowstorm, a couple of the allée trees emerged, and both the horses and the driver were reinvigorated at knowing they were on familiar terrain. It wasn't long before they were stopped again in front of the steps.

After he had helped her down from the sleigh, she turned abruptly towards him. She looked at him, and for the first time he saw that she had friendly, blue eyes, which seemed to be bordered by a smile. "I will not be cheated," she said. "You will dine with me tonight."

She turned and began making her way with difficulty up the steps, which were almost completely erased by the snow. He stood looking after her with a surprised expression. She hesitated, then stopped. She said, "Wait a second!" And he stopped. He had been following her with her suitcase. She thought. Then she pointed at him. "I forgot to say that you should go over to the estate manager and his wife and tell them to come as well. Six o'clock," she added. Then she kept walking.

It was an evening they would all look back on with only discomfort. Not because of anything that was said or done, but because of its overwhelming impropriety and lack of social convention.

The table was set with everything, with respect to service and candles, that was appropriate for a dinner celebration. The glasses stood weighty and ample in front of the plates, and on the service table, bottles of wine were set out.

It hadn't been easy for the kitchen to put together a festive meal on such short notice, but the silver serving dishes made even the salted meat—in place of a roast—look quite elegant.

It didn't amount to the usual eight to ten dishes, but the cook's maid had managed to make, on this bitterly cold day, an ice cream for dessert, even though all four of them probably would have preferred to repeat the soup, so they could have regained a bit of inner warmth.

The lord sat at the head of the table. To her right sat the

estate manager and his wife, and across from them, on the other long side, sat Jens Kristian—miles, it seemed, from the others in the party. He ate awkwardly, drank when toasts were made, and once in a while when they weren't. If only it had been beer! Or schnapps! A tinge of undecided grimace appeared in the farthest corner of his mouth when the maid served him on that side. She would be able to talk about that when she returned to the kitchen, and only down there was there anything resembling frivolity that evening. But it was an amusement of disbelief, an unsure amusement, almost anxious. The whole world order was being rocked that evening.

The lord did her absolute best—at least in the beginning. She directed her conversation to the estate manager and his wife, who was experiencing this part of the building for the first time. Previously she had helped out in the kitchen a couple of times for special occasions, but this was new to her. Her husband had been here one time at a party, but not her. She looked furtively around. A single remark was tossed her way. She nodded.

After a long pause in what was supposed to be conversation, the lord said suddenly and jovially to Jens Kristian, "This certainly is better than getting lost out there in the snow."

Jens Kristian turned red. Of course it was. The estate manager, who knew his place and his obligations, quickly started to tell about the snowstorm on New Year's Day a few years ago, which had nearly cost the priest his life when he decided to cut across the field on his way home from the church service.

"Yes, I remember that," said the lord.

Then it was silent again. And they were only halfway through the meal.

Later she did all she could to make the disparate guests into a party. But not even the wine, which could only be detected in the movements of the estate manager, contributed to that end. It was a relief to everyone when the lord stood up and said goodnight, and people could concentrate on their sentiments of gratitude.

The estate manager and his wife fought their way home to the manager's house through the snowstorm that was still raging. When they were in bed they had something to talk about – the bed was still too cold to fall asleep in anyway. "I don't like it," said the manager. "I should never have stood for it back then. Now who knows what will become of it."

Jens Kristian didn't have to go so far. First stop was the warm kitchen, where he happily exposed himself to more or less biting teasing from the maids who were hard at work cleaning up.

They thought it was hilarious to curtsey for him.

The lord went to her bedchamber, where the ice crystals on the windows nearly illuminated the room. Now her expression finally relaxed.

The next morning she was unusually terse. She cut off the manager's thanks for an unforgettable evening, gave a few random orders and sent him away.

Outside the snowstorm continued.

The snow lay over the region for weeks. A couple days of thaw followed the storm, but then hard frost returned, which created a solid crust of ice on the snow, so it wasn't blown around anymore. Then it was possible, for those who had to, to travel again, but it was still difficult. The pale white of death was painful on the eyes of those who dared go out on those frost-sparkling, sunny, cold days.

The estate manager resignedly shook his head. He said to his wife, "She still wants to be driven around in the sleigh, as if there were something out there she had to see."

"Dear God," she said. "And in that cold. She'll perish."

The manager grinned. "I'm not so sure even that's enough to cool her down." He caught himself. Not even inside his own four walls could an estate manager allow himself a remark like that. "She doesn't have it so easy," he said apologetically. "Let's remember that."

"And then to the mill," said the lord, and in the cold air her words condensed to a white fog in front of her face. Jens Kristian closed the door and crawled up onto the coach box.

They had been over at the farm of Poul Terkelsen, who was far behind in land rent. They had been in the woods—possibly to check something, he didn't know, but they had stopped where trees where being cleared. Earlier on the trip they had passed his parent's farm, but they didn't stop there. He hadn't seen his parents or any siblings about; they were probably huddled around the stove, which everyone should have been doing on a day like this. After a string of clear days, when if you were in the sun you could really feel it, a freezing fog had moved in. It deposited needles in his eyebrows and on the woolen scarf he had wound around the lower part of his face.

All the way to the mill! Half a mile at least. Oh, no. He gave the horses a little shake of the reins. He was almost envious of them. Maybe they did look like white ghost horses, but at least they didn't mind the cold.

He kicked his feet together. At least half a mile.

At the mill there was a great deal of confusion. No one had expected a visit on a day like this, and everything was a terrible mess. The bit of damage done to the one mill wing by the recent snowstorm still hadn't been repaired, and unmilled grain was piling up.

The miller and the miller's helper had read and signed, and now the lord was on her way back to the sleigh. She ought to have been satisfied that at least this trip had served a purpose, that she really did have to travel out here. But she was feeling awfully tired walking back, or perhaps more correctly, she suddenly realized she was tired. Tired of being driven around, tired of finding reasons, tired of taking care of things that really were the responsibility of the estate manager or the bailiff. Tired of fooling herself.

Jens Kristian held the sleigh door open for her. She gathered her furs around her and put her right foot on the step. She hesitated a second; then she asked, "Can you read and write?"

Sure, Jens Kristian could do both. He had even gone to school there where they used to live, and he hadn't only learned to read, but also write—even though it cost his father extra.

He was met with the hint of a smile—a smile that disclosed both relief and decisiveness at the same time. "I am going to use you as a secretary," she said. "And you can help the estate manager with the accounting."

He didn't say anything; he just bowed a little. She got inside. "Drive me home," she said.

And now the story is nearly coming to a close. It becomes almost invisible; there are virtually no third-party witnesses. The common talk between people was starved out, nourished only for a little while by some guesses, and then died. The maids could only repeat what they had said the whole time since that day, namely that Jens Kristian wouldn't be eating in the dining room any longer, but would have his food brought up to the office, and that he was moving from the room out by the stable up to an attic apartment. But that would only be natural for someone who is writing—or appears to be.

The estate manager, who was the most likely one to know something, didn't speak about it with anyone. Not even when it concerned his brother-in-law's family did he answer their questions, except perhaps one single indirect one. One day he said to Morten Andersen, "It would be good if you had money you could use to release Jens Kristian."

The estate manager reassured his wife: "Jens Kristian will never be able to do my job. Being able to jot down a few notes from the lord's dictation and add together a few numbers will never make him an estate manager." He said this so often that she realized it wasn't her he was trying to reassure.

By all appearances, Jens Kristian was enjoying his new life. In any case he seemed more self-assured when, now and again, he was able to sneak a visit to the girls in the kitchen. He had also gotten new clothes. "My secretary is not going to be dressed like a farmer," the lord had said. The maids felt his clothes and were admiring. Or maybe more than that.

When he visited his parents he was the same good and helpful son he always was. It was as if he actually enjoyed helping them with the work.

And the lord? Not too many weeks went by before people realized that now the routine was more or less the way it had been before all that restlessness came over her. Every morning she held a meeting with her secretary and her manager, but otherwise it was almost always just her chambermaid and her housemaid who had contact with her. Her conveyances were rarely seen on the roads, and she rarely took part in the region's social life. The old coachman, who had gotten his old job back, had so little work to do that he was set to doing all kinds of other things.

At first there was a lot of wondering around the manors and a lot of talk. Wondering what she was up to, the way she refused nearly all invitations. The way she was hiding herself away. She wasn't sick; not as far as anyone knew. Not in that way at any rate, the wives whispered to one another. Sad, that she never had children. They knowingly shook their heads.

Soon other things to talk about caught people's interest. Not that she was forgotten, but that she was again like she had been before—not an object of perpetual interest. *Blasted female, the way she's whipped that estate into shape* was again the remark uttered, after someone had mentioned her.

Therefore it came as something of a surprise—a shock almost—when around the estates they received her invitations. On Whitsunday she was going to be married. This was news that could even crowd out talk about Struensee's execution, the queen's exile, and the joy that, with Ove Guldberg, people again had an estate-friendly man leading the regency.

The forthcoming wedding would also help to restore the world order.

Even the county prefect, who on account of his position and descent was regarded with respect by all, expressed his satisfaction when he learned of the forthcoming wedding.

Clearly Thomas Olufsen was no cosmopolitan, and his bearing was somewhat farmer-like, but his assets were nothing to sneeze at, and uniting two fine estates in this region, where otherwise the relatively smaller estates were the majority, would only strengthen the county's reputation. And it was clever of Thomas Olufsen to increase in this way the inheritance of his son, whom he had had with his deceased wife. He mentioned this to his bride. She smiled crookedly. She said she was looking forward to it.

The prefect sent his appreciation for the invitation and his intention of attendance by himself and the prefectess at the wedding celebration.

It was celebratory. There was no question—they knew food and drink.

After the wedding, things were almost as they had been before. The wedding couple was not together all that much. They each lived at their own estates and ran them, just as they had done before. Now and then they visited one another, and they were also seen together at the region's affairs.

One thing did change however: Jens Kristian was no longer there. When the newlyweds went to Thomas Olufsen's manor a few days after the wedding, Jens Kristian was with them. When the lord returned, she was alone.

The girls missed him, in a way. Even though only one of them had had any real relationship with him—it was the young maid, and she was also sent away—he had been good to have around, both to tease and to talk about.

One of the maids garnered the courage to ask the estate manager, but he just said that Jens Kristian was working at Thomas Olufsen's. He said the same thing to his wife—and she could sense his relief—and to Morten Andersen, when he eventually showed up to ask about his son. "He is still working for Thomas Olufsen—as far as I know," he added. That was all. Morten Andersen trudged home.

Later that autumn it became obvious that the lord was bearing fruit. And at some point in December it became known that she had given birth to a son. The child had arrived ahead of schedule, one had to assume, when one counted, but they said he was completely healthy.

"So there was some spark in Thomas Olufsen after all," a neighbor remarked to the prefect at one of the Christmas parties. There was a hint of question in his tone. "Who would have believed that?" The prefect just nodded, and a nearly hidden smile revealed a couple of his chins. "So there might be two heirs," said the other. The prefect didn't respond. The other dropped it and they started talking about other things.

The subject remained a topic of conversation among the wives for a longer duration. They weren't sure if they should laugh or cry, if they should feel indignant or compassionate. Or if they should just pretend like nothing happened. There were small nuances in the tones of voice they attempted, and when Thomas

Olufsen turned up alone at one of the social gatherings, he was met with almost demonstrative, overwhelming congratulations. And he must certainly remember to congratulate his wife as well. She would be receiving guests soon, wouldn't she?

Thomas Olufsen thanked them. Politely.

But this chapter also quickly became a part of the past and the daily routine. Time passed in the region; work followed the seasons in a long cycle. A couple of years passed. The community remained much as it had been back in the seventies.

Up at the manor the lord's son was thriving and developing into a handsome child, the darling of the maids.

Out on the most remote farm, Morten Andersen travailed from morning to night and finally was getting his feet under him. They couldn't put any real savings together yet, but that might come.

Frequently they thought about Jens Kristian, and they even spoke about him occasionally; revealed to one another their anxiety. They never heard from him. They never heard anything about him.

"So," said one of the neighbors now and then, "have you heard anything about your son? He's doing quite well for himself, isn't he?"

The estate manager didn't say anything. Not even when he was asked.

When Morten Andersen's wife got sick, and no one had any faith that this was anything but the end, exhausted and weak as she was, Morten Andersen went up to the manor one day and asked for an audience.

It was denied. He could refer himself to the estate manager.

The manager said, "I don't think you should. Don't be difficult. Think about yourself and your daughters."

He also said, "You have one of the best farms. Remember that."

Morten Andersen was stubborn. He wanted to know. Marie wished to see her son before she died. That was her right.

The estate manager advised against it once more, but in the end, he promised to schedule a day when Morten Andersen could bring his request before the lord.

A few days passed. Then a farmhand came by with the message that Morten Andersen may come the following Thursday.

The room where Morten Andersen was led was the same one where the negotiations regarding his contract had taken place back then, or more correctly: where the conditions were dictated. And now it was spring, and the sowing completed. The sun was shining in through the window.

It wasn't the lord who received him, but Thomas Olufsen. Morten Andersen didn't expect this, and it ruined the little speech he had prepared. He cleared his throat, but that didn't help much.

Thomas Olufsen was standing up, leaning against the writing desk. He looked indifferently at Morten Andersen. "Well, what is it he wanted?"

"Yes, with all due respect Morten Andersen would like to ask if his son—that is, Jens Kristian—could possibly be given the opportunity to visit his mother, who is ill. She is on her deathbed it appears, and it is her dying wish to see her son."

Thomas Olufsen stood there silently. Then he said, "Neither I nor my wife have any business with his son nor do we know his whereabouts."

Morten Andersen's mouth started to run from surprise. "But we all thought that Jens Kristian was in your employment. No one had told us anything but that. We were all convinced that Jens Kristian was at your estate."

Thomas Olufsen was tiring of the conversation. "His son is a soldier," he said.

That gave Morten Andersen a start. He went quiet a moment. Then a glimpse of the once-independent farmer emerged. He said firmly, "I have a paper where it is written that my son shall not be conscripted to the military, because he is the son of an independent farmer who has been given to your wife in good faith."

An expression of irritation clouded Thomas Olufsen's face. Then he said, "His son has not been conscripted to the armed forces. His son has volunteered to serve in a regiment. He has received his enlistment fee. This has nothing to do with my wife."

Morten Andersen stared at him in disbelief. Then he asked, "If I may ask, where is his regiment?"

"How should I know? Viborg? Copenhagen? We cannot be responsible for the fact that his son neglected to notify his parents." Thomas Olufsen looked at him scornfully. Then he said, "He may leave now. We have nothing more to say."

Morten Andersen bowed. Serf Morten Andersen walked home.

In the following days Morten Andersen visited the estate manager several times, partly to have someone to yell at and partly to seek advice. The estate manager was getting sick and tired of his brother-in-law, and often regretted that he had brought him in back then. This was his reward: bother and fuss.

Morten Andersen threatened to go to the courts. He wanted the lord tried. It took the estate manager several hours to convince him not to do it. He needed to consider his family, who depended on him; he needed to consider the fact that the lord had helped him, back when things were looking their worst, when he had no other recourse. Would he really risk all that on a lawsuit that he had no chance on earth of winning? Plus, the estate manager added, "And did you consider that if you make yourself unreasonable this could come back on me?"

He was successful in getting Morten Andersen to calm down. It probably helped too that Morten Andersen's wife died, so for a while he was occupied with other things. And when he did start pestering the estate manager again with complaints, now it was with a hint of resignation. When the estate manager said to him one day, "Just wait and see. One fine day Jens Kristian will turn up and he can tell you himself how he volunteered to enlist. Maybe he's even advanced to a ranking officer and comes back in a fancy uniform," then Morten Andersen grasped the hope in the manager's tale and repeated it for his daughters. With this they were eventually able to comfort one another, which grew into a kind of habit, and as the years passed it got easier.

Because the years did pass, each resembling the other, towards a period which would bring great societal changes in the name of serf liberation.

But it advanced more slowly here. Although the years passed, the times didn't change—at least not in the time that belonged to Morten Andersen. And when the lord died, it was her stepson who took over the estate—no one had seen her own son for a long time. He was just the second son anyway, and he was set up with something somewhere—some people thought it was in the West Indies. The new lord was a modern and progress-minded lord with a knack for investing and business and with a matching need for capital. He began encouraging his serfs to purchase their farms and make them their private properties, but by then Morten Andersen had long been exhausted, and his remains were returning to the earth up at the churchyard. A couple of married daughters were there to shed tears for him—and also the youngest, who was still at home.

Morten Andersen died a serf. But he died a man of adequate means, people said.

No one could argue that he had not done well for himself.

Kirstine

A STORY OF A REGION

It certainly seemed to be a male, staggering his way from the village, leaning back awkwardly and well hidden from the road by an old jacket that he had pulled all the way up to his ears. Anyone who hadn't been outside that day themselves, and felt the weather, would have thought he was drunk the way he looked.

The Man from Overgaard—or simply 'The Man,' as most people called him when they were growing up—stood in the doorway sheltered from the wind and rain, as he saw the swaying form approaching. He himself had been on his way around the end of the barn to see if the pile of hay was still there; but he had paused in this doorway. And now he had another reason for pause, since someone was actually coming.

The stranger more or less jogged the last bit of distance and stopped, panting, before him. Then he stuck his head out of his coat. It was the curate.

"So it's you," said The Man.

So it was. The curate greeted him. But in a storm like this his words were mostly blown away before anyone could hear them.

They stood there. "There is a message from the rector," shouted the curate. "The new priest is on his way."

The Man said, "Let's go in. This is no day to be outside." And he walked in front, through the barn and into the scullery; and the curate shed his jacket and boots, and then borrowed a pair of slippers, while The Man yelled for coffee and schnapps.

The curate said, "Ten wagons have to be sent to Frederikshavn. The ship arrives tomorrow morning."

Inside the kitchen, they sat down at the table. When the maidservant girl lifted off the kettle, the fire roared from inside the stove.

The Man said, "Ten wagons? When the old priest left, eight was enough. Eight should be enough."

The curate thought so too. But he didn't say anything. He just mumbled that that's what the rector had written.

The Man repeated, "Eight should be enough."

They toasted and drank.

The Man said, "Eight is enough. I'll send two, and you can go around to the other farms and round up the last six. You can leave Laurits out of it. They have enough to see to."

The curate nodded. Yes, Laurits had enough to see to. Half their roof was blown across Vendsyssel and was probably floating around in the Kattagat by now. You could see that coming. That Laurits! The curate chuckled.

Okay, fine.

They had another coffee spiked with schnapps and sat looking at the window panes, whipped by the rain. It passed the time, and they weren't neglecting anything. The girl stood with her back to them at the stove, with a bit of coffee in a cup missing a handle. When they grew tired of looking at the window, they looked at her. Sometimes she stirred a pot.

"I guess I'd better get to it," said the curate, without rising from his chair. Even if the ship had sailed from Copenhagen as planned, it wouldn't arrive tomorrow. The Man said, "We might as well wait another day."

The curate wasn't really sure. The rector had written that the wagons should be in Frederikshavn Wednesday morning.

The Man swirled his cup with the bit of coffee left inside it. "Right, I guess so. The weather could still change." He said, "Then they can leave at seven o'clock. That should be early enough."

The curate didn't leave. He might as well stay and eat, since it was near noon. Porridge and pork. There was nothing ostentatious about the way The Man lived.

Later in the afternoon, when the curate was about to leave,

The Man said, "As soon as the new one arrives, we had better get Stefan and Kirstine taken care of."

The curate didn't look too happy. The Man said, "Why not? We need both her and the old man provided for. We need to be sensible about this." He gave the curate a couple of encouraging claps on the shoulder. "Now we have the chance. Talk with them. Tell them it's fine."

The curate left. He hadn't directly promised anything, but it was probably obvious how things stood. The Man was not someone you bandied things about with.

While he struggled his way through the storm, the curate thought occasionally about Kirstine. The Man had always had a soft spot for her, as they say. Of course, she had been a maid at Overgaard Farm a couple of years before she got married. Back then it was still The Man's father who was The Man.

She was pretty much the most attractive girl anyone could remember, but that wasn't the most significant thing. She didn't come from people whose children could get married with someone of means.

The Man—that is, The Man's father—had gotten her married to a day-laborer, a rather older man, to be completely honest.

And The Man—that is, the one who was The Man now—had gotten married. With someone of status similar to his own—or maybe even a bit more.

But Kirstine was still pretty.

And then there was Stefan. He was a jack of all trades and he fished some, too. And he had been living out there in the house by the cliff for a couple of years now.

The curate tried to speed up a little. He would really like to make it around to the farms before the evening got too late.

The thing with Kirstine could wait.

It was the weather that was the problem. It was just too much. Sometimes it came roaring in from all directions at once, swirling around the ship. You felt a sinking feeling, and all the woodwork creaked with an almost human sound.

The ship had departed at a time when the storm seemed to be tapering off, as it made its way south.

The skipper had been in a rush. A lot of people had shaken their heads when he cast off, but up through Øresund things had gone fine. Almost great.

But the storm returned in full strength. Its visit south was just a brief one; it moved westward again.

The trip north from Copenhagen to the small village ended up taking three days. A good bit of the time the ship paused for shelter below Anholt, but even that was difficult. In the cramped cabin the numerous seasick passengers were huddled together, a passive, retching pile of humans, hanging over counters and tables. Only the priest, who was traveling to carry out an errand in the west, was spared by the Lord, until well into the second day when he fainted from exhaustion, which he later described in a letter. He did his best to comfort the other passengers' suffering. The ship's sailors were working hard on deck.

In his letter the priest also wrote: "Although I miss you terribly, my own dear wife, I am thankful that your condition did not allow me to take you on this journey." And after he had described all the voyage's torments, plus the looming anxieties which only his unshakeable faith in the Creator could suppress, he continued, "But the difficulties were not over, even though we reached harbor intact. The eight farmhands, who with their carts had come to transport me and our belongings the six miles to the vicarage, had been waiting at the inn for nearly two days and were burdensome to wake up and harness the horses and load the items. But with help from some good people we were able to admonish them to seemly behavior, and later in the afternoon we departed."

It was no easy trip. Even though the rain was nearly stopped, it was still windy and cold. The farmhands were sluggish, cross and uncommunicative, and the priest totally exhausted. He was cold. Three of the wagons tipped over on the soft roads, and it took a great deal of effort to get them upright again with the furniture and boxes back in place. In his letter the priest wrote, "I am sorry to have to report that your small writing desk will probably always bear scars from this unfortunate trip."

It was nearly midnight before they reached their destination. The farmhands had demanded a stop to rest at an inn along the way. The priest, in his weakened condition, didn't have the power to prevent it.

So it was in the autumn of 1856 the priest arrived here. It was a year like many others: days with sand drift, days with rain, days with sunshine. Difficult harvest, as usual. And then there was the wind: sometimes storming, sometimes just a breeze. It was a year like many others.

In the broader society it was probably different. 1856 was one of Scandinavia's great years. Never before or since has a Nordic union been so close. In Stockholm, the Swedish king, Oscar I, went around and collected 16,000 soldiers to offer as part of an alliance with Frederik VII to defend the Eider.

There was a lot of talk about that—out there in society.

But not here. Here it was a completely normal year. And yet, in some distant future, the year would be remembered as the year the priest arrived. People were talking about him—about his journey and about his belongings.

The Man at Overgaard was expecting his visit, but a few days passed before the priest turned up. That did not please The Man. He remarked, "I had no idea that you had already arrived." The priest's expression tightened, and he explained that he had been busy organizing the household.

Yes, of course. The Man observed him more closely. He was a bony, almost emaciated person, that priest, apparently introverted and with no outward smile. He told The Man the vicarage was in terrible condition. The whole first night he had to move his bed around in the bedroom, in order to find a place where it didn't drip down on him. "First thing in the morning I sent for the thatcher and told him to put a new roof on immediately," he said.

The Man didn't think it was the right time of year for such an undertaking, and he said so. The priest was stubborn. "The vicarage has to be fixed. My wife will be arriving," he said.

The Man asked when she was coming. "When her condition allows it," the priest answered. And he didn't say anything else.

The Man offered a glass of wine, but the priest declined. The Man offered coffee, but the priest excused himself; he had a lot to do. The Man wished him luck in his new position. The priest thanked him.

When the priest had left, The Man said to his wife—the preferred address for her, "I get the feeling that the new priest is not the enjoyable sort."

When they rode home from church on Sunday, after the inaugural church service, she agreed with her husband. Although they had talked about inviting the priest over during the week, they didn't do it. He had been stern and admonishing. As if he were speaking to children.

Just after noon that Sunday, the priest was sitting in the study, as it was called. He had eaten the modest meal set before him by the housekeeper. Then he had tried to rest a bit, but loneliness distracted him.

If only Franziska were here. He dipped his pen and continued the letter he had started the day before. This day he wrote:

"Now the inaugural is over with. I think the entire parish was there; every seat in the church was occupied. Singing of the psalms was no great pleasure to the ear. It was drawling, almost moaning. The rector recommended me warmly to the congregation, and I gave a clear and emphatic sermon. I am pretty certain that I made an impression."

He took out the manuscript of his sermon one more time, and sat and paged through it. It was clear and flowing, despite the few corrections he had made at the last minute after breakfast. There was a trace of satisfaction in the firm expression around his mouth as he read a little here, a little there. He had made an impression. It couldn't be otherwise.

Then he was lost in thought. He sat for about ten minutes, staring straight ahead, before he dipped the pen again. Then he wrote, "Everything would have been perfect if you, my own, had been here."

At that point in the letter the priest was interrupted by a tentative knocking at the door. He yelled, "Step in!" and a young farmhand and a girl entered. They were still in their church clothes, but must have changed into clogs. They were in their stocking feet.

The farmhand was there to order banns. His name was Stefan Kristensen, a farmhand born in 1830 and he was going to marry Kirstine Mortensdatter, "widow Kirstine Mortensdatter," he quickly corrected himself, born 1824.

Widow? The priest looked up at the woman, standing there with her head bowed, just inside the door. No one could tell by looking at her that she had been married. She looked petite, almost delicate, as if she had never seen work, as if sun and wind had never assailed her. The priest's glance encompassed her, and his thoughts likely dwelled a moment far across the Kattegat Sea to a married woman about the same age, but from a very different upbringing—and more marked by time and vain efforts. Vain thus far. The farmhand cleared his throat and shifted his feet.

The priest sat there with his faraway stare still directed towards Kirstine, as she stood bashfully at the farmhand's side.

The priest's gaze returned to the room. Bashfully? Presumably the priest caught the poorly concealed confidential smile—the almost coquettish smile—she sent the young farmhand, followed by a quick glance at the priest. The farmhand's face was unchanging. He cleared his throat again. "Yes, we have decided to get married."

The priest nodded and looked up at him. Then he entered the desired banns in his papers. Farmhand Stefan Kristensen, 26 years, and Kirstine Mortensdatter, 32 years, widow of small landholder Jørgen Antonsen.

"How long was she married?" the priest asked, mostly directed towards Stefan.

"I got married eleven years ago," Kirstine said.

"Any children?" asked the priest.

"No."

The priest didn't ask any more. Part of his attention was probably still occupied out near Lolland. Then they talked briefly about the banns and the date of the wedding. The priest indicated that they may leave.

When he was alone again, the priest looked in the church register anyway. There it was. In '45 day-laborer and fisherman Jørgen Antonsen, who was sixty-two, married the then twenty-one-year-old girl Kirstine Mortensdatter. *Well.* The priest shook his head. His thoughts wandered; he sighed; he set the church register back in its place and continued his letter to Franziska. He told her about the couple who had just visited. "No one can begrudge her this new life," he wrote. And the priest must have felt too much alone again. "If only you were here," he wrote, "or if only I were not so far away."

He sat quietly, then put the pen aside and stood up. There was still time. The weekly mail delivery wasn't until Tuesday. "I'm going for a little walk," he yelled out to the kitchen to the old grumpy woman who had been taking care of the house for his predecessor during all the years he had been a widower.

She had promised to remain until the priest's wife arrived and they could hire maids. "I'm going out for a little walk," he yelled again. She rattled a pot as a sign that she had heard him.

The land lay open, and the sun was setting. There were no people about, but many of them saw the priest walking deep into the landscape. It was so foreign to him, that landscape. Here and there lay plowed fields, but most of the view was filled by grayish, yellowish, meager and unworked stretches, suitable only for raising sheep. And far to the west the sand dunes shone threateningly in all their barrenness. Incredible that people could live on this land. But they fished too, and some people also had said something about trade with Norway. *But still.* Behind his eyes the image of Franziska's Lollandic landscapes was still fixed, whereby he measured the rest.

Later in the evening he continued the letter he had started. He wrote, "I must prepare you for the completely different country you will find here, compared to that you grew up in and have to leave. You will probably discover it both foreign and poor, and without the mildness we hold so dear. How I wish I could have offered you something better. On the other hand there is something grand about the nature here, which we may eventually be able to appreciate. And the parish children are as they are most everywhere, once you get to know them."

As previously mentioned, it was the autumn of 1856 when he arrived—from an adjunct position in a south Sjælland market town, people said. He had to move, people said. Some people heard that he actually was forced to move away. That he couldn't get along with the school's rector and the other teachers. People also said that he had applied lots of places, and that this evidently was the place not deemed by the authorities to be too good for him.

Because this wasn't exactly a highly desired position out here; everyone knew that. The vicarage was dilapidated, and so was the entire parish, really. The priests who had been here before hadn't had much luck with them. Church attendance was generally poor, and morality in the parish followed suit, people had to admit. Over half the children held over the baptismal font were illegitimate.

But it was probably like that lots of places.

Even just the second Sunday the church was more than three-quarters empty for the service. The priest wasn't news anymore. The church was cold, and there was the usual odor of mold and musty clothing. A salty, greasy light pushed its way through the small windowpanes.

The priest's sermon was too long, but that's the way they are, those priests. And then his tone. But there was a small bit of encouragement. Surprisingly enough, he announced the wedding of Stefan and Kirstine. So people had reason to use their smile muscles and to add a couple of glad remarks afterwards.

But it was the singing of the psalms that the priest wondered about most. It was both shrill and drawling at the same time, but not without a certain fervor, he concluded. He wrote in his Sunday letter to Franziska, "Their singing—a shrill falsetto—is a strange contrast to their heavy, plump faces, which during the singing reveal a sincere leaning towards the faith, although their propriety leaves much to be desired."

What got him to write the last sentence, he later discloses in a letter to Franziska, where he tells about the congregation's reaction to the wedding announcement between farmhand Stefan Kristensen and widow Kirstine Mortensdatter. "They make a lovely couple, as I wrote in my last letter. She has a fine breeding one does not expect to see among these villagers, and the curate told me Stefan distinguished himself in the battle of Isted. But when I made the forthcoming marriage public, there was unrest in the church—laughter almost. I peered sternly at the shabby congregation." He continued, "The engaged pair sat in the third row looking modestly downward, but they were also the only ones who displayed the decorum expected in a church during a ceremonious act."

The priest added a few thoughts about the forthcoming marriage and about the congregation's reaction. "It is probably the long anticipation which drew the congregation's unseemly mirth, perhaps pointing at the fact that the pair had been forestalling for some time." He also wrote, "But we are glad that he is going to marry her before it becomes obviously necessary. The latter seems to be the common practice otherwise, here in this place."

But of course, simple well-wishing would not usually produce such a vocal expression as did occur. After the service the priest speculated that perhaps he ought not to have shamed the congregation. Eventually he decided that it probably would have been prudent to wait for a future opportunity. "It is probably best to err on the side of caution in the beginning," he wrote.

After getting this far into the letter, he apologizes to Franziska that this rather unimportant episode has occupied him so much, and that now he has taken up almost an entire letter with it. He ought to be more attentive to her, lying bed-ridden at her parents' home, weak and plagued with anxiety in advance of her third birth. And he wrote,"Every day I pray to God to give you strength, and that it will go better this time. You must also seek faith in our Creator and find solace and patience in your belief in Him." He ended the letter, "I will put the house in order in advance øf your arrival."

It was getting dark. He lit the lamp, and the study felt quite cozy. There was no longer a heavy dampness in the room as there was at first, but he had also told the housekeeper to light all the wood stoves in the house, so it could dry out. She had looked at him as if she had never heard of such profligacy, but she had done as he asked. And it helped. Dampness still seeped out of the wall in the hallway, and there was still mold in the corners, but his papers didn't curl any longer, and the books didn't seem to have been harmed. He reached out for one of them and looked at the spine. That one. That could work just as well as any other.

The farmhand who was walking across the farmyard saw him leaning back in his chair, smoking his pipe and reading a book which he supported on the edge of the desk. *That's the life*, thought the farmhand. He had woken from a rest, and he shuddered in the thin autumn air. He could hear the tenant farmer's wife already starting to milk. Now she was going to be cross, because he was late.

He heard the farmhand kick open the barn door. The priest took out his watch and looked at it. There was much too much leeway in promptness around here.

Around the farms and houses people were starting to talk about the priest in a more suggestive tone. Rumors about him had been circulating the whole time, which was only natural. It wasn't every day they got a new priest, and everyone was interested in knowing what kind of a priest he was. Even a couple of day-laborers could be overheard talking about him while they rested during threshing.

The one said, "That new priest...?"

The other one said, "They say he is pretty grim."

"Yes, that's what they say."

People couldn't find out much about him, and the less they knew, the more they talked. Felt their way. So the talk often got a bit far afield.

"Something seems to have happened back where he came from," someone said one day. But then he quickly added that, "Not because I heard anything, but...."

The strangest thing was that he was still alone. The

housekeeper, who ought to have been the one who knew the most, apparently didn't know any more than anyone else; or else she was just tight-lipped, as usual. Not even her niece, who was a maid at Overgaard Farm, had much to reveal. From that source people got only a single tidbit. The Man asked her one day, "How are things with your aunt? Is she going to stay housekeeper at the vicarage?" And the girl answered that she was going to stay on until the wife arrived. No maids would be hired before then.

When the wife arrived. Okay. Seems kind of strange about that wife.

The tenant farmer had even less substantial news to report. He had barely even spoken with the new priest, even though they lived so close to one another. "It's not like when Pastor Schmidt was here," he said. "Back then we shared many a good Irish coffee any day of the week."

"It can't be good to know so little about a man we have to be among every day," said the curate. The curate was not originally from the area, and he had retained a few curious expressions from the dialect he grew up with. "He notifies me about things by sending me letters. It's quite strange. It's like he doesn't register the other person."

There's one thing everyone agreed about: the priest was stern. And when it came down to it, that was about all anyone really did know for sure. He was stern. But most people still went around enjoying themselves quietly. People still felt they could keep him at arm's length. That softened the situation, and some people even remarked, "Maybe he won't be so bad once we get to know him."

People talked. Something would have to give. No matter who got together to talk, the priest was always brought up.

"The priest passed by here on the road again yesterday morning."

"Really; did he? I wonder where he was going?"

"Hmm –."

In one of his letters to Franziska he wrote, "I have a strange feeling of being watched when I go for my walks. I never encounter anyone; the entire parish seems to consist of deserted fields and sand dunes under a sky larger than I have ever seen. Still I get the impression of something oppressive, as if someone is continually watching me. But when I turn and look, there are no people in the windows of the houses. If it weren't for my agonizing restlessness, I would just stay indoors. I long dearly for the day we are reunited, and this vicarage will become a home."

And then once more he felt the need to warn her. "You will find the villagers here uncommunicative and almost insensitive. I am becoming increasingly convinced that emotions are poorly cultivated in a person raised under such meager and stark conditions as are the case here. Not even death evokes in them observable deep emotions like sadness and grief."

He read through what he had written, and realized that he ought to give reasons for his harsh judgment.

"I recently carried out my first funeral here," he wrote. "It was for a poor, small landholder, who had come to the end, and I was shaken when I saw his two sons of ten and twelve years standing by their father's grave, without revealing even a trace of remorse in their expressions. And almost worse than this was to witness the gladness—enthusiasm even—with which those present dug into the food that the widow had prepared for them afterwards. I heard one of them say to another, 'I wish I were a priest or curate, then I could go to all of the funerals.' And the meal evolved into an event which in its frivolity could have rivaled a Christmas feast or a harvest celebration. I felt the strong urge to shame them," he wrote, "but it didn't seem like the timing was right. I left the house as soon as I could. In your—naturally I ought to say our—region, a get-together after a burial can evolve into a kind of obligated ritual;

but it is always with a foundation of solemnity and a sincere feeling of community. And behind the expressions of common sentiment we recognize the desire to ease for the grieving ones their eventual return to daily life. But this here was something completely different. I also heard the widow say to a relative, 'It is lucky the twins died so young; for how would I have supported them now?' It pained me deeply to hear this, and even more to discover that this insensitivity is so prevalent in the parish—even moreso among those I would have thought better than that. I plan to admonish them in my sermon on Sunday."

It was The Man from Overgaard Farm whom the priest, "would have thought better than that." When the priest left the funeral dinner, The Man caught up with him. They walked together.

"Well that was that," said The Man. "A man in the prime of life, and now the widow is left behind with two half-grown rascals."

The priest didn't respond. "I paid for the funeral, of course," said The Man with self-importance. "And I'll help in the future, if need be."

The priest looked like he was about to say something.

The Man continued, "The two boys are old enough to go out and earn something, and the widow can keep milking for us. But it is still sad."

The priest gathered himself and looked sternly at The Man. "I am disturbed by the insensitivity I witnessed both by the guests and by the relatives," he said.

The Man said that he didn't understand what the priest meant.

The priest said that he hadn't noticed any sincere sadness.

"Sincere sadness," said The Man. "What does that look like?" He chuckled. Then he said, "Sincere sadness is the same as the fear of going hungry. And that was there; of that I can assure you."

The priest looked shocked. He started to say something about seeking solace through grief. Or was it perhaps God who would be sought? He spoke fervently. The Man thought it was rather uninteresting. He changed the subject and asked the priest how it was going with fixing up the vicarage and if his wife would be arriving soon.

The priest was silent the rest of the way. When they parted, the priest said he would mention something about it in his Sunday sermon. He meant the part about grieving.

Then a couple of days later, people heard that the Sunday service was cancelled. They said the priest had been quickly summoned to Lolland. The rector mentioned something to the curate. They would term it a funeral, even though the baby was born much too early, stillborn to the world. The rector hinted that it wasn't the first time. People nodded when they heard it. Perhaps this explained some of the things they had been wondering about.

"Well," said the curate, "the Lord does not spare high nor low."

The priest returned a week later. And he was still alone. A farmer who had an errand in town drove him the last part of the way.

"He seems rather distressed," said the farmer.

The days were getting shorter and the evenings too long—even moreso. In the past the priest had dreamed of having time—time for himself; time to study, and time for new pursuits, which he felt drawn to inwardly, without fully admitting it to himself and definitely not to others.

Now, time settled inside him as restlessness. During the daylight hours he set out into the landscape's infiniteness, and his wanderings in this infiniteness eventually took on the shape of habit, regarding direction, road and path. It was apparently unimportant whether the weather was pleasant or if a gale were driving sand so that it stuck to one's face and hands, or if it were raining so the air was nearly opaque. The priest took his walks—quickly, bent forward, and staring straight ahead, as if he wished to be forgotten, out of sight and without contact with others.

"He looked rather distressed," people said. That expression had spread in the parish recently. But that is how he looked: distressed—and stern; he was still stern.

His first official act after his return was to wed farmhand Stefan Kristensen and widow Kirstine Mortensdatter. The wedding had been postponed due to the priest's absence. Evidently no one had wanted to call for the priest from the neighboring parish to come and perform the ceremony, and for a moment the priest almost convinced himself that the pair actually wanted to be married by him. He was just about to register that feeling of warmth which should exist between a priest and his congregation. Or were they completely indifferent to the postponement? Did they think they could just as well be married one day as another?

There were about ten people in the church and about double that at the party afterwards. The priest was there too, even though, on account of his heavy, sorrowful mind he had naturally declined when first asked. But Stefan Kristensen's slightly older cousin, who had been the host on behalf of the couple, stated with various circumlocutions that it would cast a poor light on the wedding if His Reverence the Priest was not present. The curate attended too, of course.

The priest considered. It was his duty. Despite his melancholy, he had to do his duty; there was no way around it. The cousin, who wasn't quite sure how to fill out the dignity of his role as host, stood there with a weak smile. Then he said, "And the place is familiar with His Reverence. It will be at the building at the bottom of the large sand dune, which His Reverence passes by every day, when His Reverence takes his walks." Now he looked directly at the priest for the first time. The priest fought against his own inner predispositions. Then he nodded in a dignified manner. "Yes, yes of course." He sighed heavily, and the groom's cousin ought to have been able to discern that the priest was obviously making a sacrifice. He repeated, "Yes, yes of course." The cousin thanked him. He added by way of explanation, almost confidentially, "Everyone thinks, despite everything, that it is best the young people get married."

The party was quiet, perhaps already influenced by a certain mood, at least inside the one of the house's small rooms where the priest, the curate, the wedding couple and some of the groom's family were seated on benches. The curate suggested a psalm. The priest gave his speech about the blessing of marriage and duty, and only a few could ascertain that his heart was heavy. The bride probably noticed, he thought. Wasn't there a tacit understanding in her smile and in the way she met his gaze; and shouldn't he interpret as mutual understanding the way her hand more or less coincidentally brushed his, as she passed him a serving dish across the narrow table?

During most of the meal, surrounding the priest was a ring of oppressive silence, which now and then was shaken by laughter and shouts from the next room over—the bedroom, where there was also a table set for the day's occasion. In there the mood was almost growing gay, gradually as the evening progressed, and continually there were men exiting to relieve themselves or cool themselves down. There was a hubbub when they left and when they returned, and also when they stood outside shouting or singing, for it came through the window, which they were able to get opened when the warmth became insufferable.

In general the affair progressed rather blamelessly and properly. Only one older man, nearly geriatric, who obviously had had too much schnapps, created a disturbance. When the room was later cleared, and dancing began, and the priest realized it was time for him to leave the party, he saw the old man dancing with the bride and taking liberties with her that were far past the limit of seemliness. This displeased him. He cleared his throat loudly, but the sound was drowned out in outbursts of laughter and jovial remarks from the other wedding guests. He rose demonstratively and walked towards the exit. The groom's cousin, who rushed after him, and who probably noticed the priest's disapproval, explained apologetically, that it was just old Jørgen, whom the couple were going to support in his old age. But with his thin, forbearing laughter, the cousin was not able to soften the appalled expression suddenly spreading across the priest's face. Without a word the priest took his riding cape and made his way out to the carriage, to be driven home by the tenant farmer's hand.

The farmhand, who had become talkative from the festivities, attempted a couple of times to get a conversation started with the priest, but with no success. "That was that wedding," he said. "Everyone thinks it's best that they have the blessing of the church, as they say, even at this point." And later, with a voice slurred by either emotion or tipsiness, "She's the type you could never get mad at." The priest didn't respond. He didn't even say goodnight when they stopped in the courtyard. Silently he stepped down from the carriage and quickly went inside.

It was late that night before the priest calmed down—if he ever did calm down completely. For hours he sat in his study, before making his way to the bedroom with a candle towards daybreak.

The next day was quite extraordinary here. Under a high blue sky the air was still, clear and transparent. It made the distant houses and dunes appear closer, as if one suddenly had lifted binoculars up to one's eyes. The sounds were also different, not shrouded in wind, but just themselves, whether it was a carriage on the road or the continual gurgle of water in the creek downhill from the vicarage. And then there were these nearly unnoticeable wisps of warmth in the midst of the cold season, which made one stop in the middle of an activity and relax muscles that otherwise had been in a kind of defensive position against the increasing cold. There was an ease and a peacefulness which spread to everyone, with the possible sole exception of the priest. In the afternoon he strode at usual down the wheel track to the west, but not just as usual, for there was a perceptible violence in his movements, and it was almost as if he stumbled a couple of times. And suddenly, just before he reached the two houses out there, where the wedding celebration recently had ended, people could see that he changed his mind, paused a second, and then changed course northward, continuing towards the dunes. It wasn't until several hours later that he was seen returning home. Mads Jensen, who came plodding towards him, greeted him politely and expected a few words in return, but the priest just kept going, as if he hadn't even noticed him.

Otherwise it was the kind of day when people stood and chatted.

When the priest came home he went straight to the kitchen and told the housekeeper to send for the curate. He wanted him to stop by right after school. The woman nodded crossly. She would. Food was prepared; she said it had been waiting for quite some time. "Will the priest have something to eat? Or had he had too much the prior evening? How about a cup of coffee then? Not that either?" She poured herself a small amount into a saucer and sucked it down before she went to get her shawl.

The Man had finished his midday rest and had gotten people working. He sat with the last of his coffee in the kitchen when there was a knock on the door.

"Yes," he shouted. It was the curate.

"Oh, it's you?" said The Man.

The curate greeted him and he didn't look too happy. "It's the priest," he said. "Looks like he's figured something out."

The Man made a motion with his hand that the curate should sit down. He looked around, to remind himself where his maid was. Then he said, "You can take a cup and saucer down from the shelf over there. There's coffee in the kettle."

The curate got his coffee and was offered a hunk of bread as well. With powdered sugar, naturally. The Man had a sweet tooth and was always generous about offering to others.

"So he has, has he?" said The Man.

"I am afraid he might cause some trouble," said the curate.

The Man thought about it. Then he said, "He doesn't have to discover anything. He seems to be a pretty sensible sort."

The curate looked doubtful. "I think it was at the wedding party that he started to get suspicious."

The Man looked up, interested. "Was the priest at the party?" He laughed. "Did they invite the priest to the party?" He shook his head. "That Kirstine!"

The curate tried to smile along with him. Then he became uneasy again and serious. "That was probably the dumbest thing they could have done. The priest has gotten very strange."

The Man chuckled again. "How bad could it be?" He became thoughtful, then he continued. "He is a sensible sort, isn't he?" and then he added, mostly for himself, "But it might become necessary to talk to him and straighten him out."

Someone came walking down the hallway from the rooms. You could hear it was someone wearing shoes. The Man indicated to the curate that they ought to change the subject. The curate's expression indicated: *Naturally*.

The Man said aloud, "It's more important that we get the threshing done, than to have him sitting and nodding off in the sun."

The wife entered, nodding with a quarter-smile to the curate. The Man said, "The curate is upset that Kristen wasn't in school on Thursday. That was the day we were threshing, and Kristen had enough to do tossing sheaves down to the farmhands. That is what we hired him for."

It was obvious that this was none of the wife's business. She continued on through to the scullery, looked around, came back, and then her footsteps faded into the recesses of the house.

The Man asked, "Has the priest actually said anything?"

The curate said that he had been summoned to the vicarage right after school. The housekeeper had come and said that the priest wanted to speak with him.

"When I arrived, he stood there looking rather flustered," he said. "It was as if he weren't sure what he had summoned me for."

He continued, "In a way he seemed like a normal person. Then he gave me his hand and asked me to sit down. It was embarrassing." The curate shook his head regretfully. "He was ill at ease. He sat down and started to page through some papers. Then he got up and went to the bookshelf, came back and sat in his chair again.

"Then the priest suddenly started talking about psalms."

"About psalms?" The Man repeated.

"Yes, about psalms. About psalms for next Sunday and psalms for the Sunday after." It had made the curate wonder, because usually he was just notified about the numbers. "But after all, it might not be such a bad thing to talk about," he said.

And the priest did talk. About psalms, about singing, and about some of those newfangled psalms that were starting to work their way into the services—by that man Grundtvig. The curate didn't really have anything to add, so he just nodded when it seemed appropriate. Then the priest stopped talking, as if he were thinking about something. That made the curate feel rather uncomfortable.

"But then he started up again, the priest. About the psalms.

What he had already just said.

"Then he added, 'That's all I wanted; just to talk about the psalms.'"

"I got up to leave," said the curate. "I thought we were done. The priest was still acting a bit unusual. As if the entire time he had been thinking about something else. And then he laughed."

"He laughed?" asked The Man.

"Something like that," said the curate. "A bit shy." And then he told how the priest started to talk about how difficult it was to come to a new area. How there were so many things one had to get used to.

"I was feeling quite uncomfortable all over," said the curate, "because it seemed like now what this was all about was going to come out. The priest said, 'You have to do so many things that are different than what you are used to.' I said I understood. I said I felt the same way when I arrived here forty years ago."

Then the priest started to talk at length about the previous priest's handwriting. Sometimes he was having trouble reading the church records.

"I said I couldn't really understand that. I never had difficulty in reading Pastor Schmidt's writing in all the years he lived here."

The priest took the church register out and paged through it. Then he pointed at "Maren Nielsdatter."

"Maren Nielsdatter?" said The Man, quite surprised. "What does Maren Nielsdatter have to do with any of this?"

"It was just a coincidence that he pointed at her name," said the curate, "just to start. I said that it said Maren Nielsdatter, and he said that he could see that too, but that that wasn't one of the hard ones."

The curate paused. Then he said, "Then the priest pointed at Jesper Antonsen, and he said it was not at all obvious he wrote "Jørgen" there."

"What did you say to that?"

"I tried not to say anything, but then he asked me directly, and I had to answer," said the curate.

The Man muttered, "Then what did you say?"

"What else could I say but that it said "Jesper" there," said the curate, who then had to explain to the priest some things about Jesper Antonsen, like that he had been named Jesper Hulsig, because he came from there, like his brother Jørgen, who also was named Hulsig. And that they had lived together for a while.

The priest had said, "Now I understand. And so that is Jesper's widow, …" and there had been a heartfelt hope in his voice but the curate had to tell him that Jesper had not been married.

"And then what?" asked The Man. He was obviously not satisfied with the curate's efforts.

"Nothing," said the curate. "He just looked kind of stiff." Then I left.

"It wasn't good," the curate added, quietly. "He had been hoping, the poor man." After a pause, the curate continued, "I was wondering if maybe someone ought to go and talk to him about it."

The Man shook his head. "I'm not doing that," he said. "There's no reason to."

The curate looked as disagreeable as he could allow himself.

"He'll calm down soon enough," said The Man. "What's done is done. He must be able to see that. He is a sensible sort, after all, when it comes down to it."

And that's the way it seemed. The next morning the priest took his usual walk out to the dunes. And yet—it wasn't entirely the usual walk. Someone saw him go up to one of the houses and go inside. Stefan was at sea, but the others were home. The priest was inside a good while. They must have found something to talk about, or maybe the priest ate some leftovers from the wedding. Kirstine had always been good at calming people down, and that was probably just what he needed. Most people found out that he had been acting strangely the day before. Some people said he had berated the curate, but the curate denied that.

People waited tensely. When the priest came into view again, he hiked out to the dunes and came back a roundabout way, almost jogging, as if he both wanted to hurry and at the same time postpone his arrival home.

The neighbor's wife said to Kirstine, "Looks like you had a visit by the pastor."

Kirstine put down her cup. "I did," she said. "He stopped in."

"What was it he wanted?" asked the neighbor's wife with a touch of annoyance in her voice.

Kirstine just smiled and shook her head. "Nothing. He just stopped by."

The following days no one saw the priest. Church service on Sunday was cancelled. The priest was sick, people said.

In his next letter to Franziska he wrote neither about the wedding, nor about the curate's visit, nor about his illness. "The days here pass, each one like the next, and nothing much happens worth mentioning." And yet it still feels like an inner rebellion is seeping up from the paper. Without explanation he wrote, "It makes me almost doubt that I am surrounded by Christian folk. They cooperate around lies and deception, if there is something they don't want others to know."

Time passed. The months changed, sand blew across newly-sown fields, rain fell over sparse, mature grain, and in between, there were days so different that you could tell everything might have been less stark if the Lord had willed it so. But even the harshness had its rewards. Once in a while a ship went aground on the coast, and now and then some treasures sloshed around in the breakers. If one were lucky, one could collect some things before the beach sheriff got to them to auction them off. There were a few advantages of a harsh environment.

The priest gave his sermons; he baptized, he buried, he confirmed and he married—just as one would expect from a priest. But he was distant, and he excused himself whenever he was invited to an occasion or to a get-together after a church event. But he took his walks daily in the parish's most deserted, least populated area, and we had our daily chats about him.

"It's a bit much, the way the priest still visits old Jørgen," one person said.

"Pretty soon people will think there were no other old people in the parish," said another.

"I wonder if his wife is coming soon," people also said.

The priest's wife was still a frequent topic of conversation. She came up every time people discussed his walks. "She can't just stay away like this for years. This is the fifth holy day he has to celebrate by himself, poor man," said the tenant farmer's wife. "No wonder he's acting so restless. It would be good for him if she came soon." Eventually that became a common remark in the region: "It would be good for the priest if his wife came soon."

But Franziska was still too weak, both she and her parents reported in their letters to the priest—at least too weak for the tiresome journey to this harsh and inhospitable part of the country. Franziska's letters therefore came mostly to be about potential priest vacancies to the east. And he could apply, even though he had only been in his position a very short time. "But if you mention my illness and the climate where you are now, they will understand," she wrote. Now and then her letters also contained a little admonition. "Why didn't you apply for the position in Vordingborg which you recently mentioned?" Or, for example, "The rector was here for a birthday the other day, and he said there are several posts on Sjælland which you would have a good chance of getting if you applied. So much time has passed now. But maybe you have applied already?" she added hopefully.

The priest didn't answer the last question. Not directly in any case. But in a later letter he wrote that he felt it was too soon to think about seeking a new post. He didn't expand on this, but Franziska took it to mean that his opinion was established out of consideration for the congregation. "You could also permit yourself to think about your and my own happiness," she wrote. He didn't respond to that either. His letters to Franziska were increasingly marked by routine, and there were obviously subjects he wished to avoid completely. He wasn't planning for her arrival anymore. He wrote very little about the future, and not only did his letters become less descriptive regarding his experiences, but even his descriptions of the daily occurrences in the parish were fewer. Something quite out of the ordinary would have to occur before he found it worth retelling, like the Sunday when he wrote in his weekly letter, "Today there was a baptism, but not one of those it is a pleasure to carry out. It was Ane Petersdatter, who now for the second time in just the two years since I have been situated here, should have a baby baptized; and for the father she could only say it was a nameless salesman. This time one from central Jylland."

"Immorality flourishes here on this poor soil," he added.

The Man never actually had a real conversation with the priest. Not that The Man wasn't present at church service once in a while. "When one owns the church, one ought to show up now and then to keep an eye on the property," he said. And he used nearly the same phrase that time when he came out of the house, out there by the sand dunes, just as the priest came by on his daily walk. "This is ours from the old days," he said, making a movement with his hand which encompassed not just the two houses but also the endless landscape and everything it and the houses contained. No more words passed between them that day. Other times they met on official business, but over and above what had to be said in the presence of others, the priest was an object of silent indifference on the part of The Man. "Wasn't I right?" he asked the curate one day. "He won't be stirring up anything." He laughed.

The curate agreed, but on the inside he was still a bit sad, thinking of the miserable priest and his behavior.

The priest was still the main object of daily observation and gossip. Perhaps people didn't wonder as much as before, but they still talked and confirmed the conjectures they arrived at together. The priest couldn't have been completely ignorant of this, but he seemed to take no notice of it. He took his walks in broad daylight, and no one tired of exchanging remarks about these idyllic walks of his out to the dunes. "He is going to make old Jørgen into a saint before long." And regarding the priest's wife, who still had not shown herself: "Maybe there is no wife," some people posited, but then there were the letters that still came with regularity. People asked the housekeeper, but that didn't amount to anything. She stayed his housekeeper, even though her legs could barely hold out; and she was still as balky and uncommunicative as she had always been. They had also hired a girl housemaid now, but what help was that? She came from outside the parish and didn't know anyone.

While people talked, time continued to pass. And people noticed that the priest's sermons changed. Later, it was hard to say exactly when it happened, but people started saying that his sermons weren't so preachy and direct as people remembered them from when he first came, and definitely not as understandable. It was as if they weren't meant for the congregation, but that he was first and foremost preaching for himself, revealing his inner complaints. Yes, complaints. His sermons were complaining. The churchgoers talked mostly about that. "He seemed so tortured today, that poor priest."

Some people even said, "There goes old Jørgen's priest,"

when he walked past. People shook their heads, and gave a few regretful sighs, if they didn't show a hint of a smile instead. "That poor man; he is wasting away."

When the priest saw his reflection in the mirror, he noticed this too. He had become even more gaunt. He could also tell from his clothes, when he thought about it, but it was most obvious in his face. And he had gotten weathered. Almost like a small landholder.

"The Dune Priest," some people started to call him, but the name didn't stick. Some of the wives had thought that up. They earned a bit extra in the fall months by planting marram grass in the dunes, and there was rarely a day when they didn't see him. Sometimes he stopped at a place in the last row of dunes and stood there looking out over the ocean. There was always something to look at, whether it was stormy or quiet. But often it seemed that he was just looking at the beach. These were times when the weather was pleasant and the boats had been to sea and were just coming in, and people were bringing in the catch.

One day Stefan said, "I heard you met the priest out in the dunes." Kirstine said, "He asked me if he could carry the one basket of fish for me."

Stefan asked, "What did you say?"

"I said thank you."

"Was that really necessary? Isn't there enough gossip as it is?"

"Dear God," said Kirstine. "That poor man." And she put the food on the table and called for Jørgen, who was standing outside, trying to be useful by sawing a bit of driftwood into reasonable lengths. "I also heard," said Stefan, gesturing with his head in the direction of old Jørgen, who was slipping off his clogs by the door, "I also heard that he often goes outside when the priest comes here."

"That's a lie." She swung the pan with the fried fish over onto the table. Stefan sat with his mouth clenched, looking at her. Old Jørgen, who had sidled onto the bench, sat happily, looking with his blinking, old man's eyes from the one to the other.

Kirstine put the potato pot on the table, in such a way that you could ascertain her mood. "Go and eat," she said. "Aren't you going to eat?" Evidently she also said,, "Don't you think I have enough to deal with already with the two of you?" But it seemed as if only the old man heard it. He gave her a friendly slap on the rear.

Another day—and this was after some time had passed—half a year or so—another day, Stefan stopped by the vicarage to report that old Jørgen was dead.

The priest couldn't hide his surprise. It had only been a couple of days since he had last seen him.

"Well, it did happen kind of suddenly," explained Stefan. "It was when he came in for lunch he collapsed. It was an easy death." Stefan hadn't been home; he had been at sea and wasn't home until later in the afternoon. But with help from the neighbors' wives, Kirstine got the old man dragged into bed and set aright.

The priest mumbled something inaudible. "Yes," said Stefan automatically, "we shall all pass that way."

There was a moment's pause. Stefan couldn't quite hide his aversion. The priest most likely could tell.

Then he was the priest again. He questioned about a death certificate. No, the doctor hadn't been there, but the coroner would come the day after tomorrow, so that would be three days since. The priest asked about a burial, and they agreed on a time when the coffin would be transported from the house out there to the church. At ease again, the priest said good-bye to Stefan—there didn't seem to be any need for comforting words. If one didn't know better, one might have interpreted the priest's hint of a good-bye smile as a smile tinged with understanding and not just as an expression of pity.

Still the death must have affected him deeply, so deeply that his feelings took on a physical manifestation. In any case, it seemed to have affected his notation of old Jørgen's death in the church records. The priest's otherwise sure hand evidently abandoned him. The given name is nearly illegible; it would appear to read *Jesper* and not *Jørgen*; but then he pulled himself together. *Antonsen* is written with clear, sharp letters; the date as well.

But at the funeral the priest was again strangely unsteady, speaking low and brief; and he didn't touch on any personal details at all. There were quite a few people there. Old Jørgen had evidently been well-liked, judging from the crowd.

Even The Man was there. The priest said, "No, thanks," to taking part in the coffee afterwards. He walked straight home to the vicarage, and for a few days no one saw him.

There was a good turnout in the church the following Sunday. About twenty or so were there, moaning their way through the psalms, and bearing witness to the priest's return to how they knew him when he first arrived: a stern priest, servant of the Lord, teacher of the congregation, their guide and disciplinarian. Especially the latter. "The priest pulled himself together today," they said afterwards. "Yes, he did."

Now it is 1859. Barely three years had passed.

They talked a lot about it. The priest was returning to normal. More aggressive, sterner with others, more resolute. "He has a strong will, that he does."

"It's been some time since we've seen the priest," said the people who lived out by the dunes. "We have to go to church if we want to see him," they smiled. "Yes, that's right."

His letters started to have more content. He told Franziska

about a beaching, where only two sailors made it to land, both so exhausted that they died shortly after he made it to the house where they had been brought. And he started to write about vacant priestly posts that he could apply for. "Finally," he wrote, "I can nearly glimpse the day when we will be together again." He writes very indirectly and implicitly that he feels he has been liberated from a great burden.

His restlessness has not disappeared, but it shows up in different outlets than before. He gets difficult. He completes a complaint over the school building's increasing state of disrepair; he writes to the county manager to make him aware of the intolerable conditions regarding the shipwreck auctions; he complains about the condition of the roads; and in the continuing conflict between the dune commission and the farmers he takes the side of the commission, denouncing the farmers who let their cows graze in the dunes, thereby destroying the plantings meant to reduce sand drift. Apparently he was not aware that it was mostly The Man's livestock grazing out there—even if some people thought that that was precisely why he took the position he took. They also thought it was not just several year's pent-up energy that was being expressed now, but that the priest had initiated a kind of war with the influential people in the parish. A kind of revenge perhaps.

"Revenge?"

"Well, yes." People would have to get used to it.

The curate and The Man from Overgaard spoke about it. "He is causing me trouble," said The Man. "I always said he was not the enjoyable sort."

The curate did not argue.

"Do you think his wife will be coming soon?" some people asked one another. They tried the housekeeper. "So, is there anything new about the priest's wife?" Other people thought the priest was seeking a new post. No one could say that he had settled in, like they might have expected, and definitely not among the common people. Hadn't he also been traveling? Hadn't he been away a couple of times?

A few months passed.

People got used to the outbursts of aggression, and to the stern sermons and the uncertainty.

A few more months passed. And didn't it seem as if the priest's decisiveness and energy was subsiding? As if something melancholic had again planted itself in his behavior?

One person said, "Now the priest has started up those hiking trips again, as they say."

"Well, well."

"He passed by yesterday and also the day before."

The other one said, "So he did." They stood there quietly, lost together in thought. Then they nodded to one another and each went their own way.

The curate and The Man met at an affair. "Now we recognize our priest again," said The Man. "The other one was getting a bit tiresome." The curate nodded. So the priest returned to how he had been most of the time. "Poor man," mumbled the curate. But The Man was already starting to talk about something else.

"I have just come by to ask if perhaps Stefan would be able to stop over one day and repair the stairs to the attic," said the priest. "It needs a couple of new treads."

He stood just inside the door, slightly stooped under the low ceiling.

"Stefan isn't home," said Kirstine flatly.

"He's at sea," interrupted the neighbor's wife. She sat at the table sucking a bit of coffee through a sugar cube. "He always goes out in weather like this," she added. She could also have said, "Everyone knows that." She glanced with interest from the one to the other.

The priest mumbled something about not paying so much

attention to the weather. Kirstine asked if the pastor might stay for a cup of coffee, and the neighbor's wife slid further along the bench beneath the window. Now she was stuck there and good.

Kirstine poured—also for the neighbor's wife, who reached out her cup. Kirstine said, "I will be sure to tell him about it."

It got quiet while each of them sat thinking. Then the priest started to tell Marie—the neighbor's wife—that there were so many things in the vicarage that needed tending to, and that he didn't have anyone to take care of them. He wasn't very handy himself, and he couldn't continually monopolize the tenant farmer's farmhand; the tenant farmer would start complaining. He sat there a moment, thinking evidently that he ought to explain a bit further. "So it would be more logical to hire someone for this—and to pay what it costs," he said.

Marie understood. There must be a lot to do in such a large vicarage. And when one is alone there too. That must be hard, for sure. "And Stefan is used to doing a bit of everything," she said. She cast a glance at Kirstine, who was standing with her cup in hand again, over by the stove. "Why don't you sit, Kirstine; we're not strangers," she laughed. Kirstine sat down.

"I don't know what I would do without Stefan," said the priest.

Marie mumbled that she understood, and she started talking about what a strong and smart worker he was, that Stefan. And what a clever wife he had too. They sure kept things together.

Marie's unprovoked chuckle was the only thing audible for a while.

Then the priest said, "I just hope Stefan doesn't lose patience with me. I have a bad habit of changing my mind; then I have to come and change what we agreed upon all the time. Kirstine knows about that."

She did. And from Marie's expression it was obvious that she did as well.

Then they sat quietly drinking their coffee. Eventually

Marie said, "I guess I'd better get back to it." She gestured that she wanted to slide out. The priest stood up so she could get by.

"I had better be going too," he said. He thanked for the coffee and repeated his message to Stefan. He nodded good-bye and left. Shortly afterwards, Marie left too.

The priest continued out into the dunes in the completely transparent and stagnant weather. The ocean lay spread like a blue silken cloth, and farther out the boats were visible. It would be a few more hours before they came in with their catch.

He sat down at that spot in the dunes where he tended to take a rest. Not because there was a particularly good view right there. All he could see was dune. And then the silence, which was probably even more apparent on a day like that.

There were other days when Marie wasn't so lucky to be sitting there slurping coffee and chatting with Kirstine when the priest came by, and when she didn't think that she could just stop over on an errand.

So she watched; and sometimes she checked the clock. And when she was out and met people, she had a hundred ways she could nudge the conversation over towards the priest. Sometimes she said, "I wonder what they talk about when they sit in there like that for hours, waiting for Stefan." "It must be hard for Kirstine to be interrupted like that all the time in what she's doing," was another of Marie's comments that usually was preceded by a knowing shake of the head. Most often she ended this way: "But maybe he is just sitting there dejected, waiting for Stefan to come home."

That about the dejected expression—that they were agreed on—again. "It seems like he's changed," some people said. "Like he's straightened out."

"He certainly is sober in any case; you have to give him that," they said, when they thought they should say something nice.

He tended to his duties, in the way such things needed

tending to. There wasn't much you could say about him. His sermons were definitely not very understandable, but there weren't very many that came to hear them anyway. And his restlessness chased him out on those walks. It was as if he only wanted to be out by the dunes—or near them, you could say.

Kirstine was in the dunes quite a bit as well, people said. But she had good reason to be: a couple of sheep that needed to be moved, some fish that needed to be brought in from the boats, or some driftwood that needed carrying home for fuel.

As time passed, people eventually gained trust in the new girl at the vicarage, and so it was she who mentioned one day that it had been quite a while since any letter had come from "over there." And the priest wasn't sending out letters any more, she said.

The Man said, "That's strange." He also said, "I wonder if something happened."

The explanation spread with its usual speed through the parish: the priest's wife was dead. Now people could remember that he had left on a trip just after last Whitsuntide, but back then, people figured that he was out seeking a new post. So that was probably when. And that was also back before he starting going on his walks again. "Oh, so that was why…."

More than a year passed. The priest looked older and more hardened. Stefan also had gotten older, marked by labor. Only Kirstine looked unchanged, people said to one another now and again. She still looked young and pretty, slim and delicate, as if she didn't belong here. And she never did have any children, not all the time since back then when people wondered how it could be so; but then it didn't happen after all. Sometimes they said that Kirstine could be the new housekeeper at the vicarage, since the old one couldn't do it anymore. It was The Man who mentioned it first. They could move up there, she and Stefan, he had said. His suggestion amused him quite a bit it seemed. Or perhaps he actually was upset or a little bitter. People talked about it. He owned the house out there. He had also mentioned that he needed a place for his present farm maid to live. She was going to marry a farmhand who The Man had brought into the parish recently, and he was known for taking good care of his old workers.

But it remained an amused suggestion. Nothing happened, and certainly nothing worth telling about. There were no special occasions on which the time period could be hung. Time just passed, and the priest eventually just became a part of the landscape here—or maybe more accurately: of the nature here.

When he walked past out on the road, people still might say, "There he goes; that poor tortured man." But they said it in the same way they would have said, "It's windy," or "So, it's raining again." And when someone met him out there on the road, there wasn't a hidden smile in the corner of their mouth.

Actually, people had started to feel sorry for him.

The Man with the Cross
A STORY ABOUT SALVATION

The evening had advanced far enough so the sun reached the crest of the dunes. It hung there big and red, almost flowing from the light cool haze drifting in from the ocean, refreshing in the lungs after the hot afternoon.

Anna Katrina was running late. As usual she had been at Stina's house, helping to get hooks ready for the group of fisherman that Henrik had been a part of before the accident. The others still let her benefit from helping a little, and especially now, when Marie was about due and couldn't do so much. No one could deny that Anna Katrina didn't earn her keep. Marie was Lars's wife, and no one had expected she would go through that again. Stina was kind of shocked. She and Jørgen were past the age where such a thing would be up for discussion, and she thought that Marie ought to be as well.

In this way they sat and chatted while they prepared the hooks. "Men are not always the way they should be," sighed Stina, hoping that her sigh, despite everything, might cheer up Anna Katrina, who hadn't yet gotten over her loss.

Stina had also tried several times to get Anna Katrina to "come to us" as she put it, but she wasn't pushy. One day Anna Katrina would have to see for herself that it was a punishment from the Lord that Henrik was the only one who didn't make it in, that day they capsized in the breakers. But Stina hadn't dared to say it that way directly, not yet. The evangelist had not been quite so considerate, but Anna Katrina was totally beside herself back then, and maybe what he had said didn't quite register.

There was a lot of work for Anna Katrina and Stina to get done today, and Stina's two youngest had also pitched in quite a bit. It had been difficult work, almost unpleasant. The heat was oppressive, even though they were sitting in the shade. The bait stunk, and they had just barely managed to complete all of the lines and get them down to the boat in the wheelbarrow by the time the men were ready, lower on the beach. The afternoon had passed by the time Anna Katrina and her baby finally made it home. And then the cow had to be pulled in, and milked, and the baby had to nurse, and she needed some nourishment, too.

It was almost nine by the time Anne Katrina went out to bring in the clothes. She stood for a moment by the gable, taking a deep breath. She could hear the baby whimpering inside, but even more than that, she heard the emptiness of the house.

Anna Katrina sat down on the narrow bench, closed her eyes and leaned her head back against the house.

It sure was quiet, even with the baby's hesitant cries, and the silence felt so awful. During the day she could steel herself and keep from thinking, free herself from her inner world, and steer all of Stina's talk towards trivialities. But now, tired and lonely, she was in no shape to hide from the emptiness that poured over her or poured out of her. It was hard to tell where all of the emptiness and hopelessness was coming from.

"The Lord's punishment," was what the evangelist had said. She didn't realize it until long afterwards. The Lord's punishment.

Well maybe Henrik did used to be pretty wild. But that was before they had eyes for one another, and before he had a share in the boat. That was years ago. *Years* ago.

"The Lord's punishment!"

And it wasn't just the evangelist who might say something like that. It wasn't just him with his "death brings all to judgment." Wasn't that the same thing they all went around saying to one another? "Death brings all to judgment." Wasn't that the warning behind all of Stina's little sighs?

When she was together with other people, Anna Katrina was strong. It was only when she was alone at home that her sorrow surfaced. But tiredness could be good. It sapped the energy that she otherwise might have used to lose faith completely.

"You should come to us," Stina had said.

Anne Katrina heard the baby's whimpering again from inside the house. But still she remained sitting there with her eyes closed in a kind of half-doze, gliding in and out of a languid contentment, devoid of thoughts.

It probably didn't last more than a few minutes. She couldn't ignore any longer the baby, which was crying in its cradle, the dishes, which were waiting in the scullery, and the clothes, which needed to be brought in from the line.

They said, "It's also important to stay active."

She opened her eyes, started to stretch, just like a well-rested baby stretches when it wakes up after a long, peaceful night. Then she stiffened, not just her muscles stiffened, but also her breathing stiffened, her thoughts stiffened, and she thought an eternity passed before she not only saw, but also took in, what had given her such a start.

Up on the dune, out of the remains of the deep, red disc of sun, Jesus Christ came walking down towards her, dragging his cross.

The sound she had just heard must have been her own scream. With effort she got up from the bench and ran, or something that resembled running, because her one clog fell off, around the corner of the house and in through the door. She bolted it, and stood there for a moment, panting. Then she went down on one knee next to the cradle, hid her face in the comforter and tried to calm the baby which now was wailing, and tried to calm herself with a hodgepodge of half-forgotten prayers and psalms.

After a little while she returned to her senses. Her heart wasn't beating quite as hard. She must have seen a vision or maybe she was just dreaming. Just like when she used to dream about Henrik every night, and then when she woke up, she thought he was still lying next to her in bed, or that he was just out in the kitchen and was about to come in and wake her. This must have been something like that.

"Easy, easy," she said to herself. "Okay, okay, calm down," she said to the baby. She picked it up, rocked it in her arms, and started humming a little song for it. She did all she could, to focus her concentration on the baby, but most of her attention was still tense, listening. She should go outside and convince herself there was no one there. She could at least look out the window, she said to herself.

But she stayed kneeling in front of the cradle, with the baby in her arms, trying to lose herself in the soothing humming.

She was still kneeling there, when there was a knock at the door.

Of course it wasn't Jesus, trudging over the dune out there on that particular summer evening.

It was Mathias Jensen.

He was a painter, a landscape painter, and he had decided to use part of this summer to paint the ocean. Paint the ocean, and the people by the ocean. He wasn't that skilled yet with the people, so that was why, at his professor's recommendation, he had decided to live for a while in a fishing village, to try to work human figures and daily human activities into his compositions of wild and unpredictable nature. The professor had said. "You don't want to end up just painting maritime scenes."

It wasn't idyllic Skagen he had dreamed of, not women in white on a sun-drenched beach, not charming fishermen, who were there foremost to pose for artists. No. What he envisioned for himself was people at war with the elements, the person who survived despite the powers of nature. It was the ocean as people's fate he wanted to depict.

The professor had said to his students, "Paint rye bread and sweat." To Mathias he said, "Paint people who just barely don't knuckle under."

Now, Mathias was really exhausted. His day had gone all wrong. To begin with, when he was at the train station he had asked for directions to the wrong place, or maybe at some point he had just remembered it wrong, and after several hours walk down a rutted wheel track, he had come to a little clump of four houses, scrunched together behind a dune, where there wasn't much hospitality to be gained with the old matrons, their stooped men, and their saggy animals. And of course there was no inn there, or any other place where someone could get lodging for a reasonable price.

Finally, one of the wives had taken pity on him and offered him a meal and explained that if he just went three-quarters of a mile further north, there he would meet people who were used to strangers coming through. If he walked along the beach he couldn't miss it. She even accompanied him down to the beach and pointed him in the right direction, just to make sure he understood everything she had explained. He spoke a little differently, so it was hard to tell.

So he had walked along the beach, and it had gotten more and more tiring, walking in the sand. His duffel bag and his shoulder bag felt increasingly heavy to carry, and the strings that he had used as straps to carry his easel dug into his skin. And it wasn't even interesting to walk there. The ocean was an infinite, lifeless, flat surface supporting the motionless sky. There was not one ripple, not even so much as the echo of a wave lapping.

Maybe if there had been a bit of shade. It wasn't bearable until the last little bit, when some coolness started drifting in from the water.

He took a short rest and ate his last bit of bread. If only he had had something to drink.

It was thirst that spurred him to keep going. Finally he saw the boat launch up ahead. The boats were pulled up on the beach and a couple of sheds stood up by the foot of the dunes. But it was deserted. The town must be behind the dunes.

He started to make his way across the dunes, diagonally up and over. There was the town, if you could call it that. About twenty or so houses spread randomly and connected just as randomly by roads and paths. Mostly low, whitewashed buildings, but there was also one a bit larger in red brick with a tile roof.

He trudged along a path that led to the closest house. It stood by itself a bit south of the village. A few of his fellow students probably would have found it picturesque. A longish, low, grayish house with a heavily thatched roof. A couple of small windows up under the eave wouldn't let in much light, but that was also the back he was looking at, the west side, which needed to be as protected as possible.

Some laundry was hanging on a clothesline south of the house. It looked like there were kids—little kids.

He walked around the house to get to the front. There, it was like a totally different house, whitewashed and with regular windows in the living area. There were a couple of potted plants, and both the windows and the door looked freshly painted.

He walked up and knocked.

No one answered. He knocked again.

He checked the door, but it was bolted. He knocked again.

He was about to give up when he noticed some sounds coming from inside. It sounded like a baby crying, but there was also an adult's voice.

He knocked again, louder. Then he heard someone coming, then some anxious sounds, then a bolt being opened, and carefully the door opened a crack.

A youngish, frightened woman stared out at him. She was holding an infant as if she were guarding it.

He took off his hat and started to say something.

The woman got a strange, relieved look on her strikingly pale face.

He told her how he had gotten lost and that he had been out walking all day, and he asked if she might be able to tell him where the inn was. But first he would be so thankful if she could give him something to drink. Just a bit of water, he was so incredibly thirsty.

She hadn't said a word, yet. Now she disappeared for a moment and came back with a ladle. She must have put the baby back in the cradle. She motioned that he could follow her out to the well, and she pumped the water up and passed it to him. "There you go," she said.

He drank long and fervently. "Thank you," he said, handing back the ladle. Then he asked again, "Can you tell me where the inn is?"

"The inn?" She looked at him surprised. "There's no inn here."

He started telling her that they had told him he just needed to get to this place, but she repeated that they didn't have an inn. "Why would there be an inn here," she said, almost angrily.

"Okay, a hotel, then. Isn't there a hotel or a hostel?"

She shook her head as if she had never heard the words before. She turned to go back inside. He said, "Isn't there anyplace where I could pay for lodging, someone who rents out a room where I could buy something to eat?"

She thought for a second. Then she shook her head. She had never heard of anything like that. Strangers never came through here. She turned again to go back in.

He hurried to say, "Who lives in the big, red house at the center of town?"

She looked at him, surprised. No one lives there. That was

TABOR, the Evangelical meetinghouse.

But wasn't there even a baker or a grocery where a person might be able to get a room?

She shook her head. She was still standing as if she were holding a baby close to her in a kind of self-defense position, and it was obvious she wanted to end the conversation as soon as possible. But by asking a few more questions he was able to delay her a bit longer.

How far was it to the nearest inn? She didn't know. How far was it to the nearest market-town? A mile or so. "Your husband isn't home yet?" She shook her head. How about a shipyard? She looked at him, surprised. Not around here, anyway. There was no shipyard here. "What do you think I should do?" She didn't know.

He paused. "It's been really hot today," he said. She agreed with him, and again, turned to go inside.

He asked, "Would you allow me to sleep in your barn?" He nodded in the direction of the part of the wing that held the animals, and where there was probably something that served as a barn.

She looked terrified. Mumbled something about what would people think of her. He said, "You can just tell your husband that I was so tired I couldn't go another step."

"Of course I would pay you for it," he added. "And if I could get a little something to eat I would pay for that too."

"Please?" he asked, when she didn't answer. He asked pleadingly, though still with the hint of a coy smile.

She didn't look happy, but finally she nodded. "I'll get some food," she said. "Just wait here. I'll be right back with some food."

She went inside, while he gathered his bags and easel and carried it over to the stable door. He sure was hungry, come to think of it. And boy, was he tired.

When he woke up the next morning, he realized that he had heard something or other a bit earlier, but that he had been too groggy to wake up all the way.

It must have been the husband or the wife coming to take out the cow. In any case it was completely quiet in the stable area on the other side of the wall.

He sat up. The day must be getting on. The stripe of sun from the tiny east window suggested that the sun was high in the sky. He fumbled for his watch. Well past seven, almost seven-thirty.

He looked into the stable. It was empty, and the door leading outside was closed. He might as well use the manure trough.

Afterwards he got out his washing kit, found a bucket, and walked outside. Over by the well pump there was an overturned fish crate, and on top of that something with a towel over it. A couple of stones were holding the towel down, though it wasn't windy. Underneath the towel he found a couple of pieces of bread and a cup of milk.

He looked over towards the scullery door. It was shut. It was also totally quiet, as far as he could tell. He went over and knocked anyway. No one answered. He shrugged his shoulders and returned to his breakfast. He noticed there were also a couple of slices of cheese. He sat on the well cover—the grass was still wet from the dew—and started eating.

She would look pretty if she didn't go around with that ugly scarf on her head. Again, he looked over towards the scullery, the closed door, and the lifeless window. Strange that he hadn't seen any man around. Maybe he was at sea.

Anna Katrina was very quiet when they started working. She barely said hello. Calling her pensive would not have been stretching it. And Stina couldn't bring herself to ask her a question, not yet anyway, even though it was burning on her lips. Someone had seen someone go by her place last night, or something like that.

It was still good weather for fishing, even though the catch could have been better. And there were lots of lines and hooks to organize and put bait on.

They worked more or less in silence. Stina's chance came a bit after noon, when she saw someone she didn't know walking over towards the grocery.

First she cleared her throat.

Anna Katrina didn't say anything.

Then Stina asked, "Who could that be walking over there?"

Anna Katrina looked up. "Who?" Then she said, "Oh him. I guess he's a stranger."

"A stranger?"

"Yeah, he was looking for lodging, a place where he could stay for a while," she said as casually as possible.

"A place to stay," repeated Stina. Then she asked sternly, "And where did he stay last night?"

"Last night?"

"Yeah, last night. Where did that stranger, who was looking for a place to stay, stay last night?"

"In our barn," admitted Anna Katrina quietly. "I gave him permission to sleep in our barn. It was late, and I didn't know what else to say."

"And on top of that you probably fed him too?"

She said, with a touch of self-contempt, "I put some food out for him, like he was a hungry dog . Like he was some stray mongrel that would only get a hunk of dry bread before being chased away."

Then she broke down. Sobbing, she said, "At first I thought it was Jesus Christ coming in from the ocean. It looked exactly like Jesus, bearing his cross, walking down towards me."

Stina looked shocked. "Jesus!" she gasped. She looked sternly at the sobbing woman. Then her expression softened. "There, there," she said comfortingly, giving Anna Katrina a few, almost tender, little pats on her arm and shoulder. "There, there," Anna Katrina, "tell me all about it." And Anna Katrina sobbed her way through the whole story. As it progressed, a flash of understanding appeared on Stina's tanned face.

After Anna Katrina had finished her account and sat blowing her nose, Stina said solemnly, "It's a sign. It's a sign that you need to come to the Lord, Anna Katrina."

Anna Katrina was silent. She resumed working after the interruption.

"You need to come to the Lord, Anna Katrina," said Stina again. "You should join us."

Anna Katrina was silent, steadfastly continuing her work, and Stina resumed working, too. No good could come from being neglectful. For a long time neither of them said a word. Then Stina couldn't restrain herself any longer.

"So you saw Jesus in a vision," she said, and her expression was a combination partly of humble gratitude and partly of triumph. But still she felt anxious. She looked over at Anna Katrina, but decided in the end, not to continue with her line of burning questions. That would have to wait until more trust was built up between them.

After school let out, the youngest children came and helped them, so then they could only talk about things the children could hear. Stina could only refer to the subject indirectly. A couple of times during the course of the afternoon, she tried to speed up the children by telling them, "We have to make it to the meetinghouse tonight," with a sidelong glance to Anna Katrina.

Later she said—and this time directly to Anna Katrina, "If you need someone to watch the little one so you can join us, you just have to say so. Our Anna would be glad to help you."

When Anna Katrina made it home that evening, she was more than a little perturbed to see that Mathias Jensen was still there. He was standing a short distance from the house, and the strange apparatus, which was not a cross, but an easel, was set up in front of him, and there he stood with his long brushes and his paints, sketching the house.

He smiled and waved, but not too intrusively. He laid down his brushes and started walking over towards her, but most of his attention was still concentrating on the play of colors in the thatched roof.

She stood there hesitantly. Almost anxiously. He said, "I'm sorry I'm still here. I hope it's not a problem. And of course I'll pay you for it. Also I have to pay you for last night and the food you brought me, but you were gone by the time I finally got up."

He explained that he had tried to find lodging with someone, but that he was unsuccessful. "So I guess I'll get back on the road tomorrow."

She looked at him with aloofness. No one could tell what was going on in her mind, if anything. Then she said, "I'll fry up a plaice for you."

She entered the house, and he went back to his easel. On the canvas the house was low and closed, almost eerie in the bright, sweltering afternoon. The small windows were blind spots on the neglected backside, but when he looked over at his model, the sun had gotten just low enough that a warmer, brighter glint had appeared on the windowpanes.

That wasn't what he was looking for.

He started to pack up; he was done for the day.

Mathias was invited to eat inside. He was placed at the table in the kitchen with a fried plaice, a hunk of bread and a cup of tea. When she was sure that he didn't need anything else, and when she had communicated that he needed to be quiet since the baby had fallen asleep, she left.

So he sat alone in the kitchen while she brought the cow in and milked it. Also while she was over with the family that didn't have any land, to whom she sold milk. When she returned, she mucked out in the stable. He noticed that he blushed a little at the thought that she was also mucking out after him.

He finished eating, and finished drinking his tea. He sat waiting, but then he realized that she probably wouldn't come back inside until he had left.

He cleaned up after himself, wiped the table with the cloth hanging by the stove, set the chair neatly under the table, and went outside. She was standing near the corner of the house, tidying something up. "Thanks for the meal," he said. She mumbled something and went in the house.

He paced back and forth outside. He had gathered that it should be obvious they were not in the house together at the same time, that it was important for one of them to be visible at all times to anyone who felt it was their duty to keep an eye on things.

She came outside to get water. Lightly, almost conversationally, he said, "Your husband gets home late. Is he at sea?"

She looked at him, and there was fear, hope and despair in her eyes. She said, "Henrik stayed out there."

Then she pumped until the bucket was full, and carried it back inside, before he had gotten himself together to help her, as a polite young man certainly ought to have done.

He walked over and sat on the bench by the gable end of the house. The landscape was blurred by the light shining in his eyes. A large flock of young starlings landed in the distant heather, took off and flew a short distance, landed again and flew off again—a great wave of birds passing through his field of vision.

He ought to be writing a letter. There was someone who really wanted to know where he was and how he was doing.

He stayed sitting there. It could wait.

In the morning he woke early.

He listened. The cow was standing in the room next to him, intermittently interrupting the quiet. He looked at his watch. It was six.

He got up and straightened his clothes. Then he took a bucket from the stable and got water from the well, so he could get washed.

When he later emerged afterwards with the dirty water and tossed it, Anna Katrina came out from the scullery. She took the bucket from him and started cleaning it. He realized, too late, it was the milk bucket that he had used. He mumbled an apology; she wrestled with the bucket. She hadn't put on her dark hair scarf yet, and even though her blonde hair was tied tightly in a bun behind her neck, suddenly she looked young. She might be about the same age as him.

She noticed that she was being watched. She said, "I set out oatmeal in the kitchen."

He thanked her and went inside. It appeared that the baby must still be sleeping. Mathias sat down and eat. He took a small second serving and chewed slowly. He took his time over each of the last spoonfuls.

She didn't come in.

The baby started to stir. Quickly, Mathias cleaned up his plate and went outside. Anna Katrina was waiting. Without looking at him, and without answering his "Thanks for breakfast," she hurried inside.

He probably should pay her, or at least make an agreement of what he should pay.

He stood there thinking about it. But it would have to wait. He snuck up to look through the window, and he saw her sitting with her back to him, presumably nursing the baby. He would have to wait.

So he might as well set up the easel and continue with the painting he had started the day before, even though the light was a bit different now, since it was earlier in the day than when he painted yesterday. But the west side of the house with the neglected masonry and the small, dark portholes were in shade again, like repudiations in an otherwise sun-filled landscape.

He became absorbed in his work, and when after a good while he remembered that he actually was waiting for the chance to get to speak with his landlady, it was too late. She had already left.

Who knew what she was going out to do.

"People are saying the stranger is still there," remarked Stina sternly.

Anna Katrina didn't respond. She was busy, bent over her work.

"Some people are saying he goes in and out of the house like it was his," added Stina.

"That's not true. He sleeps out in the barn, and twice I have let him eat in the kitchen when I was outside. He has only been inside when I was out milking the cow."

Anna Katrina was mad. And conflicted. "What should I have done?" she asked. "I couldn't just send him away. It was late in the evening when he showed up. Where would I have sent him? Would you have taken him in?"

Stina didn't answer. She wasn't comfortable with Anna Katrina, and not with herself, either. She showed it by not offering morning coffee. Instead she went on at length about the latest evangelical meeting and about the beautiful psalms they sang, and about the beautiful sermon the evangelist had delivered. "It went right to the marrow of people's bones. It made people tremble inside."

Then she added, now almost friendly, "You should come join us, Anna Katrina. We all want what's best for you." She sat quietly for a moment, and then she added, more ardently, "You received a sign, so why don't you accept salvation?" And then Stina realized that she couldn't have said anything worse than that, considering the situation. She launched into a long monologue about confusing the Savior and the Tempter, and she ended by once more encouraging Anna Katrina to "come to us."

A little later, carefully she asked, "So when is the stranger leaving?" When Anna Katrina made no answer other than slightly shaking her head, Stina said more sharply, "You have to get him to leave; or else you will have to bear the consequences."

The was a long silent pause. Stina tried to keep up her stern appearance. Then she let it out: "But dear, Anna Katrina, don't you understand? I have laid awake all night thinking about you and your poor son. What will become of you?"

Anna Katrina looked over at Stina. Stina had tears in her eyes. A couple of them made their way down over her cheeks. Suddenly she looked not just sad, but also totally defenseless.

Anna Katrina turned her face away. It took all she had not to start crying herself. She pursed her lips together and clenched her face.

Stina saw how Anna Katrina apparently had turned away from her. Angrily, she dried her eyes. "Have you already forgotten Henrik and what happened to him?" Then she said it again, fervently. "You have to make him leave, Anna Katrina, for your own sake and for Poul's. What do think everyone is thinking about you?"

But "the painter guy," as they named him eventually, evidently hadn't given any thought to leaving. People still saw him around, mostly on the beach, where he stood spreading paints on a canvas. Sometimes one of the fishermen snuck up to look. Oh, so he was painting them! Only rarely were any words exchanged. It certainly wasn't goodwill or friendliness that Mathias felt himself surrounded with, there at the boat launch. One day, while he had to take a quick walk up the dune, someone had come by and thrown a handful of sand on the picture he was working on. That's how it must have happened. Even though the wind was blowing hard that day, so hard that he had to tie down his easel, the wind couldn't blow that precisely.

He swallowed his anger, attempted to remove the sand with his knife, and was mostly able to repair the damage. He made a demonstrative point of staying there working until late that day.

It wasn't until he was back in the kitchen with Anna Katrina that he expressed his anger, his restlessness, and the anxiety which got a hold of him once in a while. Like this afternoon, for example.

Anna Katrina understood. She had had a difficult day too. Stina had been totally closed off, but then suddenly she had asked, "Are you eating together now?"

Anna Katrina hadn't answered at first, but when the question was repeated, she had answered, a bit fresh, "Yes, but he still sleeps out in the barn, in case you're interested."

She probably shouldn't have said it like that. Stina seemed very embarrassed and started going on and on about the evangelist and the evangelist meetings. And almost pleadingly she had asked, "Why are you turning away from us? Why are you turning away from God, Anna Katrina?"

Anna Katrina had answered that she should mind her own business.

They talked about it for a long time that evening. About their problems, about the fishermen, and about Stina.

"I should leave as soon as possible," said Mathias. "I can see it's bad for you that I'm staying here."

Anna Katrina knew he was right. But on the other hand she was afraid of the emptiness that would return, the day he left.

She said, "Let them talk."

How they came to eat together happened gradually.

It most likely started the evening that Anna Katrina came inside after milking the cow, and he hadn't quite finished eating. She walked briskly towards the bedroom door. Then she stopped. "I thought I heard Poul crying," she said.

Mathias explained that Poul had been completely quiet and was probably sleeping. At any rate, he hadn't heard anything. Anna Katrina remained standing there, uncertain. "It sounded like it," she maintained. "It sounded exactly like he was crying."

Then she started straightening up around the stove. She stood with her back to him moving pots and pans around.

Mathias started talking about how nice it was that it wasn't quite so hot anymore. Then he said he wished the wind would pick up, so he could get a better look at the power of the ocean.

She mumbled something, but he couldn't make it out. "Sorry," he said, "I couldn't hear what you said."

"Nothing." She stood there. Then she turned around to face him "I just said that when the wind is really blowing, the fishermen don't go out, and then I'm not able to earn any money."

"That reminds me," he interjected, "that we haven't decided what I should pay you for room and board."

"Oh, that," she said. Her voice was relaxed, but there was something tense in the way she was looking at him.

"I would like to stay here a little while longer, but I think I should pay a few days at a time."

Anna Katrina couldn't help but say that she would like that very much.

There was a long silence. "I don't know what people usually pay around here," said Mathias.

Anna Katrina didn't know either. He tried to get her to suggest an amount.

She shook her head. "You know more about that," she said.

He asked if there was someone he could ask for advice,

but there wasn't. "What have you paid other places?" she asked instead.

He made a suggestion, realizing full well that he hadn't thought of paying that much. It was close to the price of a hotel.

She looked at him uncomprehendingly. He wasn't going to make her look like a fool. If she got one *krone* per day, then she would make sure he had food to eat.

That's what she said. And the rest of the evening they discussed back and forth the reasonableness or unreasonableness of the amounts they had each suggested.

At one point, Anna Katrina made coffee. She gave him a cup, and took one for herself as well, but then remained standing by the stove, sipping it.

"Won't you sit down," Mathias encouraged her. "What harm could that do?"

It actually made her blush, but still she pulled up a chair and sat across the table from him.

They bargained for the longest time. Evidently she was glad to have something to talk to him about.

In the end they agreed on one and a quarter *kroner*.

"But then I'll make sure you have decent food every day," she asserted.

A few moments passed before he realized, that just then, she had used the familiar "you" form instead of the formal, more stilted "you" form that she had used with him up until then.

He looked at her, but wasn't able to make eye contact. He said, "Thank you. It's a deal."

He got up, but she stayed seated without looking at him. He took a few steps towards the door, and was just about to say goodnight, when he stopped, turned around and returned to the table. She looked at him questioningly, perhaps a bit anxiously. He said, "I had better pay you for the days I've been here." And he got out six and a quarter crowns.

For the first time, she looked directly at him. And there was a gentleness in her expression when their eyes met.

"There you go," said Mathias, laying the money on the table.

"Thanks," said Anna Katrina. She took the money and went into her bedroom with them, evidently to put them in a drawer. Mathias stood, watching her go.

After a bit, he could hear that she had picked up the baby, probably to nurse him for the night.

It had been a nice evening, a full evening. And that was the way, more or less, in the kitchen and with conversation, that their evenings came to unfold, though with one addition. After a few days it seemed only natural that they ate at the same time; and together, at the same table.

Sometimes Mathias sat and drew while they chatted. One evening, while Anna Katrina was in the other room nursing Poul, Mathias started what looked like a letter, but he got stuck and didn't finish it.

She had changed, Anna Katrina; Stina was sure of it. While they were together, working the hooks, it was like she was distant, as if the whole time she was making an effort not to show that she was feeling happier. And every time Stina tried to steer a conversation towards something serious, Anna Katrina either became too distant or she redirected everything Stina said, so it all became pointless. She was almost out of reach, Stina thought. She lay awake at night, horrified, thinking: *Lost.*

She brought it up at one of the meetings at TABOR. The evangelist had a long talk with her afterwards. It was obvious that Stina was beside herself. She groaned, "She thought she saw Jesus, but it was Satan she took in."

The evangelist nodded, talking about tragic delusions. "We must be very strict," he said, "then she will find her way to God." He also talked about the necessity that Anna Katrina feel their disapproval, so there would be no doubt about it.

The next day was windy, and before Anna Katrina left home— they had sat talking for a long while over breakfast that morning, and Anna Katrina was running late, so he had promised to clean up—Anna, Stina's youngest, arrived, to say that Anna Katrina didn't have to come to work today. No one was going out on the ocean.

"What about tomorrow?" asked Anna Katrina.

Anna said that her mother had said that there was no need for Anna Katrina to come unless she was sent for.

Anna Katrina looked worried when Anna had run off home again. Mathias looked excited. "Then you can come along with me today," he said. "I'm going down to paint the ocean. We can make a picnic out of it."

"A picnic?" Anna Katrina looked worried. "A picnic?"

"Sure. We can take some food with us down to the beach, and I can paint while you and Poul enjoy the fresh air and scenery. We can make a day of it."

In the end, Anna Katrina let herself go along with it. But it was obvious that a "picnic" like that was the strangest thing she'd ever heard.

Mathias was in charge of the picnic basket, so he visited the grocery to buy small beer, since of course they didn't have real beer, and lemon soda. And in the end, that was all he could get Anna Katrina to agree to take with them. "We can't do that, not on a regular day," she said again and again.

But they both felt it was more than a regular day, with their being together in a strangely serendipitous way. Even though there were periods when Mathias concentrated on his painting, and even though Anna and Poul had made camp away from the wind, behind one of the farthest dunes, still there were moments when they both felt the other's presence with an almost palpable joy.

Part of the way home—the part that was well-hidden—they ended up walking hand in hand. It just happened. Almost unavoidably.

They walked in silence for a long while. Almost as if there was nothing to say.

Then Anna Katrina said, "I feel bad for you, having to still sleep out in that filthy stable."

Mathias mumbled something.

Anna Katrina continued, "But we could never change that."

Mathias gave her hand a little squeeze. He understood. They could never change that.

There were several days like that. Even though the weather changed, and even though the boats went out again, no one came over from Stina's to tell Anna Katrina they needed her to work. Even though she hardly expected it, it still made her uneasy.

"It's fortunate you make some money from your boarder," said the grocer pointedly one day, when she was shopping. "You do, don't you?"

"What am I going to do when he leaves?" she asked herself numerous times, observing his peaceful expression in the late evenings and early mornings, when they sat across the table from one another.

"You were the savior who came to me," she whispered, when he couldn't hear her. But she felt inside herself that it was dangerous to even think that way. And dangerous to have expectations.

Still, one day she said, "What will happen to me after you leave?"

They were sitting at breakfast. At first he looked confused and uncertain, then he patted her hand and was as reassuring as he could be, without saying anything. Because he couldn't say anything, he didn't dare. He tried smiling, but for the first time, he wasn't able to get her eyes to smile back.

The end of the summer was approaching. It was the day he finished her portrait.

The next few days he was out again, working on the beach. Anna Katrina and her son were there too. Anna Katrina knitted all day. And she sat at the foot of the dune, where she was visible, if someone from the fishing village happened to look that way.

And of course they did. They knew they would. Of course they followed with great interest what she and "the painter guy" were doing, as much as they possibly could.

With every day that passed, Anna Katrina was more and more convinced that she was lost. Her ability to see into the future became shorter and shorter. She didn't talk about it.

Mathias didn't talk about any period of time that lay farther ahead than tomorrow, either. Often he thought about that letter he had once tried to write.

One evening while they sat eating, Stine, the evangelist, and the grocer came by. The evangelist was the one who knocked, and he was the one who entered first and directed the conversation.

He said, "We are here to insist that you come to TABOR tonight, Anna Katrina. You cannot turn away from the Lord any longer. You must repent for your sins and come to us."

Anna Katrina shook her head. The evangelist continued, "Anna Katrina, think carefully about who your true friends are in the Lord. We will receive you in TABOR tonight, and we will help you to receive the Lord's forgiveness, if only you are willing."

He also said, "You must clean out your house and your soul and come to the Lord your God."

Anna Katrina looked at him defiantly, but said nothing. Mathias shifted his weight uneasily. Stina sent him a critical look and added a few comments on the side, about how lucky he was to be sitting there when it was only eight months since Henrik was called to his final judgment. The evangelist shushed her, and the grocer was not pleased with her interference either. He said quickly, "You know that we miss you, Anna Katrina. You belong with us. We would not want you to end up as an outcast." He demonstratively turned his back towards the side of the table where Mathias was sitting.

Anna Katrina shook her head. "I have nothing to be ashamed of," she said. Her gaze sought Mathias'. He was staring down at the table. He sat thinking, nervously, barely hearing how, more and more, the conversation around him came to resemble an argument. Sometimes the three of them talked over one another, but what they were saying didn't register with Mathias.

He was trying to think of the future. Trying to imagine his future. Trying to leave a future behind.

His attention didn't return to the room until he heard Stina say, "And how will you survive all alone with the baby and one poor cow and no help from us?"

There was an almost frozen expression on his face when he caught Anna Katrina's gaze and said, "Yes, Anna Katrina, you are going to TABOR tonight, and I'm going with you. We have to clear something up." And he got up and said right to the three imposing guests, "We will be there tonight, Anna Katrina and I."

It got quiet. The grocer looked uneasily at the evangelist, and the evangelist collected himself for a few moments. "That was not how we had planned it," he said.

Mathias went over and put his hand on Anna Katrina's shoulder. "That's the way it's going to be," he said.

They said goodbye and left. Once they had gotten away from the house, Stina recovered her voice. And Mathias and Anna Katrina could see from the window how the conversation became very animated.

"You don't know what you're doing," said Anna Katrina doubtfully.

Mathias didn't answer. He made himself useful by clearing the table.

They walked down the wheel ruts towards the Evangelical meetinghouse. The summer was still warm and dry, and all the hues were pale and sharp. The black-clothed figures they saw along their way in the landscape were elements almost screaming for a painter.

Anna Katrina carried Poul, and she had pulled her black headscarf far down over her forehead. They didn't talk as they walked along.

The evening was quiet. Anna Katrina had thought it was best if they arrived a bit late, just as the meeting was about to begin.

"It's best if we don't have to sit and wait too long," she had said.

The meetinghouse windows were open, but there were no sounds coming from within. No one else was arriving but Anna Katrina and Mathias, no one who could observe them walking the last bit of the path.

They stopped for a moment just before the steps. Anna Katrina took a deep breath, and she caught Mathias' gaze. He nodded. She went first through the door.

The second she went in, two men appeared blocking Mathias from entering. The one shook his head, and without really touching him, pressed him backwards, back out through the door which immediately was closed behind them.

Mathias protested. The one man gently put his hand on Mathias' shoulder and said, "Come on. We're going over to Anna Katrina's." They headed that way. The other man disappeared, returning quickly with a horse and cart that had been parked behind the meetinghouse.

"What do you want?" asked Mathias. Humiliation burned on his cheeks. He had tried carefully to pull back from his guards, but they kept him in place. Now he was afraid.

The man didn't answer directly. He said, "It's not that we have anything against you—not really."

Nothing else was said. Mathias could barely hear singing emanating from inside TABOR. The voices blended with the wagon wheels creaking and with the distant sound of breaking waves.

He asked again, "What do you want?"
Silently he let himself be led along.

It didn't take long to pack. The men had told him to pack his things, and now they lay on the cart—his bags, the easel, and a roll of paintings. One of the men walked into the house. He looked around the kitchen, walked into the bedroom, and returned with the portrait of Anna Katrina.

He handed it to Mathias. "That's not mine," said Mathias. "I gave it to Anna Katrina."

The man said, "It's yours and you will take it with you."

The rage, that until then had been suppressed by his anxiousness, now rose to the surface. He yelled, "That is Anna Katrina's and it's staying here."

The man, who was still standing there holding the painting, just shook his head and handed it towards Mathias again, who again protested. So the man walked into the kitchen over to the stove. He lifted the cover and saw that there were still glowing embers. So he pulled the painting free from the frame and stuffed it in. Soon the flames flared up and he replaced the cover. "That is how it burns down in hell," he said. Then he broke the frame up into small pieces and threw them in the kindling box.

"I guess we're done here," he said. "Let's go."

They indicated to Mathias that he should get on the cart. He did as they said. It was no use resisting. Not now. Maybe later, he thought, and that thought bolstered his morale. He felt himself shaking a little, and he wasn't sure that he had full control over his voice. Still he asked, "Where are you taking me? What are you going to do with me?"

"To the train," answered the one. "We're driving you to the train. You will sleep at the inn tonight and then take the train in the morning. The innkeeper is expecting you and it has been paid for." He smiled weakly. "We're not beasts," he said congenially. The other one nodded. "It's not that we have so much against you," he said. "But you don't belong here. You lead others to sinfulness."

They drove past TABOR. Inside, they were singing, "Greet your Savior and Reconciler." Mathias tried to catch a glance through the windows, but he couldn't make out anyone.

The singing died out in their wake.

One of the men, the one who was driving the horse, hummed something that sounded like it must be some kind of psalm melody. Mathias didn't recognize it. The other one cleared his throat once in a while. Then he said, "We only want what's best for her. We are leading her to the Lord."

Slowly the landscape around them changed. The scorched dune country changed to greener fields, and well-manicured four-sided farmsteads lay spread out in the landscape. Trees grew here and there, and there were yards around the houses. Here was a more abundant world, a more colorful world, a world of nuance.

The sun had gone down a while ago, but the evening was still warm. As they advanced deeper into the bright evening, gradually something worked itself loose inside of Mathias.

"I'd like to walk," he said, jumping down onto the road. The one fisherman made a movement as if he wanted to go down after him, but decided not to.

For a while Mathias stayed beside the cart, but imperceptibly, he sped up, until eventually he was a good bit in front.

He looked back. They were still there, like a sharp silhouette against the bright northern sky. A horse, a cart and two bent figures.

He started running.

On average, about every other month someone's history gets buried here at the cemetery. They die, the old folks, and one last time—for some of them the only time—they are the stars.

That's because we treat one another with respect, especially when it's the last time we have the chance. When someone dies, it gets noted by flags flying low at the property where the deceased lived, and likewise at the neighbors. And if it happens to be someone who was at the nursing home the last few years, the flag is at half-mast there as well. So it can add up to six or seven flags in all, reporting with some certainty, to people who know the area, who it is that now has departed this life, which some still consider a life of waiting down below.

So it's not all that easy if it should happen to be a burial day when one, for example, returns home from vacation or some other trip. Because on that day everyone's flags are out, though there are a few younger folks who don't have flagpoles, and then there are a few transplants who don't want to be intrusive, and then there could also be from time to time an old enmity that wounded so deeply, that also has to be noted one last time. But in general: everyone's flags are out.

Then one either has to ask around, or page through the old newspapers.

But anyhow. The flags at half-mast report that now we are respectfully remembering a person who had a place in our common consciousness. And when the flags later in the afternoon are raised to the tops of the flagpoles, it is a visible sign of the uplifted mood, which a good memorial gathering in the meetinghouse can bring about, and of the lightness, not to mention frivolity, that spreads at that opportunity. Only now and then the mood is dampened a brief moment, when we notice the island of silence that the eventual left-behind spouse might find themselves in, and we remember in a flash the actual reason we are sitting here drinking coffee. But then we can assure one another that the deceased absolutely would have requested no downcast faces or other assumed expressions of sorrow. There is certainly no one who ever would have attributed to a deceased anything other than the heartfelt desire that people should be cheerful at the burial coffee.

By observing the flags and their placement in the landscape, or by the process of elimination, it is relatively easy to establish who just died, or to figure out which farm or which house it befell. "So Christen Jørgensen finally met his end," or "Helga must have given up the ghost," or "What do I see, something unfortunate happened to someone at Ballegaard Farm; it's probably that son, isn't his name Erik, the one who just got his drivers license?" That's how the remarks surface as if by reflex. But there was that one day, when there was only one flag—the one at the nursing home—and people were at a bit of a loss. They had to ask around.

"It looks like someone died."

"I saw that too. They say it's that guy Poul."

"Poul?"

"Yeah. Poul Poulsen."

"Poul Poulsen?"

"The one they called 'The Graduate.'"

"Oh, him." A brief pause. A chuckle. "I can't believe it. Was he still alive?"

And at the bakery, all day long, questions and answers were exchanged. Towards evening a recent transplant came in. He had a shopping list, and in addition to a rye bread he needed ten rolls and three long unsliced pastries. The baker's wife explained that the board of the lecture association was holding a meeting at their place, and she ought to know. She also knew that he was new on the board, so she said that he needed to bring cookies too. She explained that that was what they usually had.

He bought two kinds: vanilla rings and shortbread.

After he paid, the baker's wife said, "You saw the flag, right?"

"Flag? No, actually I –?"

"At the nursing home. They're flying half-mast at the nursing home."

"I guess someone died there." He collected his bags and turned to leave.

She quickly said, "It was Poul, the one they called 'The Graduate.'" And with satisfaction she saw what seemed to be a questioning expression in the eyes of her customer. And she had already begun a little preparatory laughter when the telephone rang, and the lecture association's new board member quickly nodded good-bye and disappeared.

And that was the reason the story of Poul Poulsen was not told on that occasion.

The new guy didn't get to hear it, and since there would go many years before he would have frequent visits to the cemetery, it is uncertain whether he ever would get to see the stone that could perhaps arouse his curiosity. And even if he did see it, and even though if it did make him a bit curious, it's doubtful that he would run into someone at that time who could tell him about the person whose name is engraved on that stone.

Because by that time both the very last eye-witnesses and the all-knowing narrator would be entering a greater and silent cycle.

Poul Poulsen was born in 1908, and even though it had been hard for the mother, it was a good birth, they thought back then. As the next-oldest son on an above-average farm, he couldn't have had a much better start in life, especially since after that there was no visible blessing in his parents' marriage.

Poul grew up a quiet and thoughtful boy in the shadow of

his bigger and more duty-encumbered brother. His brother had to take part in chores almost since he could toddle —"Well it will be his one day." Meanwhile Poul sailed through, almost unhindered, past the age when a boy in the country normally had inescapable duties. Lord knows he was kind of small, and he had been sick the first few years, since he had a tendency to catch everything possible within miles around. And he also had a tendency towards clumsiness, when he was set to helping. "Stop pestering him; he will meet the seriousness of life soon enough," said his constantly worrying mother, when someone like his father or older brother made remarks.

"Well he does have a pretty face," said the neighbors' wives, when talk turned to the spoiled boy, who, unlike his contemporaries, was not sent out to earn money in the summer. "He looks like a girl," his classmates said of him, and let him know it. "He appears to be quite a bright boy," said the curate a bit uncertainly. "He will probably amount to something, if only –." This "if only –" referred to an introversion that the curate perceived in him, and which was in contrast to the ease with which he apparently could learn anything. "He computes fractions in his head," he told his wife, "but he doesn't tell anyone. He just sits there staring into space, as if it didn't matter."

"That spoiled kid," he said, just like others did.

"He ought to get out of that house," he added, "and the sooner the better."

And since the curate was a man who knew his duty, and since he had a pretty good idea that the solution was not to send Poul out to work, he staked all his prestige on Poul getting into private middle school, and later, when middle school was surpassed surprisingly well, to Viborg Catholic School. It was the first time in the history of the parish that anyone but a child of a priest had taken that step, and that of course led to a bit of commentary.

"So a regular diploma wasn't good enough for him." The dairy chairman looked at his card buddies. He had a hand that would have benefitted from the others' losing their concentration, but they weren't led so easily astray. It wasn't until the cards were gathered up and Kristen Østergaard started shuffling, that comments were made which, spoken at the opportune time, perhaps could have kept the dairy chairman from folding.

Meanwhile the wives sat, having coffee in the other room. "And now he's going to graduate," said one of them, and for a while the talk centered on what that could lead to—when he was such a little weakling.

Then Margrethe, the dairy chairman's wife, said, "We were saying what a shame it is for his parents. And then how much it costs."

And that was probably the most common opinion in the parish. That it was a shame for the parents to have a son like that.

But actually, Poul's mother quite liked the thought of a son who was going to graduate, even though she was from a liberal home, and as a child she had gone to public school in the neighboring parish. The father hadn't been so easy to convince. He had a number of objections, but he also had trouble coming up with a different path for that wimp of a son, which the creator had granted him. In the end he relented. It was probably best to get Poul out of the house, the way his mother coddled him, so it was worth a try. The father didn't say this directly, but that was what made up his mind.

So Poul was boarded in Viborg. *He was sent away* to Viborg, as his contemporaries termed it. That was where they sent all the loony ones.

The next few years no one saw very much of him. When he came up in conversation, and his parents weren't there, often someone thought that he might have developed "other interests," as they say. Naturally he was home at Christmas, and sometimes for other holidays too, but since he didn't visit anyone, and since no one visited him, it could be said that there wasn't really any contact between him and the people he grew up with. His brother rarely mentioned him, and when his parents felt they ought to say something, all they could say was that Poul was doing well. "He must be settled in, there where he is," people said, adding that it was probably best that way.

One day people found out that he wasn't in Viborg any more, but in Copenhagen, and that he was studying. Not for the priesthood, but there were plenty of other things to study.

Once he had a friend, or study partner, or whatever he was, home with him on vacation, and they were seen now and then walking or biking down to the beach. It made an impression. It was during haymaking season, when everyone could have used an extra hand.

He came home for his parents' twenty-fifth anniversary, and he was completely natural and friendly at the party at the meetinghouse. And when his father died—that was in '30—he came to the funeral. On top of that, he was the one who thanked people at graveside and invited everyone to the memorial gathering. He carried it off quite well, though he was obviously weighed down by the situation. And people could sense a tension between him and his brother, when the future was discussed. The mother wanted to keep running the farm with the eldest son as manager. The neighbors didn't comment, but an uncle noted that it was probably best if Bent took over the farm right away. The mother didn't agree. "Poul needs to finish his education first," she said—decidedly.

What was Poul studying? Oh, he had alternated between a few things, he told people who asked.

A rumor circulated that he had failed out.

Other rumors began circulating, which perhaps weren't rumors. He had gotten more strange, people said. Mogens Østergaard, who was doing his military service with the Royal Guard, said he had run into Poul one Sunday in Copenhagen. Mogens said that Poul was keeping company with unusual people. Poul had taken Mogens to a pub where Poul apparently had friends. "They were all a bit crazy," chuckled Poul. "One of them was an artist or a communist or something. But Poul, he was really nice; it wasn't that," he added.

They only got together that one time. Mogens was soon made corporal and re-enlisted. But the picture he had painted of Poul, as someone who had gone off the rails and gotten a bit artistic, was preserved for a few years, and was perhaps embellished a bit each time it was aired.

Then Poul came home and stepped into it.

It fit.

It was in '33 that Poul arrived, drawing attention with his sailor's pants and his beret, which were even more conspicuous than his slimness. People talked about him, but not so much at first. At that time people were talking about his brother Bent, for a change.

Bent had hung himself. It was the mother who found him, out in the barn, and it was the neighbor who cut him down. Poul was called home—not just for the funeral, but also to be there for his mother. That was only fair, considering everything he had cost her over the years; but on the other hand it was naive to think that he could help. First, he had no talent for sensible work; and second, at that point not even a skilled farmer could have averted the bankruptcy that Bent had just succeeded in escaping.

They had to leave the property—the mother and Poul—and without a penny in their pockets. The mother left the area and became a kind of housekeeper—for an uncle, I think it was, whose wife had tuberculosis and was in a sanatorium. And Poul returned to the capital and probably had to assume that he wouldn't be getting the monthly amount from home anymore.

On the rare occasion that someone met the mother in the city and asked her, she said that Poul was doing just fine. He was with a newspaper, she said. He made sure things were spelled properly. And he was still studying.

Whatever that would be good for.

As the thirties progressed and the years of occupation began, both Poul and his mother slid from that part of memory which was in daily use. For memory to be kept up, a small infusion of news is necessary, and there was none of that available. The fact that many of them who knew the family the best were dead probably also played a role, besides all the dramatics of those years which sort of covered up the previous ones.

But one day, in spring of '46, we realized that the somewhat strange man who had been living for about six months in the shed by the river, down among the scrub, must be Poul.

"Right, that guy Poul Poulsen, the one who absolutely had to have a diploma."

"The ones who had Lars Jensen's property?"

"Yes. And the brother hung himself."

The strange man had been placed, and he wasn't so strange anymore.

It wasn't so easy to see that he was someone we knew. But it was probably the beard. When he was asked, he didn't deny that he was Poul Poulsen, but he seemed kind of upset. He had moved back for some peace and quiet, he said.

We respected that. Lars Jensen, who of course was the owner of the scrub and the shed, didn't make a fuss over Poul's living there. He had pretty much given him permission; at any rate he didn't throw him out when he realized one day that someone was living in the shed. But he didn't have any use for it himself, and that bit of scrub was no use to him either. And actually Poul improved the shed some. He replaced a bunch of the boards and installed a new door, and even though it wasn't totally professional work, it looked good. It cost him 87 *kroner* and 45 *øre*, he told Lars Jensen's son, who sometimes passed by there, on his way to fishing in the river. "87 *kroner* and 45 *øre*—including hardware," he said, with emphasis.

Quite a few conjectures had to be made before people returned to a state of equilibrium. At first most people thought Poul was wanted, and that he was trying to hide out there. The most obvious explanation was that it had something to do with the court proceedings after the occupation, and that in one way or another Poul had ended up on the wrong side. For that reason people didn't speak to him directly, even though Mogens, the one from Østergaard Farm, who wasn't exactly one of those who would put on an armband for the fifth of May, but who had been part of an underground weapons-collecting group, and had been part of things that were told about in the newspaper after the occupation, acted as if the thought that Poul was wanted made no sense to him.

But they had known each other before in Copenhagen, people remembered.

We all felt the urge to protect Poul. It was as if it were unavoidable that he had ended up becoming someone like that. Poor guy. We almost liked him because of it. It was a kind of proof. We had always thought there was something wrong with him. And then the way he looked.

"I think it is best to let people take care of themselves and not get involved," said the dairy chairman.

It became apparent that Poul was not wanted. He registered as a resident just like people were supposed to.

It was a bit of a disappointment.

And of course that raised the question: Why did he move back? What business did he have here?

And why did he act so strange? On the rare occasion he was shopping—and at first we had no idea where he got the money—he walked back and forth outside the store until there were no more customers left. Then he went inside, and usually he just pointed at what he wanted to buy. As if he were afraid of his own voice. And he hardly ever said good-bye when he left.

By the way, it turned out he got his money from the savings and loan in the city. Peter Madsen had a daughter who worked in a dry-goods store on the corner across the street, so she saw him once in a while when he passed through.

Ten miles each way—quite a walk. But it was a way for him to pass the time.

Eventually it got to be old news that he was living here, so it wasn't anything people mentioned much. Not even when he started to work the ground around the shed. He set potatoes, planted cabbage and sowed peas. The part he took over was a patch at the top of Lars Jensen's meadow, but Lars was never stingy about his land, so it didn't amount to anything. And it could be that Lars recognized, despite everything, that that ground once belonged to the farm where Poul was raised. Some people feel a tender spot for the family whose farm they bought at auction.

A few remarks were made. "Looks like you've got a sharecropper," someone said to Lars.

Lars didn't know how to answer when people teased him about his indulgence.

"Oh, that," was all he said.

Actually we liked him for it. In a way, Poul was like a prodigal son, returned home to a warm welcome. Better than he deserved. We didn't actually come out and celebrate it, but we gave him what he wanted: peace and privacy.

But then something happened which changed our picture of him. One day suddenly everyone knew that, far from being a traitor, Poul had been in a concentration camp. Was kind of a freedom fighter, one might say.

We felt like we had been deceived. People spoke carefully about the topic.

"Could that be true?"

"I would never have believed that about him."

"Wasn't there something about him being a communist or something?"

There were also a few who tried to get him to answer an almost direct question.

"During the war, I think most of us didn't have it so horribly," was a pretty good start.

You couldn't really tell if Poul reacted to the statement, but it more or less just hung there.

"But of course some people had it worse."

Then a kind of nod appeared in Poul's eyes.

Peter Madsen, who, up till then, had been a bystander, pensively contributed this: "We've heard a lot about those concentration camps. But could they really have been as bad as people say?"

Three pairs of eyes looked at one another and not at Poul, but people still felt a hint of tension in his facial expression. Then there was a slight twitch of a couple of millimeters, and then Poul left. Without a word.

The three watched him go. *Who did he think he was. And his clothing.*

Then Martin Clausen said, "He walks around thinking he's above everyone else."

And then Mogens, the one from Østergaard, who had been an actual freedom fighter without it going to his head, tried something he called 'an approach.' He was probably the one best suited for it, in more ways than one.

He used the National Guard Association as an excuse. Mogens had become one of the local leaders. He worked zealously to increase support for it, especially recruiting people who had focussed on keeping the wheels turning during the war, as they say, to help Denmark come through it as unscathed as possible.

"When it comes down to it, we all wanted the same thing," as the dairy chairman said, when people talked about the years of occupation. "We each worked against the Germans in our own way, and some of us had to do it quietly."

Mogens never confronted him. That's the way he was. "He knows how to handle any situation," maintained Ivar Mikkelsen, who during the war had felt obligated to sell sod to the German military installations. In order to survive, as he said. And Mogens didn't look down on either Ivar or the rest of us, simply because he was the only one from here who had been involved with illegal things. Quite the contrary.

But as I was saying: Mogens used the National Guard Association as an excuse and bicycled out one spring day to the meadow to have a look at his hedge and then did a detour around Lars Jensen's brushy area.

Poul was setting potatoes. He didn't react to the rather prominent greeting with which Mogens approached him. Mogens stopped anyway, put down his bike and walked over to Poul.

From a distance it looked like they stood there talking together.

And that's what they did, Mogens explained later that evening, when the Venstre Party had a general meeting, and people had the chance to ask him about it at the coffee table.

"We talked a bit about the old days. And about potatoes and things like that." Mogens smiled—a bit teasingly, it seemed—and said: "He's planting bintje."

"And what else?"

"Nothing else. I think it's his nerves."

"So was he really in it?"

Mogens didn't think so. Not really. He had been in a concentration camp, all right; but a real freedom fighter?—no, he didn't think so.

Much later it was rumored that the money Poul was living off was a kind of pension from the Freedom Fund.

We agreed it must have been a kind of handicap pension he received, since he happened to be a prisoner of the Germans and his nerves had been shattered.

We all thought the most merciful thing would probably be for us to leave him in peace.

So he was left in peace. We got used to the idea that he was living in the sheep shed down in the scrub, and that he worked a plot of ground which wasn't his; and we got used to seeing him along the road or in the village. We got so used to it that we almost didn't notice him.

Now and then a bit of talk flared up anyway. It might occur late in the evening, when other conversation topics were used up, and people sat at the table with their third or fourth cup of coffee. Is it alright to let a person live like that?

"He picked up an old stove someplace."

"He probably should be in an institution or something like that."

"I always thought we should let people manage their own affairs for as long as they can."

"Pass those cookies around, Laurits."

"And that seems like the way he wants it. People are happy when they get their way."

"I've heard some people donate their old clothes to him. He should have enough money, since he hardly uses any."

"Maybe I should try loaning some from him." A remark

like that might release the bit of laughter which was a suitable closure to their considerations, and at the same time it was a signal for people to get up, say their thanks for the coffee and the evening, and each go their own way through the winter darkness.

But talk like that also got to be old hat and petered out.

And the years passed. Naturally, once in a while there were children who wondered about the strange man living down there in the shed, and who asked the adults, and the adults told them whatever they could remember or wanted to remember.

Eventually, as the older people died or got dementia, clear memories about Poul's grandparents and parents disappeared. Later, as his contemporaries started to decline, memory of Poul's childhood, and gradually his entire past, disappeared down into the earth up at the cemetery. At first, certain information changed over from being direct reports of an eyewitness to being "people say that –" which in the end caused the answers that were given to the questions of younger generations to veer substantially.

Still there was one fact which survived intact, although most people came to regard it not as a fact, but as a joke.

That was one day towards the end of the fifties when a couple of the village boys went down to fish in the river, and on the way passed the place "where the strange guy, that Poul in the shed" sat on the edge of a ditch looking out over the meadows.

They nudged each other, and the youngest of them, who of course wanted to swell his standing with the others, shouted, "Hey, what are you doing over there?"

"I'm studying the birds."

The boys laughed and started running. *Studying the birds!*

When the event was reported back home in the evening, the one boy's grandfather remembered that Poul actually was a graduate. "The Graduate is studying birds," mumbled his son. And some time later the remark was made, when several people were in a car on the way to the dairy general meeting and they passed by Poul walking along the road: "I wonder what The Graduate is studying now?"

As can happen with remarks like that, it was remembered and recycled and gradually Poul came to be referred to as "The Graduate" just as often as he did "that guy Poul" or "the guy in the shed."

"Don't you know, here comes The Graduate," one might hear, and one could almost hear a smile and an "Oh, dear Lord" afterwards.

The sixties were a time of upheaval in the parish. One farm after another went bankrupt. People found work other places, in construction or in an industry. The remaining farmers bought more land, built and modernized. Most houses underwent changes as well. Especially attic spaces were renovated with tax credits which nearly covered the cost of converting the spaces into rooms, some with wood stoves; and quite a few people put balconies on their south or west gables. The remaining gravel roads were paved shortly before the municipal reorganization started, so the parish, which always had demonstrated an admirable frugality and thereby had saved up a small fortune, could enter the larger county in as defensible a position as the city it was going to be combined with. The scene changed in the village, too. The paper dealer disappeared, the butcher disappeared, and the little store, where Mathilde had sold thread, cloth, and underpants with fleece lining, died along with her.

Only two things remained unchanged through the decades: the church and the shed down in the scrub. The scrub didn't belong to Lars Jensen anymore—now it was part of the property merged with Svenning Søndergaard's—but Lars had gotten Svenning to promise to let him stay, that guy Poul. Svenning used the opportunity to knock the price down a couple thousand.

"Lars is something of a softie," some people said afterwards. Other people thought Svenning had acted a bit too overeager. Lord knows he—The Graduate—wasn't going to live forever,. He didn't look so good. It was only a matter of time.

And time did pass. But Poul kept up with it longer than anyone thought he would. He more or less crawled along with it. It was a shame to see him. No one would have thought that he was somewhere in his sixties, and seeing him became an increasingly rare occurrence. In one way or another he had gotten one of Severinsen's boys to do his shopping for him, and he had long ago given up his trips to the city for his handicap pension, which became an actual one. The mailman brought it now. Once a month he had to make the walk around the pig sty, as he called the shed down there in the scrub. He shook his head. *That anyone could live like that.*

It was the Conservation Commission who ended up intervening. In 1976, one of the employees at the county conservation office discovered in that scenic area that there was not just an unsightly shed, but also that the shed was being used as a habitation. He said this was not only unacceptable, but also illegal.

It became a court case, and the case got fatter and fatter. The municipality received letters, but it apparently was not intending to do anything about them. The owner, Svenning Søndergaard, received letters as well as phone calls, but he said that he could not care less. Even if they wanted to go ahead and burn down the shed, he would not lift a finger. Nothing they said would make him do anything about it.

In the end, two men, Schmidt and Hansen, were sent out

in a car to tell the resident that with the owner's knowledge they would be starting the process of removing the shed. They agreed to give him two or three months, and that by that time he should be moved out.

They reached the shed, stopped and got out of the car. It was a cool and sunny spring day with a breeze, but here in the shelter of the brush, the coolness wasn't as noticeable. A dog barked somewhere. It was as if the sun was slightly buzzing, and from a lead pipe in the shed roof a weak smoke rose. When it reached the tree tops it was dispersed by the wind and disappeared.

They stood there. "I wouldn't mind having a cabin here myself," said Schmidt. He took a deep breath and noted the spicy fragrance of the firewood smoke.

They approached the shed. The smell changed.

They found him on the floor, halfway between the stove and the bed. Evidently he had lit the stove and put on a kettle of water, but then he couldn't hold himself up. When they entered, he opened his eyes and asked them to help him into the bed.

Hansen stayed back at the cabin while Schmidt got the ambulance. At the hospital they said it was a miracle Poul was found still alive. Pneumonia, 105.8° at admittance.

People in the area talked about it.

"He sure was lucky they came on that day."

"I don't know."

"No, we'll see what happens."

Poul survived the visit from the two men, but the shed down in the scrub did not. Even though the shed had been there for so long and its use as a habitation extended back so many years that conservation law couldn't be used in this case, the two men were still able to get the owner to enter voluntarily into an agreement. He said that if it didn't cost him anything, they could take away the whole thing.

It took five minutes to write down the agreement, and Schmidt, who was out there alone that day, drove home to the office in good spirits. Not only had he recently saved someone's life, but now he had saved the environment as well, from the aesthetic pollution which that horrible shed had been causing.

Only a couple of days passed before an contractor arrived with a bulldozer, two men and a truck.

"What about the belongings?" the contractor had asked, and he had received the answer that you couldn't call them belongings, the junk in there. "Just get rid of it all."

And that's what they did. It took a couple of hours, and then after that the bonfire burned for four hours—everything of no material value was reduced to ash.

Nature—or perhaps more accurately stated, culture—was restored.

In the village, people talked about it some. Some people didn't really think that Svenning had shown enough resistance. *Dear God, when he liked living in that rathole, that guy Poul, how was that bothering anybody? He was no burden to anyone.*

"There's not much you can do once the authorities get a hold of it," Svenning defended himself. "They have the clauses and the police on their side. I didn't want any part of it."

Society provided for the homeless. When the hospital declared him well enough, Poul was admitted to a nursing home. It would be good for him; most people agreed on that.

He didn't say. He didn't show relief or gladness; actually, for a while he seemed unhappy. He kept asking where his things were, and the director had to call the conservation authorities, and then the contractor, to ask if some of the things belonging to the man who had been living in that shed were stored someplace or other.

He was told that there had been nothing of value. Just a few pieces of furniture that fell apart when they moved them, some clothing which wasn't decent enough to wear, and a pile of old papers that lay in a big mess. And the books were totally ruined by moisture and grime. Everything had been burned.

The director thanked them quietly, and later told Poul that there had not been anything of value, and in any case, nothing that he could use now. He lacked nothing. The director pointed around. New furniture, new bedclothes.

Poul started to make a commotion about wanting his things. It could be heard down the entire hall.

They calmed him down, but the next day he asked for his things again, and again he was quite upset. Yelling about thieves and robbers.

It must have been his nerves. He had always been a bit strange, some people told the superintendent.

"It's a shame when they get preoccupied like that," remarked the director to the nurse, "but it could happen to anyone."

They agreed that he would need something to calm him down.

Poul became a kind of hermit at the nursing home, too. After that initial period he got very quiet and couldn't be coaxed from his room except when they forced him to get washed. During the day he sat in a chair looking out the window, eating at intervals, but that was by the window too.

There were a couple of old guys who remembered Poul from their childhood. They tried to get him to join in when something was going on in the day room, but he refused, angrily even. Sometimes they came and visited him for no particular reason, but then they stopped. "It's no use," they told the director. Soon Poul was forgotten, even by those on his hall. People got used to the fact that one door was always closed.

And the years passed.

So that was the Poul who died recently and who was now going to be buried. It won't be a very large funeral. Not many flags will be raised; most likely just the nursing home's and the church's.

Poul left behind some money, but there don't appear to be any descendants. The child of a cousin is his closest relative, though it is uncertain she will inherit anything. Still, people did check with her before using his money for the funeral. The gravesite is already there. He should at least have a gravestone, and it would only be fitting that there be coffee and cake at the nursing home that day.

A small committee, consisting of the director and couple of spry seniors, took it upon themselves to organize things. And among those, the most difficult thing to decide was what would be written on the stone.

So they went on an outing the hundred yards or so over to the cemetery and looked at the gravesite. The grave manager was there, and he showed them where it was. It looked a bit neglected. The manager explained that he does a little bit now and then, but since no one is paying for it, he can't make it as nice as the ones that pay him for their upkeep. They understood. And considering the circumstances it was pretty nice.

They looked at the stones. There was a large one with the parents' names. "Farmer" was written over the father's name and dates, and over the mother's it read "and his loyal wife." To the left of the large stone there was a smaller one. That was the brother's stone—the one who hung himself. The stone read "loved and missed."

To the right of the parents' there was room for a matching stone. And something had to be written on it. It would look too strange if there was just his name and the dates.

"Loved and missed," would be nicely symmetrical, but then, there wasn't anyone living who loved Poul, and no one who would miss him.

One of the seniors thought that it didn't really matter, that it's just something on a stone. But the director didn't agree. They discussed the matter when they returned and were drinking coffee in the director's office.

Then something was awakened in the back of the director's mind. Something someone said to him once. Then he remembered. "Wasn't there something to do with that he was a freedom fighter?"

"A freedom fighter?—nah –?" The one senior looked at the other, and he shook his head too. "I don't think it was that. Not really."

The director thought it was. He said, "How about 'Veteran from Denmark's fight for freedom'? That would explain plenty."

The others shook their heads. "We can't write that," they said. "He wasn't a real freedom fighter. Not like Mogens Østergaard, and there's not even anything about that on his gravestone."

They sat in silence. Then one of them said suddenly, "But we could write 'Graduate.'"

Now it was the director who looked not only dismissive, but also rather appalled. "You can't just write someone's nickname on their gravestone," he said.

"Well, he was a graduate. He really was a graduate," confirmed the other old man. "He studied in Copenhagen, people said." He added with a wondering tone, "Just like almost all young people do today in one place or another."

They sat quietly. Then the one chuckled, "He definitely was a graduate!"

The director wasn't convinced, so they called in a couple of the oldest residents, and one of them confirmed that that's the way it was. "It was hard for his parents back then," she said.

Finally the director yielded. He actually was happy to have the information, since now he had something concrete he could tell the priest, who could use it at the funeral. She could probably use it for something.

The next morning the director would drive to town, choose a stone, and tell the engraver what to write:

POUL POULSEN
GRADUATE
1908-1993

Actually we were all happy about the outcome. Now we had given him a decent life, that guy Poul.

Actually, we liked him.

SVEND'S STORY

1

So now we have reached the story about Svend. It begins one April day in '68, when, late in the afternoon, he got up after sitting and thinking for an hour or so. He walked to the entry to get his nice cap, and then out through the utility room to his car, which was parked just outside. He got in and started it up.

Magda came out. "What are you doing?"

"Nothing. Just going into town."

"Into town? What are you going to do there?"

"Nothing. Just an errand."

He drove off.

The mail had come late that day, and it wasn't due to the weather. Even though it was only the beginning of April, it was a warm, dry day with a bright sunny sky. The reason for the delay was that on that particular day there had been a handful of certified letters. They required receipts, and receipts involved having coffee at more places than usual; so it was already after twelve by the time the mailman reached Svend's house.

They sat at the table. Magda got out a plate, silverware and a glass. "Won't you have a bite to eat, as well?" she asked. The mailman would like that. Magda's meatballs had a nice heft to them; he knew that from previously. For appearance's sake, he paused a moment. Then he said, "Thanks for offering."

He took two meatballs, five or six potatoes, a ladleful of sauce and a couple spoonfuls of strawberry marmalade on his plate, and the others gave him the peace and quiet he needed to catch up to them. Svend read some of the newspaper that the mailman had laid on the table. "Those damned college students," he said. "They deserve a whipping." The mailman

135

mumbled in agreement. Then Svend got around to saying, "You're late today."

The mailman explained that there were so many certified letters. "From the county," he added. Svend nodded. "I saw the two stakes in the ground," he said. "They sure are a bunch of varmints." There was a hardness in his voice. "But me they are not going to…" he began. Magda got up and started collecting the dishes. "Easy," she said. Svend gave her an irritated look. Then his expression relaxed again. "There is probably one for me, too," he said quietly.

Svend took his letter and opened it, while Magda signed. She was the one who always took care of those kinds of little things. Svend sat there, lost in thought. Magda looked at him anxiously. "Expropriation," he mumbled. "Grounds inspection." He got up and walked noisily into the living room without a word. Magda quickly asked about the mailman's children. "Well," he said, "my daughter is going to be an intern at the bank this summer, after she gets her diploma."

So it was a bit later in the afternoon when Svend drove into town. On the way, he stopped by the blacksmith to get a few squirts into his Morris 1000. "So you're going on a trip?" asked the blacksmith. "No," said Svend, "just to town. But go ahead and fill it up."

In town he parked at the center and cut across to the land surveyor's office. He left his clogs outside the door and knocked.

He wasn't visiting the land surveyor because there was any special relationship between them. Actually, Svend had only been in contact with him once before. The reason was that Svend knew, as did everyone else, that a lawyer earns his money sitting behind a desk, while a surveyor earns his money tramping around in the fields. A visit to the surveyor's office rarely necessitated a bill. He had just come to ask a question. "Are you the one who put stakes in my land?" was his opening.

The surveyor ensured him that it wasn't. He said it must be the county. Svend knew that already, but still he sat there a moment and thought. Then he said, "I need your help. Do you have the Constitution?"

"The Constitution?" The surveyor had a hard time hiding his surprise, but he said of course he had the Constitution. "Once I even had to sign that I would follow it," he said. This didn't seem to make an impression on Svend. "Can I see it?" he said.

The surveyor rummaged around in his shelf and eventually handed a heavy dusty book across the desk. "Is there anything special you want to look at?" he asked. Svend shook his head. He just wanted to look at it, he said, and he asked if he could stay there and read it. He took out his glasses and started reading.

It took a while. The surveyor assumed that his client was sitting there looking for clause 73, but he didn't say anything. Instead he carried out a couple of phone conversations, and he turned to his calculator a few times and got an equation to add up. This didn't bother Svend. The surveyor walked out to the front office and came back with a pile of cards and papers that needed signing. He passed the time with that, while Svend kept reading.

Finally Svend found it. "Here it is." The surveyor looked up. That was it. Svend sat with his finger planted on clause 73. "The right of property ownership is inviolable," he said. The surveyor nodded and said, "But expropriation is permitted, when the public good demands it." And he quickly added, "with full compensation, naturally."

"The public good!" There was an obvious tone of contempt in Svend's voice. "Nonsense," he said. "In this case it's the good of Oskar." He reread the clause. Then he asked, "Can I borrow this?"

The surveyor thought a moment. The Constitution was not a book he often used, so he could do without it, even though there were other things in that edition by Karnov. On the other hand, a legal document like that wasn't meant for laypeople, not without thorough commentaries and explanations. He said, "It could be that the library has a more suitable annotated edition. You might like that better."

Svend said he didn't need any notes. "This is the Constitution, isn't it?" he asked.

"Well sure, but—" The surveyor didn't get any farther. "Can I borrow it, or are you on their side?" Svend was looking right at him. Then Svend said suddenly, in a different tone, "I'll take care of it. I'll wrap it in a cover so nothing happens to it."

The land surveyor nodded. "That's fine," he said, and he also offered to explain the issue in a bit more detail. He told Svend about the process of expropriation, about taxation and about legal practices, and about anything that might be of interest to a person who was going to be subjected to action by the government. Svend listened, with a little closed smile on his lips. Then he said, "I'd better get home." He got up from his chair, taking Karnov too. "He's going to have trouble," he said firmly. "This is a land of law and order. We live in a free country." The surveyor sighed. "Now, listen," he started to say, but Svend was not disposed to hearing any more. He offered his hand and left.

Svend's full name was Svend Agner Vestergaard. Despite his name, he lived in the eastern part of the parish, and the farm was called Nygaard. It had gotten that name at the start of the previous century, when Svend's great-great-grandfather split his farm in half, and let the youngest son build on the farthest piece. The other half, the original farm, had been out of the family for some time.

"Svend came by it too easily," was Oskar's judgment many years later. "No siblings, and he took over the farm debt-free. He never had to fight for anything, not like most people. He never imagined that things could be any different." The consultant nodded sympathetically. Oskar continued, "Some people think they have more of a right than other people. And Svend has always been like that." He toasted with the consultant, and, as if on command, they poured some schnapps into their coffee after a quick sip. After a good drink and an "aah," the consultant agreed: "He's never asked for my help. He hasn't kept up with the times. He's never invested as much as one penny." This was bit unfair, but Oskar didn't see any reason to be preachy. The consultant was quite young. Back in '58 he had just been a big kid, when Svend had renovated his cow house and put in a feeding aisle. It wasn't until later, when Svend had gotten shaken up, as they say, that he gave up on cows and pigs and scratched out a living just through raising a bit of grain. No, he decided, it would be too diffuse to veer off into all that. He would have to be satisfied with just shaking his head regretfully and stating that it was a shame when people ruined their own prospects.

Then they changed the subject to discussing field plans.

Oskar and Svend were neighbors. They had been neighbors since the mid-fifties, when Oskar married Lilly, the daughter from Søgaard Farm. In contrast to the grocer's Magda, whom the farmer's son Svend some years previous had snatched up right from under the nose of the farmhand's son Oskar, Lilly was sturdy and fertile, and the same could be said about the farm, which followed her a couple of years later. The farm became Oskar's springboard. And while Svend more or less isolated himself with a bruised pride, after having lost one election onto the dairy board, it was as if all the trusted posts that Svend, in another and more stabile era would have seemed to be born to assume, systematically were taken over by Oskar. Not just the place on the dairy board, but also in the slaughterhouse and the feed cooperative, not to mention the parish council, where Oskar became the chairman after the vote in '62. "He'll be a politician one day," people said about Oskar.

About Svend, Magda once told the schoolteacher, "He's too proud and sensitive to deal with other people. He can't bear losing."

So Oskar and Svend were neighbors, even though they weren't the kind who stood at the stone wall talking. Oskar didn't have time for that anyway. His time was taken up off the property. The parish, the feed cooperative, the dairy and the grocery demanded most of his attention and presence. Once— that was in '63—Oskar borrowed a container of gasoline from Svend, when he was in a hurry to get to a meeting and his Saab had run out of gas. "In my position I can't risk using tractor gas," he explained. Svend nodded sympathetically and didn't say anything about the container being full of tractor gas. Another time—and that was when Svend had broken his arm—Oskar had offered to drive together to the meeting at the slaughterhouse.

Svend let him know that his wife had a driver's license, but that he hadn't given a thought to going to the meeting anyway.

The relationship between Oskar and Svend is part of the story, but it's the changes in society that set it all in motion. The changes occurred in such a way that, after the land couldn't support as many people as before, entrepreneurial folks began occupying themselves with other types of commerce. Therefore, the parish council, together with the neighboring townships' parishes, had pressed the county into constructing a new highway, intersecting the lines that had marked the landscape for centuries. This would bring the region closer to the big world outside, and also lure a greater fraction of modern society's business development and flow of money in their direction. It was no trivial amount of work for the parish leadership; especially Oskar had been indefatigable. "We need a new life artery," as he expressed it, at every opportunity.

They succeeded in persuading the county as the sixties came

to a close; that's how long ago it was. The county council resolved that the road would be built, and the county road surveyor directed his construction department to take care of the details. His name was Jensen—the construction department, that is.

It was Svend's fate that a couple of houses were located in the way of the road, if it were going to follow a somewhat straight line. It wasn't Svend's house—the closest one was a quarter mile from his property, and due to the terrain they couldn't even be seen from there. But just that, that the reason was hidden, made the effect even stronger.

Tearing down a house is a costly affair, and strong protests came from a powerful owner of one of the houses. Regarding the other house, its owner would have probably preferred compensation to being allowed to keep it. In any case, that was the engineer's understanding, when he did the introductory measurements and started to deduce that the house was rather in the way. Magnus protested, of course, but very quietly. He remarked, with only partially hidden eagerness, "This is going to cost you plenty."

Engineer Jensen was a competent engineer, and the county road surveyor liked curves. So, with the aid of a curve table and a slide rule, they were able to reroute the said road, using soft curves, around the endangered buildings. It looked beautiful on the map, and there were no problems getting the project finally approved. The parish chairmen were looking forward to it. They were about to construct a monument that would impact the landscape and development forever. The parish leadership's elation and expectation trickled down over time throughout their neglected community, and was soon shared by all their subjects. With a single exception: Svend.

Svend was not happy—to put it mildly. The elegant curves that saved the two houses from demolition had caused the road, not as originally planned, to follow the boundary between his property and his neighbor's. But it lay entirely on his side of the line, and askew, relative to the boundary. If you looked more closely at the public plan printed in the newspaper, it was evident that Svend Vestergaard would not only lose to the road a strip of land nearly a half-mile long, but he would also lose a wedge of land of nearly three acres to his neighbor. The neighbor—that was Oskar, of course.

Everyone was talking about the plan. "So you will be coming into some money," said the dairy chairman to Svend, when they met in the grocery. "and Lord knows you can do without that tiny bit of land." Svend didn't answer.

That was when the certified letter with the notification of inspection arrived.

"It's hard to forget that day," said the land surveyor. "The strangest day I have ever experienced in my career.

"It started in the usual way: the long column of cars arriving with the county board members, technicians and other individual experts; the many handshakes exchanged; and the county road surveyor, who pointed out the future roadbed in the terrain—it was all routine. And there was nothing new in the way the ramifications were outlined. Such and such an area, establishment of a new driveway to the farm, drawing of new setbacks around the new road. My job was to confirm the areas. Otherwise most of the people present stood around in small groups, chatting about other things, while the project was being explained to Svend Vestergaard.

"He stood there with a blank expression on his face. He looked like he usually did. Then he was presented with a settlement offer specifying precise compensation for the amount of land surrendered, for additional burden, and for the required easement. All of it was routine; one of the county board members was already on his way to the warmth of his car to wait there for the completion of the transaction.

"Then Svend spoke: 'You are breaking the law. The right

to property is inviolable.' and he took out the book and read aloud, in a clear voice, the Constitution's clause 73, word for word: '*The right of property ownership is inviolable. No one can be required to surrender their property, except when demanded by the public good. This can only happen according to law and with full compensation.*'

"It was very quiet for a few seconds after the reading. Then the head of the technical committee started to say something, but Svend Vestergaard interrupted him: 'Show me the law that has been passed by Parliament, where it says that Svend Vestergaard has to surrender some of his property.'

"It was to no avail that seven or eight people tried to explain to him, all at the same time, that a new law didn't have to be passed for every separate instance, but that according to transportation law, the state, county and municipality were permitted to expropriate property for the purpose of building roads. 'Now listen,' the county road surveyor began, trying to get the undisciplined crowd of politicians and subordinate technicians to shut their traps, 'now listen to me,' but I think that that was the moment, right then, when the storyline became inevitable. Svend Vestergaard lost his composure briefly. He pointed his forefinger at the county road surveyor and asked him, in a voice so loud that no one could miss it, how much Oskar had paid him to place the road as far south as possible. 'This is my land; you are stealing my land,' he shouted. 'You could have put the road on the property line, that would have been understandable. Or why not on Oskar's side; he's the one who wanted the road, not me.' We heard the insinuation, of course, but the county road surveyor took his time explaining to all present, that due to technical reasons, it wasn't possible to follow the property line. That would have resulted in the demolition of several houses further east.

"I stood there looking at Svend Vestergaard. He had regained his composure. His voice was nearly normal, and he attempted a smile, which could best be described as condescending. 'You are breaking the law, but I'll win in the end,' he declared. Then he left.

"A county council member remarked afterwards, shaking his head: 'It's impossible to deal with people who take the law literally like that.'

"'And who believe in it,' I said."

A couple of days later, the land surveyor stopped by Svend's place on an errand. The parish chairman had called him and hinted that it might be a good idea if someone spoke with Svend, and the surveyor agreed: "This is an unfortunate situation we have here." But the surveyor thought it would be best if it were a local who did this, someone Svend knew and would listen to. Someone who had some local standing. The parish chairman didn't agree. "Svend and I have never been on the same wavelength," he explained. Then he added, "Just send the bill to the parish council."

In the end the surveyor let himself be talked into it, and after having rummaged both in his memory and in some papers, he put together a question about an old easement, which could be used as an excuse for a visit. He took a couple of maps and a briefcase too, so it would look credible.

When the land surveyor found him, Svend was standing in the barn, talking to a sow, who was lying amid her litter of pink piglets. Svend didn't seem all that welcoming; he took his cane and started scratching the sow on her back. The surveyor explained that he was examining some old easements, and that he was hoping he could get Svend's help in locating one of them. Svend appeared a bit skeptical, but he followed him outside. When the surveyor led him south, away from the part of the property involving the road project, Svend became himself again. They had a good chat about the spring weather, and the grain, and about milk prices. "Everyone says that we should join EU," said Svend. The surveyor nodded: "That's what they say." They walked for a bit without saying anything. "Well, I don't know," said Svend, turning his head so he was almost looking at the surveyor, "people say a lot of things."

Now they had arrived at the part of the field that once had been called reg. nr. 7d. The surveyor made a big show out of looking at maps and papers and mumbling aloud to himself, but after explaining the problem to Svend, it wasn't difficult for them to agree that the easement concerned a previous owner's property rights to a long-ago demolished house with a vegetable garden. It was registered in 1863, so it hardly had any bearing anymore. "That was who my great-grandfather bought the parcel from," explained Svend. "It was like a wedge into our land." On the walk back, the surveyor learned the history of the farm in the smallest details. Not just the great-grandfather, but the grandfather as well, had added a number of acres.

"A person feels responsible for it," said Svend. "In our family we always understood to hold onto what what we were given."

They were back in the farmyard, and Svend said that Magda probably had coffee ready. The surveyor thanked him, and it wasn't long before they were sitting at the table. The land surveyor talked about some of the unusual easements he had encountered before.

That passed the time, while they had some cheese and bread, and the first two cups of coffee. Svend sat quietly. When they arrived at the cake, Magda said, "Svend doesn't understand how they can treat him like this." Svend mumbled something about varmints and criminals, and the surveyor quickly began his well-prepared explanation. He said that in a case like this, it was important to make the encroachment as small as possible. And though of course it might be felt as unfair to the individual person, the path of the roadway seen as a whole is the most favorable. "And the law treats the public good as superior to the property right of the individual," he said, and he continued on a long tangent about all of the things that could never have been done if it weren't this way. "We would never have been able to create the society we have today, if the public good didn't have the highest priority."

Svend just said, "The devil can have the society that takes away my rights." Magda looked worried. "But now Svend," she said. Svend straightened himself even more. He banged on the table. "The devil can have the society that takes away my rights," he repeated, "and lets itself be told what to do by someone like that." He made a movement with his head in the direction that pointed right at Søgaard Farm.

Now the surveyor was starting to look a bit worried, too. "You have to be realistic," he said. "No one wants to bother you. It's unfortunate that it has a greater impact on your property, but you'll have to make the best of it. You're going to get a nice compensation, and you can use that money however you want. It's tax-free," he said. "Expropriations are tax-free. You could buy bonds with it. Current interest rates aren't too bad."

Svend looked at him, so he almost felt ashamed of himself. "You don't understand," he said. "I don't want money. I just want my rights. And it's my right to keep my land." He sat there, while his face returned to its normal hue. Ceremoniously, he said, "This land has been my father's, my grandfather's, his father's and his grandfather's. And that incurs responsibility; but you don't understand that. And the others don't either." Then he glanced at Magda.

The land surveyor said that of course he understood, but now we were living in a developing society, and Svend said some unflattering things about development and then he asked, "Why didn't you help me? You were there that day." The surveyor explained that he was only on the job as an expert, to answer questions about land area and registration numbers and appraisals and things like that, but that he had no influence. "I'm like a book that the politicians can open if they need some information," he said. "But," he added, "I can give you a piece of good advice. You should have your lawyer or consultant with you when the appraisal commission comes. They can protect your interests."

Svend shook his head. "I've talked with them already. They say the same thing as you; that nothing can be done and that I should try to get the biggest compensation I can. They would help me with it, but it would be a waste of time."

A bit later he said, "You're all against me," and he started listing everyone who was out to get him: the parish chairman, the neighbors on both sides, and the county's people, who danced to the parish chairman's tune. "They're all out to get me," he said. He sat there, gathered himself, gave up, then gathered himself again. Then he said, "And, of course, you're also in his power."

Magda quickly offered a second piece of cake, but the surveyor said no thanks. He had to be going. He thanked them for the coffee, got up and put out his hand.

"The book," said Svend. "I'd like to keep it a bit longer. They say a judge, the head of the commission, is going to be coming."

The surveyor nodded. He probably ought to repeat the whole thing again, but it wouldn't help. Instead he said, "And that easement, I guess that can be deleted from the records." He gathered up his briefcase and maps, thanked them for the coffee, and left.

When he was sitting in his car again, about to start it up, Magda came out the utility room door with a bucket of garbage. He could see that Svend was still sitting at the table.

She walked over to his car; he rolled down the window. "You'll have to excuse him," she said. "He gets excited so easily."

She glanced at the kitchen window and continued over towards the pig barn.

In the coming months, Svend and his situation were the talk of the area. Regardless of whether it was coincidental meetings at the grocery or at coffee tables or after confirmations or funerals, eventually the conversation turned to Svend. "He's gone stark raving mad," said the grocer. "He's always been a bit different; he was like that when he was a boy," said Enok's Gerda, who was evidently qualified by having known him better than most—from what people said. "He has plenty of land, that idiot," said Holger to Jens Christian, and Jens Christian agreed. "And he doesn't even use it to it's full potential as it is," he said, and then they repeated the story about how Svend stood in front of the judge and the rest of the appraisal commission, reading aloud from the Constitution, and blaming not only the commission, but also Oskar, the county road surveyor, the land surveyor, and everyone on the county and parish councils who he could remember the names of, for being criminals. Finally Magda came and dragged him inside. "But he got a nice compensation," they agreed. They also agreed that something like that was always welcome.

What was unusual about the story was that it developed over a longer period of time than local stories normally did. It was as if it didn't want to end; new developments were always arising; but where they came from, no one knew. Who would have known, for example, that Magda had threatened to go live with her sister in Copenhagen, if Svend didn't stop being so obstinate? Magda hadn't told anyone that when she was in town, but still everyone knew about it. It was as if it spread through the air, like hoof and mouth disease. People also knew that Svend's lawyer had thrown him out, when Svend visited him to get the lawyer to sue the authorities, and that Svend had written to the Prime Minister, and later to the king himself. But that information originated with the mailman, who was keeping an eye on the correspondences.

"Too bad about Svend," said Oskar, when the issue came up in his presence. "It's sad when people don't have a vision for the future, and they put their own interests above that of the whole." And one evening at the coffee table in the meeting house, Oskar let slip that Svend had refused to accept his compensation. "When he sent back the check, he wrote that he wanted his land back." Oskar looked around. "So the county deposited the money into Svend's bank account, but wouldn't you know that he mailed a check for that amount back to the county and repeated that he wanted his land back." Oskar chuckled. "But he subtracted the cost of postage from the amount," he said to the person next to him. Then Oskar regained his official facial expression. "The county commissioner decided that the amount would be deposited in a special account, which Svend can draw from, when he comes to his senses."

"Is it a lot of money?" someone asked. Oskar nodded knowingly. "The number isn't official," he said, and around the table they discussed the unofficial amount.

The third or fourth act, or however many we are up to, unfolded when the contractor's road-building trucks reached Svend Vestergaard's eastern boundary. It was the year after the expropriation and not the most favorable time of year. Even the ones who were doing the earth-moving were bothered by having to bulldoze a field of grain just before harvest.

Saturday around noon they reached the boundary line, and when they arrived Monday morning to start a new workweek, Svend was standing on the stone wall with his hunting rifle over his shoulder. The men were a bit hesitant. They took a little longer than usual preparing their machines. They were extra careful in checking the oil levels; they tightened a few bolts. But when the contractor's car came into view behind them, they got into their trucks and started them up. The bulldozer approached the boundary. Svend swung his rifle into place and shouted: "Stop in the name of the Constitution!"

Jens Madsen couldn't hear anything, but he could see plenty. He stopped the bulldozer, crawled down from the driver's seat and gingerly approached his good friend, Svend, who had played halfback, back when Jens Madsen was the left wing on the level five team. "What's wrong, Svend?"

Svend explained to Jens, that according to clause 73 of the Constitution, the right to property is inviolable, and that no underhanded tricks were going to strip him of even one square foot of land. "I'll shoot anyone who trespasses on my property without my permission," he said. Jens Madsen started by saying, "Now look," but Svend continued the sentence for him, "When people aren't respecting the law, a person has to defend his own rights." He said it as if it were something he had memorized.

Jens Madsen tried to explain that it wasn't him and his work buddies that had done anything wrong; they were just doing what they were told, to earn their paychecks. But Svend didn't budge. "Cross the line and I'll shoot."

Jens walked back and waved the others in. They stood in a group discussing what to do. Jens walked over to Svend again. "You're going to get yourself locked up," he said. "Why don't you go home to Magda and have some coffee."

"Come any closer, and I'll shoot. And it's in self-defense." Jens retreated. The contractor, who had arrived, and who had been oriented to the situation, asked Jens if he thought it would do any good if he talked to the crazy guy—as he called him—himself. Jens didn't think so, and the contractor walked relieved back to his car and drove to the nearest telephone. The men drove their machines a couple of hundred yards back from the roadbed. A decision was going to have to be made, and they would have to wait until the situation was cleared up.

Svend remained standing on the wall.

An hour or so later the police showed up. It was Olsen, the local policeman. He walked over to the stone wall. Svend pointed the gun at him, but he kept walking. Svend said something about the Constitution and his right to property, but the policeman didn't respond. Svend shouted with an unsteady voice, "Stop or I'll shoot," but the policeman kept coming closer, right up to him. Svend was having trouble holding his rifle still. His torrent of words was becoming more and more incoherent. Now the policeman was just a few inches from the muzzle. Tears were increasingly audible in Svend's voice, but it was still possible to hear words like "constitution" and "right."

The policeman looked at him pleasantly. "You must have looked at the calendar wrong," he said. "Hunting season hasn't started yet." He put out his big mitt and took the rifle. He opened it and discretely pulled out the shells and put them in his pocket. Then he looked down the barrel. "It's empty," he said, loud enough that the contractor, who had returned and was standing behind his car a little ways off, could hear it. Then he said, "Let's go," and he started walking with the open rifle in his hand, through the grain, towards the farm's buildings. Svend followed him. "He was walking kind of unsteadily," Jens Madsen said to everyone he met.

The next day the newspaper reported: "Owner tries to stop roadwork in vain with rifle in hand." According to the article, there would be no legal action taken, since it was decided to treat the episode as a demonstration, and since no one was harmed in any way. The rifle was not loaded, it read, and the man would just be fined for creating a disturbance.

By the time the newspaper came out, the machines were deep into Svend Vestergaard's property. The contractor's workers didn't see Svend at all, and the people in town didn't either. Magda let it be known that he had caught the flu or something like that. For a while people asked about his health. At the harvest festival in the meeting house, where neither Svend nor

Magda were present, the high point of the entertainment was a song about a hunter who went hunting without shells, but who read the hunting ordinance to Oskar's pheasants. Also, quite a few remarks about "creating a disturbance" released not inconsiderable merriment.

Some time later the land surveyor received a package, and inside the package was the book with the Constitution. It had what a book dealer would call 'signs of wear.' And across the pages where the Constitution was printed, in thick pencil was written, "Abolished in Denmark."

Time passed. It passed every day at Svend's property, where a sense of isolation grew unhindered. Magda was gone, and the cows and pigs were too. Only the changes in seasons brought some variation to the picture. Svend sowed and harvested at the appropriate times, but otherwise not much activity was observed there. He wasn't in attendance at meetings or events, and other than seeing him now and then in his fields, he was only seen every two weeks, riding his bicycle down the nice new highway to the neighboring town to do his shopping. Evidently he had given up his car, but he had mounted a wooden crate behind his bicycle seat and a basket on the handlebars. The only local person he kept in contact with was the blacksmith, a man of few words, where Svend bought his tractor gas.

His property taxes, his more or less symbolic VAT, and his modest income tax he payed on time.

No one heard anything different, and not even the credit union loan, which was from the renovations in '58, caused him any apparent difficulty. Interest and payments were no more than a couple hundred *kroner* each due date. And it stayed that way. There was no one who had the opportunity to convince him that his interest was too small to declare. And while the region's other farms acquired new barns and silos, and had their attics renovated with assistance from the VAT exclusion,

Svend's property came to resemble more and more a future farming museum.

No one tried to pull him back into community life. No one did much to invite him out or even just to go over and talk with him. "Too bad about that guy, Svend," someone would say, but that was about all. People were unsure if it were a situation they could handle. It would have been different if it had been an accident or a case of bad luck. If the farm burned down, or if Magda hadn't left, but was dead, then people would have known how to behave, whether they were good friends or just neighbors.

But this—that the man obviously had gone stark raving mad—meant that people couldn't predict how he might react if someone tried to do something. It could be embarrassing.

So he was left alone, and gradually people stopped talking about him. His story was too well-known, and the lack of direct contact with him prevented new ribbons from being tied on. Although the year he didn't harvest the farthest parcel, and apparently decided to let it go out of production completely, reignited some talk. But the sight of that, too, became an everyday occurrence. All people heard about Magda was that the teacher had bumped into her at Tivoli, back when the senior class was visiting Bornholm and had spent one night in Copenhagen on the trip out. A few of the children had talked about it; the teacher never engaged in social talk.

Soon after that we knew that she was working at Tuborg.

2

It was one morning about twenty years later in October, one of those October days when it's not raining, but everything is still wet, as if the moisture were rising up from below.

He turned into the driveway and drove slowly towards the

buildings. For many years he had had a strange feeling when he drove by the place. Something was left undone and waiting, and at the same time he knew there was nothing he could do. "I have nothing to feel bad about," he thought each time, yet that stretch of highway seemed filled with reproaches. He had an errand to carry out, and, truth be told, he had been on his way out there several times, but always had something else to do on the way, so the trip wouldn't be wasted, as he said; and these other things always took up all the time he had. But now he couldn't put it off any longer. It was something he had to do.

He parked in front of the utility room door and told his helper to stay in the car. "It could get a bit uncomfortable," he said.

He stood there, looking around. The property didn't look neglected, actually. Things were neat, almost overly so around the buildings, but it could still use some basic maintenance. And as decent as it looked on the surface, it really wasn't. When he opened the utility room door he had to really push to get it to open. Dampness. He knocked on the door to the kitchen. There was a voice that clearly said, "Come in." That door stuck, too.

Svend was sitting at the table. He was done with his morning coffee and he was playing solitaire. He looked up. He didn't look like the eccentric or hermit that one would have expected to see, judging from all the rumors. Somewhat newly shaven, nice work clothes, and he might have even had a haircut recently. Svend said, "Welcome." The land surveyor said, "Thanks," and asked if this was a bad time. It wasn't. He was invited to take a seat.

Svend gathered up the cards. "I lost anyway," he said. Then he looked up: "Is it about an old easement again?"

The surveyor didn't answer. A hint of a smile was enough. He said, "It's about a question."

Svend got up and walked into the rear living room. He came

back with a box of cigars. "I don't smoke any more," he said, "But I have them, so I can offer you one."

It was a Paragana, and it became obvious that it was not just the doors that were marked by dampness. It was hard to get it lit and no easier to keep it that way. "They're going to put in high tension lines," the surveyor said.

"Okay," said Svend. "I don't care, not in the least."

His guest relit his cigar. "It's going to cut across your southwest corner. One tower is going to be located on your field."

That didn't seem to make an impression either, and the surveyor continued telling how he had been asked to design the line, and that he was going to have to come by one day and measure for it. "I thought I should give you plenty of advance notice. In a few days someone from the electric company is going to come by with an agreement for you to sign."

"It doesn't matter to me," said Svend.

The land surveyor had to give up on the cigar. He leaned back. "I was thinking about what happened back then," he said. "That time with the road. It bothered me that it had to happen like that."

Svend made a motion with his hand which probably was meant to indicate that he didn't feel like talking about it. His guest continued anyway: "I've often been involved in projects that could have been interpreted as unjust against the people they affected, and also projects where I didn't like what had to be done. But generally things got ironed out with the affected parties with tolerable consideration. The people understood that, whatever it was, was going to happen regardless. But it was different with this road. That was one of the most unpleasant situations of its kind I've ever been involved with. I've always thought that I probably should have explained the whole thing better back then; that I should have spent more time on it that first time we talked."

Svend sat there, as if he hadn't heard a word. Then he looked up, about breast-high: "There's nothing to talk about. It was my fault." Now he looked directly as his guest. "You rattled me. You did. I was too weak. I should have fired that day. That's what a free man would have done."

He sat quietly a moment. Then he said, as if by way of explanation, "But I don't have any children."

"So go ahead," he said. "You do whatever you want anyway."

The land surveyor left.

And while he was driving along, lost in his own thoughts, in his just a few-weeks-old Morris Oxford, he didn't just hear a bump, he felt it too, when it was transmitted down from the seat, up through his spine to his brain, telling him that underneath him, underneath his car, there was something that was not supposed to be there.

He stopped. He got out. Well!

It was one of the potholes that was quite a bit deeper than the others, so deep that only a tractor could go right over it. He had hit that hole. Here was another place he had to remember.

He got in and drove on. But only a short way. Then he stopped again. Something about the way the motor sounded.

Out again. Around the car. Down on his knees and looking underneath. There it was. Hole in the exhaust just in front of the muffler. Dented muffler. The pipe hung down dragging on the road.

He stuck his arm under the car to get a hold of the exhaust pipe, to try and reattach it to the muffler. He groped for it, so far under that he wasn't able to put his arm in and look at the same time. Then he found it—and with a gasp pulled out his hand. He blew on it, then placed it against the cool car door. Well, that was stupid.

He looked under the car again. It was still there. It would probably stay on until he made it to the mechanic's and had it fixed. It would probably be fine, as long as he didn't back up. If he drove up to Kresten's, he could turn around in front of their house, and then he wouldn't have to go all the way home and tell Kristine what was wrong All he had to do was make it back to town and have the mechanic fix it.

He got in again and started it up. It didn't sound too good. It was so noisy, he was almost afraid to press on the accelerator. It sounded like he was about to break the sound barrier, even though he was just creeping along. And strangely enough that, even though the motor was wailing, he thought he could hear and feel over the noise, how the exhaust pipe hopped along over the road's unevenness.

He turned into Kresten's driveway and regretted it only after it was too late. Because Kresten was home, of course, and now he was going to have to stop and explain what was wrong, and that it wasn't the Morris Oxford there was something wrong with. Kresten will sure gloat over this. He might not say anything, but he'll be thinking it. He'll think, that's what happens when you put yourself above others. And then he'll be sympathetic and say, "What a shame with that nice, new car, that it already has to be fixed."

Kresten was home. And his wife. And his two young children. And they all came dashing out to the driveway, from the barn and from the yard and from the utility room, as he arrived in a cloud of noise. They stood gaping, watching him while he used the entire width of their front drive for his u-turn. And they gaped even more, if that were possible, when they saw him continue on, after it had seemed like he was going to stop, waving them off as if to explain that it was all a mistake, that he didn't have time to talk now after all.

"Doesn't look so good," said the mechanic. "You'd better do something about that road. This is going to be expensive. New exhaust pipe and new muffler."

Thomas looked grim. "It's that parish council," he said. "None of them live near our road. They make sure the roads are fine where they live."

"Hm. Couldn't you throw a little gravel in the holes," said the mechanic. "Then it wouldn't be so dangerous."

"It's a public road. It's public all the way to Kresten's driveway. I take care of it from there." After a bit, he said, "And it's fine there. My road is fine."

"Maybe the parish council hasn't given it any thought," said the mechanic. "They're not thinking about your new car. The road's fine for horse-drawn wagons and Fergusons, which is fine for most people."

Thomas got the message. Then he asked, "When can you have it done?" And when he found out that it wouldn't be ready until the next day, since the parts had to be delivered, he just said good-bye and left. Out on the county road and down the pot-holed lane to his house, by the edge of the pond.

Kresten approached on his bicycle. He stopped and stuck the tip of his clog down to the ground. "You walking?" he asked.

Thomas grumbled. "It's that damned road. It's hazardous." He just stood there. Then he looked to one side and said, "Yeah, it must have looked a little strange, driving by your house without stopping, but I couldn't really –"

"Couldn't you stop?"

"Of course I could stop. It's just that damned road plaguing me. How can we keep on living here? They should fill it in with a couple loads of gravel," he added.

Kresten looked down the road. "Yeah, maybe," he said. "But— is it really that bad? The veterinarian doesn't complain when he comes out to us."

"The veterinarian! That speed demon. The way he drives he barely even notices the road." For the first time, Thomas looked directly at Kresten. "It might be okay for tractors, but when you're driving in a car, it's terrible." And then he nodded abruptly and kept on walking, upset, while he prepared what he was going to say to Kristine when she noticed. It was the parish council. It was all their fault.

The next day he picked up his car, and drove it home carefully. There was a burnt smell from the new exhaust system, and that bothered him. He called the mechanic. That was normal. It's supposed to do that.

Fine.

It was raining. It was good for the grain, here in June, but not so good for the Feast of St. John gathering at the community meetinghouse. But they still had to go. He had been a member of the board at one time, and he couldn't just stay home because it was raining. And the priest needed an audience to give his bonfire speech to, and of course Kristine usually sang as well.

Sure is strange, thought Thomas, how when there was only one teacher at the school, he always came. He sang, he read telegrams, and he gave a speech. Now there's a bigger school with six teachers. And they never see them. Not in the meetinghouse or anywhere. And the priest can't sing. If it weren't for Kristine, he thought, they might as well get rid of the songbooks.

He looked out the window at the heavy sky. "I guess we'd better get on with it," he said, and went and drove the car out of the garage, the former henhouse, and Kristine emerged with the picnic basket and sat down next to him. And then they drove off, quickly down their own well-maintained road, but when they got to the public section, Thomas slowed down close to a walking speed. To a distant observer, their progress would have appeared both strange and tentative.

Inside the car, Thomas was swearing, and the coffee cups were tinkling in Kristine's basket. "Shouldn't we be bringing Kresten?" asked Kristine suddenly.

"No," said Thomas, "We didn't talk about that."

A few hours later they were on the road again. Homeward. It had been a good Saint John get-together. True the bonfire didn't burn, even though they had poured plenty of gas on it, but then they moved inside the meetinghouse and had their coffee, sang some songs, and the priest had read a couple of stories.

So now they were on their way home. It was almost completely dark, and there was water in all the potholes, so it wasn't easy to see which ones were really potholes and which ones were just irregularities in the road.

He felt a bump. Not as bad as the one the day before, but still. Carefully he pressed the accelerator. It sounded fine, thank God. If something had happened it would have pushed him over the edge. He had seen the looks that Kresten and the mechanic had exchanged with some of the other guests.

They were nearly past the worst of it. But this was ridiculous.

"We pay taxes just like everyone else," said Kristine suddenly.

Thomas nodded. Yes, they did. Just as much as everyone else.

"They're going to hear about it."

The next morning he repeated what he had said. Then he added, "I'm going over to his place. I'm going over to Peter Overgaard's when I'm done milking. You'll have to feed the pigs," he said. "I'm going over at nine." And Kristine said fine and then repeated how they pay taxes just like everyone else. Just like Peter Overgaard does even.

About three hours later he made his way on foot over the pasture, down the farm road past Karen Madsen's place, and up the county road—the paved county road—to Peter Overgaard's place. He stopped for a second at the driveway and pulled out his watch from his vest pocket. Just past nine. That was good. Everyone knew that the parish council president didn't receive people before nine. Before nine he was in his barn or on his own time.

But that particular day he was running a little late. Normally by nine o'clock he would be inside having coffee, but there was a problem with one of the calves that he would have to get the veterinarian to look at. So just as Thomas walked into the front yard, Peter Overgaard emerged through the barn door. "Howdy, Thomas," he said.

Thomas mumbled a greeting. They met. They stopped.

Thomas said, "I just cut across the field." Peter Overgaard nodded.

They stood there a moment. The sun was shining. They were sheltered from the wind. "Luckily it's drying out," said Peter Overgaard. They both looked up at the sky, where delicate, white clouds were speeding across, before a crisp southwest wind. And they looked across the green landscape where, here and there, flocks of black and white Holsteins were about to complete the day's first round of filling their stomachs. Thomas said, "If this holds, things will really get going."

And there they stood, hands in their pockets, each of them in their own pensive silence, which now and again was broken by a remark about the price of milk or the price of piglets. Things weren't as bad as they could be.

The conversation ground to a halt. One of them cleared his throat. Then Peter Overgaard said, "I guess you should come in and have some coffee."

Thomas mumbled a thanks and walked into the utility room, took off his clogs, and continued into the kitchen. On the table, cups and bread were laid out, and there was a pot on the stove. The pot was boiling. A lot. The lid was jumping; it seemed like the whole pot was jumping.

Peter Overgaard said have a seat, make yourself at home, and he sat down too, and Thomas glanced at the noisy pot and asked carefully, "Shouldn't you—?" Peter Overgaard shook his head. "In this house we each take care of our own domains," he said. "I'm sure she'll be along." And she was. She came in, took care of the pot, greeted Thomas, and took out a couple of additional cups. She poured his coffee, and the farmhand came in too, sat down and got a cup.

A cat came walking in through the kitchen with its tail held high. The parish council president's wife asked how Elsa was doing. And Thomas, looking both shy and proud at the same time, answered that it wasn't going too badly. She was done with her teaching certificate, and the guy she was engaged to was also done. And even though he had to do his military service, they were thinking about getting married. "They're kind of young," he said, "but what can you do?" And the parish council president's wife said that Elsa wasn't any younger than the grocer's daughter, Grethe, who has already been married for a few years. Thomas mumbled something about Elsa not having to get married.

He had another cup, and he might as well have some cheese after the piece of bread with the liver spread, and the conversation turned to weddings and silver anniversaries. When his twenty minutes were up, the farmhand got up and left, and Thomas thought it was about time for him to be getting back too. Kristine would wonder what happened to him. He thanked them for the coffee and got up. Peter Overgaard got up too and followed him out to the utility room. And just as Thomas was going out the door, Peter said, "They'll be coming over to put more gravel on your road next week. Now that you've gotten a car," he added. And, pensively, Thomas said that, come to think of it, it probably could use some, but he didn't give it much thought. They had gotten used to it. Then he said good-bye again and left, humming contentedly, through the still-warmish summer breeze, down the gently sloping hillside, to his farm.

After he had turned off the tractor, climbed down from the cab, and taken off his hearing protection, the air was filled with a real sound, namely, the sound of birds.

Unfortunately it wasn't jubilant larks that afternoon, but a long line of seagulls that crowded into the plowed furrows, and contentiously, almost riotously, had taken up the fight against the sound of the motor, but had not yet realized that it had been shut off. He looked at them. In a way they looked decorative against all that black.

He clambered with difficulty across the ditch and walked towards the farmstead to make his way west around the barn and into the farmyard. It was easiest to just leave the tractor there until he went back to work after lunch, and then he got to move his limbs a bit, too. And he got to breathe, too. It was one of those days that when he took a deep breath it made him feel like he was floating up beneath the blue sky.

He washed his hands in the utility room and then brought the newspaper with him into the kitchen, with the letters and all the advertisements that the mailman had tossed on the counter. He sat down in his usual place on the built-in bench just inside the door.

"Well," asked Bente, "have you thought it over?"

Lars didn't answer, at least not right away. He was in the middle of an article about the region's last remaining dairy, which the dairy company wanted to close, and which the employees wanted to keep open. So he just rattled the paper a little. Bente repeated, "So have you thought it over?"

He looked up over the newspaper and quickly said that of course he had thought about it, he thought about it a lot, but he just wasn't done thinking about it yet.

"You're not?" Bente set a plate before him. It sounded like something, not exactly anger, but impatience. "We have to decide soon," she added. He nodded indulgently.

What Lars had thought about, but was not finished thinking about, was their silver anniversary. Their twenty-fifth anniversary was in a couple of months, and Bente was eager to celebrate it. In the town meetinghouse no less, with lots of friends and neighbors and relatives and acquaintances and with a cook and music and printed invitations.

"We can afford it," she had said not just once, but many times; and not just once, but many times, Lars had to admit that sure they could. Even though they didn't flaunt it, they weren't doing so badly.

Lars mumbled something about, that at his age, he wasn't much for being made fun of. But if it were meant for Bente, or just for the newspaper, wasn't obvious. Then they heard the farmhand enter the utility room. "Tonight," he said. "We can talk about it tonight."

Lars was of that generation that took naps. Bente was not, and as soon as she had put the dirty dishes in the dishwasher, cleaned the pots and wiped the table with the rag, she poked her head into the bedroom and whispered, "I'm heading into town. There's a couple of things I want to take a look at." Lars pretended he was sleeping. It was safer that way. He wasn't in the mood to resume the conversation. Bente waited, but just for a moment. Then she said aloud, "See you later," and was gone by the time Lars, for appearance's sake, grunted and opened his eyes. Then he lay there listening. After a bit he could hear the car outside. She always kept it in first gear all the way up to the road. This always bothered him, but he stopped saying anything about it, not directly anyway. He made his point by demonstratively putting it all the way into third gear when he was driving. He might also add, "The motor has such a nice sound when it's driven the right way."

Then his thoughts got muddled and he slipped into sleep for half an hour.

Bente had set out a thermos with coffee for Lars and the farmhand, and there were also a couple of pieces of cake from Sunday. They sat down and had a good conversation. The farmhand was an enthusiastic hunter and enjoyed telling about the buck that had eluded him every morning for a week. And Lars was pretty familiar with hunting—truth be told, he had been treasurer in the hunting club many years back. And the time started to get away from them; they had work to do. So a quarter to two Lars was back in the tractor seat, and all afternoon he drove back and forth, back and forth. And half of his conscious mind was on the furrows and and other half was even further behind, turning over the past that suddenly had intruded on him.

Twenty-five years is, of course, a good long while; but when one has passed the seventy mark a year back, it's not one's whole life. Actually it's not even the majority. And even though he could certainly have found arguments to the contrary, he couldn't let go of the sense that, by celebrating the past twenty-five years, it made the previous amount of time seem more meaningless. The years with Ellen, the years with his son, Viggo, until the split those twenty-five years ago. "Well, okay," he says to himself when he thinks about the word "split," that in a strange way appeared to have both meanings back then. "It was just that we both realized it would probably be best for him if he moved. A kind of joint agreement for everyone's benefit, even though Viggo hadn't seen it that way, of course." He nods to himself someplace in the back of his mind. "I sure did sacrifice myself," he thinks, trying not to lose the thought. "I sure did sacrifice myself for him, for my son, Viggo." Somewhere under that thought another one squeezes out. "I sacrificed myself to get revenge," he thinks, shocking himself, and wincing. "No, no, no," he quickly thinks, "I really cared for her. Despite everything."

The afternoon was waning, as they used to say. The sun neared the horizon, leaving room for a couple of degrees just below freezing. He could see it in the colors on the western sky and he could feel it in his lungs the couple of times he had to crawl down from the cab, either to position himself out of sight of the road or to tip up a rock so it was easier to spot when they collected them and drove them out to the boundary line.

He is still thinking. He crosses the boundary line, the one lying there for twenty-five years, and he goes down on the other side back to his younger days, when he and Ellen and their son Viggo—and he tries to force his thoughts to stay back there, but not even his will can make time stand still, and inevitably his thoughts go forward to the day when Ellen flipped the tractor in the ditch and Viggo found her, and there was nothing they could do.

Later, a few years later, when he couldn't deal with all that cooking anymore, they got a housekeeper. That was when Bente arrived, young, strong and cheerful. And on Viggo's nineteenth birthday they had people over for the first time in two years since the funeral. There was family, neighbors, and a couple of Viggo's friends.

The evening was a little sad, actually. But still: Bente had brought something new into their daily lives. Or maybe more accurately: Bente had brought back their daily lives. They were both happier. "I allowed myself to be happy again." thought Lars. "I guess that's what it was."

And it was like that; it lasted almost a year. Until that upsetting day. Until that day, when he had to tell Viggo that he probably should leave home, and that he was going to marry Bente. He had told Bente his decision. She had made a fuss, was angry almost, but he was able to make her understand that it was the only solution. He had also said to her that she wasn't going to live the rest of her life looking for housekeeper want ads with the line "children no hindrance." "And Viggo is going off to study. That's been decided. I'm not going to put his future in jeopardy. We'll be alone here."

And that's how it went. But they were only alone for half a year before the twins arrived. Twins no less. Girls. But they really enjoyed them, no doubt about that. One went into education, the other one was still finishing her degree. But then she had both a husband and a child.

"I think they look like Ellen," said one of Ellen's sisters, always with feigned surprise, when she saw the twins. She also added, "What a strange coincidence."

Lars always ignored it. And Bente did, too. "We really didn't make out so badly together," he thinks, "after it all fell into place." And he allows a warmth to spread through his body. It wasn't Bente's fault he couldn't forget Ellen or his jealousy. She had certainly done her part, there was no denying that.

He noticed that Bente was back, and it was also about time to stop for the day. He lifted the plow and sat still, turning his head from side to side. It was the kind of afternoon that could lead to a stiff neck.

Then he drove in. He parked the tractor in the machine shed and puttered around a little. When he emerged into the farmyard he could hear that the farmhand wasn't quite yet done in the barn.

Now it's completely dark, and there are only lights on in the utility room and the kitchen. He sees Bente standing, doing something at the kitchen counter, maybe mixing dough, it looks like that. And he sees her, like he has seen her for over twenty-five years now, always busy with something, always engaged, almost a little domineering, but she has been like that right from the start. That's her way. He always thought it didn't matter that much.

The farmhand still hasn't made it in from the barn, so Lars goes back out to the machine shed, turns on the lights and starts moving some things around. Then suddenly he realizes what he actually had been thinking about all afternoon, in the background of all his other thoughts. "It can't have been so easy for her all these years, either," he thinks; and he also thinks that maybe it has been just as hard for her as it has been for him. Now he stands completely still, like his thoughts. They are stuck in his body.

A bit later he goes back out to the farmyard. The light frost cools his eyes and cheeks, and when he regains his sense of balance and feels like a man who damned straight is seventy-one, but still can take care of business, he goes in.

"So," he says, "I see you're back."

He sits down. Bente sprinkles a bit more flour on the dough and starts rolling it out on the counter.

"I was thinking," he says. She doesn't look up. "I think we should do it the way you wanted." He feels the warmth inside him again. Then he says, "I was also thinking that maybe we could invite Viggo and his wife."

Now Bente looks up. Surprised. "Sure we can," she says, and her eyes are suddenly smiling. "There's no guarantee they can make it, being in the middle of the week, and them coming all the way from Odense, but then maybe we could invite them over another time," and as if by accident she brushes his hand, leaving a white stripe. He clears his throat a couple of times, is just about to say something. Then they hear the farmhand come in, and Lars gets up and goes into the living room, while Bente sets the dough to rise and starts putting out supper. Lars puts on the six o'clock news.

There is probably also something that's happened in the world out there, something he should know about.

A Dress for Astrid's Confirmation

He could have said it didn't matter. More than three thousand *kroner* go through this property on a daily basis. God knows, what's the difference if we use a couple hundred more or a couple hundred less once in a while? But he didn't say that. He didn't get that far.

They had sat over their evening coffee and had started talking about Astrid's confirmation. Ingrid said, "Of course we're going to the confirmation. I can spruce up the black outfit from when Ellen and Einar celebrated their twenty-fifth. And you have decent clothes."

At first he had said, "I think you should buy a new dress." And she had looked at him with the hint of a bitter smile, but chose to interpret the statement as a joke. "Sure I could."

"Really, I mean it," he assured her. "Why shouldn't you get a new dress, since we have this confirmation. You have just as much right to look good as anyone else."

"You know what people will think." She cut off any further discussion by leaving for the bedroom to get out the black dress. When he went in to go to bed, she was standing in front of the mirror, trying the dress on with a white tatted collar and with pins marking how much to take it in around the waist.

"See how slim I've gotten?" she said. "A lot of women would be happy to look like this."

"Oh, cut it out." he said. Then he added, "You know I like it when you look a little sharp and snazzy. That's why I said that."

And come to think of it, she thought—the next morning while she was collecting the cups after breakfast—anyway, I earn my own money. Her mouth took on a resolute expression, and she had a sense of how it would feel to hold her head high. I do earn my own money.

She drank down the last bit of coffee in the pot, then walked out to the hall and put on her windbreaker. Then she walked back to the kitchen, ripped a page out of the notepad, and wrote: Dear Hans— I'll be back a little later today. I'm shopping on the way home. Can you turn on the potatoes?

Quite a while before, Hans had locked himself in, behind the barn door with the sign "NO ENTRY without owner's permission" signed by the National Pork Producers Council. So he would be removed from verbal contact for the next few hours.

I do earn my own money, she thought again, as she started up the little red Fiat 127, that they had to pick up for her when she became a home health aide. They figured it would be adequate. I've done my part. She accelerated and changed gears a little too quickly. The gravel sprayed out from the front wheels as she drove from the farmyard.

From inside the barn Hans heard the faint sound of the motor. Muffler, he thought. I'll have to remember to tell her. Strange that women can't hear those kinds of things. Standing in the sanitary entry room, in his barn clothes and his disinfected barn boots, he perused the medical refrigerator's contents. Yet another pig had gotten weaning diarrhea, and a different one had produced a single sneeze, but otherwise everything was looking okay. No deaths and no real signs of illness. His schedules showed that it was time to inseminate a couple of sows.

This was one of the easier days. No moving, no deliveries, just daily routine, almost.

Of course he could just call his daughter, but that would have to wait. He didn't have a telephone in the barn, even though the consultant had recommended it, back when it was renovated to meet SPF standards. "You'll be completely isolated for hours at a time," he had said. "It would be good to have a telephone in here, or at least a bell, so your wife can call you."

He had chuckled and said that actually he would enjoy being out of reach. And that's what happened, for a while anyway, and in a way he hadn't predicted. That was back when all their letters were either collection notices or threats, and back when every visit could have been one of those that could presage an "arrangement," however theoretical that could turn out to be. He knew then, as did everyone, how badly they were doing. Back then it was nice to be able to legally hide behind closed doors all day, and his workdays got longer and longer. He had had a table and a chair in the entry, and he brought his lunch and his coffee and his radio with him, so he only had to show himself outdoors during the day when absolutely necessary, only if there were outside work that he couldn't postpone. Back then he behaved much like a sick cat.

Towards noon the first part of the day's work is about done. The one sow is still too early into heat and has to wait, while the other one is ready for her "test ride"—as they call it in the instructions. He straddles her and injects her with the allotted portion of semen. That was that. He cleans his barn boots, removes his barn clothes and walks in his stocking feet over the grate to the unsanitary area where his work clothes are hanging. Out of habit he sits down on the chair. Eleven-thirty, well, okay. Too early to go in for a bite. He'd be done before the radio news if he started eating now. Better to sit awhile and plan.

That crazy woman, he thinks, feeling at the same time a warmth up around his throat. It's been hard for her too, maybe even worse for her. She was always the one out in the public eye.

But that's over, goddammit. He emphasizes this thought by slapping his right hand down on his knee. A cloud of dust envelops him, and even though he's sitting in the unsanitary area, it's still not too good. But now that's behind us, he thinks again, and he'd better get a hold of his daughter before she goes to lunch, even though she doesn't like being called at work.

Okay. He gets up, lets himself out, and walks across the yard to the farmhouse.

He gets through to his daughter. She works in a law office, where taking private calls during work hours is frowned upon. But this is important. And the daughter listens at least, even though she doesn't say very much. But that's okay.

"It's your mother," says Hans. "We're going to Astrid's confirmation on Sunday, and she doesn't want a new dress."

"What doesn't she want?"

"She doesn't want a new dress. She wants to take in the old black one." And he continues with an involved explanation about which black dress and when she got it.

"I know which dress," says the daughter. "It's very nice."

Hans nearly moans, lamenting his daughter's obliviousness while trying to explain to her that it's all that from back then that's still bothering her mother. She won't allow herself to spend the money. She thinks that other people think that she can't spend the money. She's never gotten over it.

The daughter sighs. "Shame," she says. "Huh?" asks Hans. And the daughter says that Henrik calls that kind of thing shame. "You both have it," she says, sighing, and he can almost hear how she is sitting there shaking her head. But finally she promises her father that she will go out and get a very nice dress for her mother—she knows her size—and put it in the mail later that afternoon. She'll do it, though she ends with a parting shot, that her mother probably won't like that someone else is buying her a dress.

So that was that. A little irritated with his daughter, but satisfied with himself, he pulls lunch out of the refrigerator. A beer for the occasion? What's got into him? He pours a glass of milk. It's good to support his neighbor, who still has cows to tend.

The dress comes in the mail the next day. For once he's

outside of the barn at that point of the morning. It's that day of the week when the butcher's truck has been there to pick up pigs for slaughtering, and Hans is in the middle of cleaning and disinfecting the expediting room which lies the regulated distance from the barn. He notices the mailman's yellow Kadett turn from the road. He waves and observes with satisfaction that the mailman is carrying, along with the newspaper, a package into the utility room. "How did it go?" shouts Hans. "Two-two," answers the mailman. He still plays, even though now it's only on a level five team. "Almost had 'em," he shouts. He pulls up a bit on his right pants leg, edges back into the car, gives a honk, and disappears.

Hans takes the chloramine spray and gives the room an adequate once over. Good. And now he has to go through all the rigamarole and go back into the stable to the sow that he didn't inseminate the day before. Today she's got to be ready, by God. Or else nature has gone awry.

He had been looking forward to the evening. As usual, they eat late, and of course they have to watch the TV news, before he says, "By the way, I have something for you." And he comes back with the package that he had hidden out in the front entry and hands it to her. "For you," he says.

Ingrid looks at him, surprised, trying to say three or four things at once. "For me? What for? I mean it's not"—and whatever else springs from her bewilderment. Then she looks at him and asks, "What is this?" He nods encouragingly, and she starts to open it.

It's reddish, he can see. Maybe almost purple. With large but discreet flowers. He thinks it looks really nice. "It's for you," he says, "for the confirmation."

She stands there looking at the dress. She holds it up and looks at it. Then she lets her arms fall, standing there with a strange expression on her face. Is she about to cry? That never happened before. Then she turns to him, and it's not a particularly friendly expression on her face. He can almost feel how his own face must look stupid. "You big idiot," she says. "You great big idiot."

"But," he begins, but there's no reason to say any more. She slams the door behind her.

"But," he says out into the air.

He picks the dress up off the floor and stands there feeling it. It's cool and smooth, and it is really pretty. She has taste, that daughter. He hangs the dress over a chair back. She doesn't get it at all. She can't keep getting stuck in all that. One day things have to go back to the way they were before.

A little later she comes in quietly. "I'm sorry," she says. "It's just crazy."

"Why don't you want me to—" he starts to say, but she interrupts him. "I bought one myself," she says. "I bought one yesterday. That's why I was late getting home." He stands there looking foolish while she continues, "I earn money too, you know."

He quickly agrees with her, adding that he doesn't know how they would have gotten by without her. But that's probably not really what needs saying right now.

"The one I bought isn't nearly as nice as that one there," she says obstinately, "but it looks just like the old black one would have looked if I did a nice job altering it. They all will think it's the old dress."

"Ingrid," he says, "can you—" but she keeps talking in a voice that is halfway between contempt and despair. "They're all going to be there, the whole family, and they all say how great it is that we made it through, and they don't say one word about all the money that Dad and Mom had to co-sign for on our behalf. But what do you think they're going to say and think if I show up in that thing?"

Hans sits there quietly, shaking his head. "They're not like that," he says. "You're being unfair."

She looks at him, now almost lovingly. "You are so dumb," she says. "You have no idea. But on the other hand they are *my* siblings and parents." She sits there for a little while, then adds, almost frightening herself, "Sometimes I think it all would have gone more smoothly if we didn't make it, if we had to move. Away from everything."

Suddenly she starts crying. And he sits there not knowing what to do. Anything rational would be no use. Not to her. Or to him either.

"That was nice of you," she whispers.

And Hans feels again that warmth in his throat, and he's just about to say that they should take a trip together. To Mallorca, for example. They could hire a temp and screw them all and take a trip to Mallorca, and she can bring her new dress and they can do what other people do. But of course he doesn't get the words out and lucky for that. It would just have made everything even worse.

Then he thinks, we could send our regrets about the confirmation. One of us could get sick. And he imagines how they have their own party instead, just the two of them, with new clothes and wine and everything, and no one else would ever need to know.

He clears his throat, but doesn't say anything.

She does. She answers. She says, "This is really nice of you, Hans, but I can't help it. I'll take it back myself tomorrow."

Celebrating Birgit's birthday was kind of a tradition, even though we didn't do it every year, since it wasn't such good timing with the harvest. Sometimes we had to skip the evening if the weather suddenly became just the kind we had been waiting for. It was rare, but it did happen.

We would have appreciated a cancellation like that this year. We still hadn't gotten to the farthest stand of barley, and there was quite a bit of hay that hadn't been baled yet; but what could we do? The radio had predicted good weather towards the end of the week.

Erik and Lone came as usual. They weren't quite done either. They still had to do the greater share of their parcel down by the creek, but that field was almost always a bit late.

We had roast, and ice cream; then hot chocolate. That was kind of a tradition too. And then plenty of coffee afterwards, to wash down the hot chocolate.

It was raining, but we pretended we weren't thinking about it. Birgit showed us the jacket she had bought as a gift from me, and Lone said, "That is so nice." Lone felt it, and the material must have reminded her of something, because she said to Erik, "Do you remember the one I got, the year that Evald and Sonja got married?" And when Erik evidently didn't, she said, "Yes, you do. it was the one that got stuck when we were going to drive to the church because we were in a hurry and you slammed the door before I was all the way in." She chuckled. "It got so wet and filthy I couldn't wear it into the church?" And Erik said, "Oh, that one," while glancing at me as if he were shaking his head.

I said, "How about a round of cards?"

We don't play to win anything; it's just to play. And actually we don't even play to play; it just feels good to sit there with cards in your hand.

Cards are pretty new for us. But since we're four people, it just feels natural. It's cozy, and time passes so easily.

Then Lone asked, "Do you ever see Evald?" Erik flipped an ace down on the table. Obviously it wasn't his question.

Birgit shook her head. She started to say something. I said, "Of course. He's done harvesting. He was out driving until after midnight on Sunday." And Erik said he stopped about eight o'clock, because he thought the good weather was going to continue, and he wanted the moisture content to drop some more.

It was still raining. But we agreed it still wouldn't be such a bad harvest this year. It had come together at the end of the summer.

"It could still use some drying out," said Erik.

I turned on the television, so we could listen to the late news and the weather.

So that was that birthday. When we were in bed, Birgit didn't say anything, but she made up for it in the morning.

She said, "Why can't we ever talk about that? It's not right. We can't keep on pretending he doesn't exist."

I said, "Now you're exaggerating."

But she kept going. "I've been lying there thinking about it all night. We should be ashamed of ourselves."

It wasn't the first time we had had that discussion. I said, "I know. But it's not that easy."

"Well, it's not getting any easier."

And it wasn't. But I said we couldn't be sure Evald felt the way Birgit thought he did. And of course we did go to Sonja's funeral back then, and each of us was as much to blame as the other. There was no reason for her to blame me for anything. Who was stopping her from calling up Evald and inviting him to something or other, huh? And in a way, things were completely fine now. She knew that. Neighbors don't have to continually darken one another's doors.

I was having a little trouble controlling myself, so I left. Shortly after that, Birgit drove to work.

It's always now, around Birgit's birthday, that we can't get around it. Otherwise, months can pass when we don't have the feeling that something should be different than it is; when, without thinking about it too much, we accept that things are the way they are.

But we couldn't skip a birthday. If we stopped celebrating it suddenly, it would seem strange. Like we were admitting something. And now we can't invite him, not now. And everyone says he's isolated himself. He never attends meetings; he doesn't get a newspaper anymore.

The whole thing is so awkward.

The rain has stopped, but the humidity is still too high. Way too high. It's windy, but we'll need some sun too, and we're short on that. The clouds, gigantic and dark, drift by overhead. Karup weather station will probably be right with their talk about showers.

It was in '82 that everything changed. From one day to the next.

We had been living here for five years. The others had been here longer. Erik and Evald were among the ones who bought properties before they even finished their management degrees at agricultural college. That was back when the teachers started every class by saying we should buy as soon as possible, "because it gets more expensive with every day that passes." "Don't be afraid of debt," they said. "Inflation will take care of that. What you need is a large operation."

Erik and Evald bought. They were from this area, so it was only natural that they came back home.

I guess I was more cautious. But six months after I

graduated, Evald called me one night and said that the property neighboring his was for sale.

"Don't you want to buy it?" I asked, half-teasing. He didn't want it. He was in the process of building a big, new pighouse and renovating his farmhouse. That was plenty. "And with grain prices the way they are," he said, "I can buy all the barley I need at a cheaper price."

So I got the property, and shortly after that we got married, and we were lucky that Birgit was hired at the accounting office in town.

Of course we didn't get together every day, but the six of us stayed close. We saw more of Evald and Sonja naturally, since we were neighbors, but Erik and Lone were part of our group, and they only lived a mile or so away. It was actually the four of them who had known each other longest.

We didn't get together just for birthdays and things like that. We got together on regular nights too. Once we went to a movie together; another time to a show.

Those kinds of things go in cycles. Erik and Lone had a couple of kids, and for a while it seemed like they had their hands full. All six of us still got together, but for a couple of years it was mostly the four of us—Evald, Sonja, Birgit and me.

Evald and I drove to a few meetings together, too.

It's clearing up a bit. Over to the southwest there is so much blue you could make it into a pair of hussar pants, as my grandmother always said that her mother said. It looks promising, but you can't help but be a little nervous when you've still got several acres standing.

We drove to a couple of meetings together, Evald and I. We were there in Herning when the LR 80 farmer protest movement was founded. To show solidarity with them, we said. We had asked Erik if he wanted to go, but that wasn't for him. "It's just the bad farmers who're getting up in arms," he said.

On the drive home, I said, "The skilled ones will survive. But there will be some attrition."

Later we didn't have anything to do with LR 80. I didn't, anyway.

Birgit and Sonja painted ceramics on Wednesdays. And it became a routine that we had coffee together when they got home. Sonja appreciated getting out. She was one of the only housewives left, and she did her share of work with the pigs. And she enjoyed it. "It saves us from hiring a farmhand," said Evald. Sometimes he said, "This is the only family farm in the area."

Back then they also had a child on the way. And they had bought more land in '79 just before prices peaked.

After 1980 we talked about it sometimes. "A lot of properties are going up for sale," we said. "Now's the time to buy."

I mentioned this to Birgit. She said, "Haven't you learned anything?"

It's been a while now—a couple of years or so—since the day I discovered the mailman wrongly delivered a letter here to us; it was for Evald.

A few times I had chatted with the mailman about him. "Do you ever see Evald?" "No," he said, "I never see anyone nowadays." Another time he said, "It's gotten to look kind of abandoned over there. And he moved his television into the kitchen."

It was shortly after that when I saw the letter. It was a Friday, and I probably should have left it lying there, until the mailman came back on Monday, to kind of show him that he shouldn't get involved. But it could have been something important, so I let my son run over with it.

"What did he say?" I asked, when he got back.

"Nothing."

I can hear that Evald has started plowing, and the truck has been there for his pigs. The sounds are quite distinct when the wind is from the southwest. Sometimes I think I hear him walking across his farmyard in his clogs.

So now it's four years ago. Yesterday and today.

We had celebrated Birgit's birthday as usual, the six of us. Birgit and I, we'd had a few problems with a couple of recent payments, but that was behind us then, and only the bank knew about it.

Anyone could see that we were six happy people enjoying one another's company. Sonja seemed particularly glad, I think. She had just been released from the hospital and she just had to be a little careful. So things would probably work out this time.

One way or another we got to talking about Anthon's property. There was going to be an auction in a couple of days.

Lone said, "That must be so horrible."

"It was his own fault," Erik said. "He wasn't quite skilled enough."

"Maybe he was just unlucky," I said.

"I feel so bad for them," said Sonja. Then her expresson changed and she smiled at each of us. "I'm so glad for our good luck—all of us."

She gave Evald's hand a little squeeze.

I said something, and Erik said something, and Evald got up and said it was about time to go. It was late, and tomorrow was a workday.

The next day we saw the announcement.

I was out in the barn. Birgit had just gotten home, and I was about to go in when I heard her come running. She had the newspaper.

"It can't be true!" she yelled.

But it had to be. There was no name, but the address and registration number and all the other information was obvious.

It was for Evald and Sonja.

"I don't get it," I said. "I just don't get it." Birgit was beside herself, worse than back when we had to go to the bank. "We have to do something," she stammered. "We can't just stand here."

I got her inside. "We have to do something," she said again. "Should we go over there?"

We called Erik and Lone. They hadn't seen it yet. "It doesn't make any sense," said Erik. "They didn't give any hint of this happening."

We decided that it was probably best to give them some space to deal with this. Not go rushing at them right away. "Like we demanded an explanation or something," said Erik.

"Better if it happens naturally, on its own," I said.

"Lone agrees," said Erik. I told Birgit, "Lone doesn't think we should intrude right now. On a day like this it's more considerate not to go barging in on them."

Later that evening, Erik called and said that maybe he and I could help Evald by buying up his place before the auction. "We could probably make an arrangement," he said, " and we could split the land, and sell the buildings."

Maybe not such a dumb idea. "But we'll never be able to sell the buildings for what they're worth," I said.

Erik laughed. "Trust me," he said. He said he had already talked to someone who would be interested in just the buildings, so the pork production could continue as a stock venture. "It'll all work out," he said. "So are you in?"

I didn't really know; but I guess I was. If Erik thought it would help Evald and Sonja, I guess I was in.

"Great. We can talk to the lawyer tomorrow."

Birgit had gone to bed, so I didn't get to tell her about Erik's idea. There was no guarantee that we could do it anyway. But if it did work out, maybe it wouldn't be so bad. Maybe Evald and Sonja could walk away without too big of a loss.

And you had to admit that convenient land doesn't grow on trees.

We talked about it the next day and next. We spoke with the lawyer, the bank, and the vice-chair of the farming commission.

I told Birgit about it, of course. She didn't like the idea, but I told her it would be the best solution for everyone. "And there's no use going around being sentimental about it," I said.

"Well we at least have to talk to Evald and Sonja about it," she said.

I said that we would, of course, but that we had to be more certain first. We didn't want to give them false hopes.

"Hopes?" she asked. "Hopes about what?"

"Well, okay."

"They have to leave in any case," said Birgit. "Don't you think they need friends more than anything right now?"

I didn't say anything. We didn't really disagree. It was just kind of tricky. Some things are just difficult to talk about. If they had just said something, before all this, it would have been a lot easier.

I think it was the next day I went to the grocery store for some tobacco, and someone said to me, "I hear you're expanding." I acted like I hadn't heard it.

But when I got home, I called Erik. "Everyone in the parish knows," I said. "We have to tell them what we're planning on doing."

Later that same day we heard that Sonja—well—that Sonja was dead. There was a lot of talk.

We went to the funeral. We didn't say anything, but still we thought we had to be there. We had been good friends, after all.

Sonja's parents were there, and some of her siblings. Evald looked like a stranger among them. He was very pale, and he didn't greet anyone. There weren't that many from this area, but it had said that it was going to be a quiet gathering.

There was a lot of talk leading up to the funeral. Everyone knew a lot about what had happened. That Sonja had gotten a real shock when she saw the announcement about the auction in the newspaper, and that she wasn't herself after that. And that no one could hardly get a word out of Evald; he receded into himself even more. The only thing he said was, "I had to protect her."

There was no memorial gathering afterwards. We drove back with Erik and Lone and had coffee. It was better to do it somewhere that couldn't be seen from over there.

We talked a lot about Evald and what he might do now. He would probably leave the area; we all thought that. That would make sense.

I told Erik I didn't really like the idea we were going to buy his property, not now. I know it didn't really make any difference, but still. Birgit nodded, and I think Lone understood too.

But we agreed to go ahead anyway. Convenient land doesn't grow on trees. And the lawyer was interested and he didn't seem to see anything wrong with it.

And it wouldn't harm Evald in any way.

We also said that Sonja's mother might stay with Evald for a little while, to look after him and to help with moving.

It's not the most pleasant thing to remember. The couple of times we got to talking about it, Birgit said that we went about it all wrong from the very beginning.

"You went over there one day," I said. "Did you forget that? You went over, but you didn't go in."

"I didn't try the door," she said. "I just knocked. I was almost glad that no one answered. And then I rushed back home." Then she said it again, "We were cowards and we acted all wrong from the very beginning."

It's easy to say things like that afterwards. And then she admits, every time, that the way it all happened, it probably couldn't have been helped. And I remind her again, that when we were in a bind, we weren't so crazy about the idea of people flocking over to comfort us. It would have been embarrassing and wouldn't have helped one bit.

We showed our sympathy by going to the funeral. It was a raw, cold rainy day, and we weren't finished harvesting that time either.

And then Erik and I wanted to talk to him and tell him about our plans. We had decided we would. Erik figured it would look best if we told him before we told the lawyer to go ahead with it.

But then there was another newspaper announcement. About cancellation of the scheduled auction.

Erik called. "Did you see that?" he asked. "Who's that idiot sold it to?"

I asked the mailman the next day but he didn't know anything. No one in the grocery said anything. Erik spoke with the lawyer, but he just said that everything had been worked out. He had to follow some kind of professional confidentiality.

It wasn't until a few days had passed that people started to find out. The property wasn't sold. Evald was staying.

There was talk about an uncle. Sonja's evidently. It was hard to imagine.

I can still hear him plowing over there. The wind is picking up, the clouds are dissipating, and there is some sunshine breaking through. If this holds, I can harvest the rest tomorrow.

I have never admitted this to Birgit, but there was a time when I couldn't bring myself to work the field out by the property line if he was working near there. Maybe he felt the same way, but that's in the past now. About a year and a half ago, in the spring, I drove out there, sowing, and suddenly I saw that he was driving right on the other side of the stone wall. I felt a bit awkward but then I raised my hand and waved. I don't think he waved back. He might not have seen it.

Still, it felt like a bit of a relief.

"Dagnabbit! How did it get so late?" Plus he had to get washed up first, even though he was only going to the dentist.

He jogged in from the barn and slipped off his clogs in the utility room. Then he got out clean underwear and went into the bathroom. It was freezing cold. She had left the window open to let out the damp air.

Obviously.

Why did she absolutely have to take a shower every morning. Except for Saturday and Sunday, when she stayed home with him. She could just get washed in the evening like everyone else who did an honest day's work.

He took off his clothes and grabbed a bar of soap for the shower. All that nonsense with shower gel, or whatever it was called, made no inroads with him. And all that other stuff: moisturizers, body lotion, scouring cream, toning cream, cleansing milk, balsam, something in a very foreign language for removing callouses (as if it were shameful to be marked by one's work), and the devil and his dandruff, as he once blurted out, and it still made him chuckle. She did get a bit short with him, saying that he shouldn't think other wives didn't all use the same kind of things, but she seemed to get the message. All that crap—no, a bar of soap was a bar of soap, and that was good enough for him. And then a good, stiff nail brush and a scrub brush for his feet.

He dried himself off and thought again how unfair it was that she wouldn't let him have the car today. He had alluded to it the night before. He had asked if she knew the bus schedule, since he had to go to the dentist. But she just went and looked up the times for him. There was a good connection, she had said. Eleven minutes past nine from the grocery. And home again at eleven.

He was still cursing her and the missing car as he started making his way down the road towards the village center. But it's not at all like she didn't suit him—everything had been pretty good, up until she started working. And it still was, he quickly added, in his thoughts. But still it wasn't exactly as he had envisioned it, back when they got married, fourteen-fifteen years ago. Back then she did her share of the work, and even though they didn't end up with kids, it was a good solid marriage—everyone said so. And their age difference wasn't that much.

But it was the times. "Shouldn't I try to get a job?" she had said. "I could probably work in an office again," she had also said. He hadn't protested, not enough anyway, and the money would be nice.

But she had changed. She bought more clothes, wore shoes with heels, and did things with her looks. As she said, "A person has to look presentable." It happened gradually. Lately it was her hair. She had it all teased out. "A person has to look presentable," she had said again, and evidently, she had become that. He was sure the other wives were talking about it. They looked at her anyway, when they were out at something.

As if they were thinking, "What is Inger doing now?"

Then he realized that he forgot his health insurance card. He looked at his watch. He might still be able to make it, so he turned around and trotted home.

Where did she keep things like that? He rummaged through the drawers and found it in the end. "Women," he mumbled. "Why do they never leave things out where you can find them?"

Out again. Now jogging. He was getting sweaty. A shower is kind of useless when you have to rush around like this. It didn't bother her; she had the car. She wasn't sweating, even if she had to hurry. He more or less sneered out the words, "she has to be presentable," as if he were trying to make an impression on someone.

Horrified, he halted his train of thought; tried to rewind it back to the place in the darkness where it came from; tried to keep it down there, where he didn't have to think it anymore, down where he had been able to keep it at bay, up until now.

He would have to get hold of another thought instead, but there was only one other thought available, and that one wasn't any better. *Department head*—something about a department head that she seemed to mention all the time. It didn't bother him, and he didn't really listen when she went on about it. He just buried himself in the newspaper—even if it was one from three days ago, he just buried himself in it.

All the wrong thoughts kept weighing on his mind, until he made it to the village center. Then they departed from the lower level of his consciousness, as he saw the backside of the bus driving away.

He stopped, looked at his watch. Well, there was nothing to complain about there.

Now what? Call a taxi? Too much money. Go back home, now that he finally had an appointment? Definitely not.

He started walking. If he were lucky, someone he knew might drive by; then maybe he could get a ride.

He made his way briskly along the road. When he heard a car approaching behind him, he made a little motion with his left arm that could be interpreted as an attempt to get a ride, or maybe as a little greeting when the cars drove by without stopping—or without noticing him. He wasn't too animated in his attempts to get attention. But after half a mile his arm motion increased by a little bit. Now it couldn't be deemed coincidental, but still perhaps as a wave, or maybe even somehow as a motion up towards the brim of his hat.

It worked. He heard someone slow down. It was the priest.

"Do you need a ride?" she asked. "I'm going to town." He explained that he would be much obliged. He had to go to the dentist, and Inger had the car, and he had missed the bus. "There were so many things to take care of before I could get away," he said.

He got in and fastened his seat belt. "Lucky I came by," she said. "I thought that was you."

They drove for a bit in silence. He looked at her out of the corner of his eye. Her name was Ruth; everyone called her by her first name. And she had only been here about a year or so. No one called her Pastor Svendsen, like they would have, if she had been a man. And not 'Pastor Ruth' either. Just Ruth. And when she was in attendance at some occasion or other, no one went around overly conscious that the priest was there.

And she looked just like a regular person, you might say. He snuck a closer look at her. Young, he thought,—and all alone at the rectory. But she was a no-nonsense woman; everyone said so. She turned her head towards him, as if she could sense he was looking at her. A brief moment their eyes met, and he blushed a little. He quickly looked straight ahead, but still could see her face on his retina. She looked like a regular person. Proper almost. And her hair was plain and flat, not all puffed up like Inger's of late.

But this female priest only had to make an impression on the Lord, and He probably didn't care about things like hair styles.

He was a bit shocked at the thought that now completely uninvited was trailing other thoughts along with it, which he otherwise had just swept out of the way. He quickly asked when the painting of the church would be all done. She explained that the restoration would be completed in the fall, and that the bishop would come and give a sermon on the occasion. "But you and Inger probably won't come, will you?" She chuckled. "It's not so often church wins out. If I didn't see you in the meetinghouse, I wouldn't know you at all." She still chuckled, and he could tell that it was the kind of laughter to smooth over a statement that maybe was a bit too direct. He mumbled something about how the animals still needed to be tended to on Sundays, and how Inger was away all week, so there was more than enough to catch up on when she finally was home.

"I didn't mean it so seriously," said Ruth, giving his nearest hand a little squeeze.

Then they talked a bit about the weather, which was great for people who were about to have Easter vacation. "But that doesn't include us," she said in a confidential tone. "Priests and farmers do not go on vacation during Easter."

He nodded. No they don't. Priests and farmers have commitments. She had to lead the congregation, and it wouldn't surprise him if he would be sowing the upper fields.

It started to smell a little in the car. At first it was so faint that you couldn't really tell what it was, but it developed into a rather strong scent of liquid manure, which is of course entirely normal for that time of year. But still not very pleasant. It was the kind of thing that could be a topic of conversation if there were city people or urban transplants in their company.

The priest didn't say anything. She wasn't the type who made a fuss about the environment, even though she was against EU, as far as people knew. Instead she quietly rolled up the window; and he felt like he ought to do something or other on behalf of farmers, like explain that maybe it didn't smell too nice, but at least it was being spread at the time of year when the ground could really use it. But he kept his mouth shut, afraid that it might be interpreted as defensiveness on his part.

Instead he quickly said something about the recent amateur theater performance, which they both had seen, and which the priest had written about in the church newsletter. She had praised the actors, and about the piece itself she had written that it was modern and relevant, and not like usual amateur shows. He said, "That Elisabeth was really good as the young girl who didn't want to marry the young farmer, but wanted to 'live her own life,' as she said. I can totally understand that. That could be even better than getting married." He mumbled, "Live her own life," followed by a quiet grunt.

Even before he had finished the grunt, he realized that maybe that wasn't the most appropriate remark, and that she might take it as a discrete little nudge. A subtle revenge for her remark about his and Inger's church attendance, or lack thereof. Maybe it would have been better if he had said something about the manure. He sniffed and said, "When you really know what it takes to grow good grain, it doesn't smell all that bad."

The priest didn't answer. She thought it was funny, he could tell. Luckily they had made it into town, and he asked to be dropped off at the center square. He had plenty of time, he said. His appointment wasn't until ten.

She said, "Enjoy," which she had a right to, considering what he had ended up saying. He said thanks for the ride. "That sure was better than walking the whole way," he said. "Anytime," she said, and drove away. He walked away, wondered what she would be doing in town on a morning like this. She didn't mention it, and after all, it really was none of his business.

Of course he missed the bus at eleven, and he had to wait for the one that ran an hour later.

The woman at the clinic said that it was an emergency, when she had to explain to him why it would take a bit longer before he could be seen. Now he was walking around with his half-numb head unable to make himself go into any establishment, neither stores nor into the cafe, when it would have been nice to get a cup of coffee. It must be okay to drink, even though it was impossible to eat or drink with a mouth, where only half of the machinery was functioning. So he just walked around, down the main drag, down Railroad St. to East St., through K. Olsen's Alley and down to the marina. He stood there for a while, looking at the store where they sold rope, nets and fishing equipment, and other sporting goods to the tourists. There was a big sign on the door: "Live Sand Worms—10 kr. per pack." Beneath it there was a smaller sign, stuck on less carefully, attached as if in haste: "Closed on account of death." He made a clucking sound and almost forgot that only half his head was working.

He walked back the same way.

When he got on the bus, the shrew who used to run the phone switchboard in the old days was sitting in the second row. She had retained that operator voice from back then, as well as a smile that could just nearly hide her bitterness over no longer knowing everyone's secrets. It was the kind of smile you didn't just return, but that you also replied to verbally and preferably with confidentiality. It was that smile she used now, when she saw him.

He tried to just smile back, but she was facing his numb side, and her reaction alluded to a sense that his smile was more a grimace than a smile, which she seemed to have taken in a way that did not put him a good light. In any case, she gave a sniff, followed by a demonstrative stare at the back of the driver's neck.

He sat in the far back. Now the inside right of his top lip started itching, and he couldn't make it go away. He rubbed it back and forth with his index finger, but he could have just as well have been rubbing another person, or no one at all. And it still itched. He tried biting his lip, but he couldn't feel that either. He figured he'd better stop. He didn't want to end up at home with half his top lip gone. He would just have to put up with the discomfort, as usual, and at some point the numbness would wear off. He tried to distract himself with his surroundings. There was Jens Christian's Peter in his Mazda. He was unemployed; at least that's how the talk went. And his wife had her own car too; but that's the way things were today.

Boy, did that itch.

The afternoon didn't go so bad. His half face turned back into a whole, normal face again, and the pain that had been rummaging around in the eastern corner of his top jaw for the last month or so, and which had been keeping him from sleeping well the previous few nights, was completely gone. There was just a bit of soreness left, but nothing worth mentioning.

The cows gave their milk and got their feed. He got a shower, and meanwhile, he focussed his thoughts on that cow which seemed on the brink of getting an udder infection, and he was going to have to do something about that. That was why it was only registered within the outer reaches of his consciousness that Inger was running late again. In theory they would eat on the hour, although of late it wasn't that infrequent she had overtime or a workshop or a meeting, or whatever they called what was going on.

Then the phone rang. It was her. "So there you are," she said. "I've been calling and calling."

He didn't have time to explain to her that he happened to have cows that needed his attention, and that he wasn't the type to run around with a mobile phone, like he heard real men did these days. He thought it would have been a clever reply, but he barely started getting the words out before she interrupted him. "I got it!" she just about cheered. "I got it!"

He hesitated. He could tell by the hush in the receiver that she was awaiting a reaction.

"What did you get?"

"The position. I got the position!" He still didn't know what to say. He thought about it. Then she lost her patience: "The position as department head. I told you we were going to get a new department head, because the one we have is going to be sales manager."

"Oh, that position," he said, sounding like he knew all about it, while he stood there thinking silently to himself that she had hinted about something or other recently.

"I didn't want to say too much about it before I was really sure," she said.

Then he pulled himself together. "Congratulations," he said. He tried again with a bit more enthusiasm: "Congratulations, Inger!" She didn't even get to say thanks before there was a voice asking something in the background and then she said, "And you know what, Kristensen is springing for dinner to celebrate, and he says you should come too. You can come, can't you? In an hour at Royal's."

He didn't answer. Instead he asked, "Who's Kristensen?"

Now she was irritated. There was no warmth in her voice when she said, slowly, as if she were talking to someone with mental disabilities, "Kristensen is my boss. I'm going to get his job, because he's going to be the sales manager." Then she changed course and pleaded, "Please say yes. Tell me you'll be there."

"But I don't have a car," he said.

She was thinking; he could tell by the silence. Presumably, she was thinking if she should offer to come and pick him up. But the words didn't come out like that. Instead it was: "You can call Petersen for a ride. For once in our lives we can use a taxi. Especially today."

Taxi! Is that what you call Petersen's old diesel jalopy. He said, "Sure, I could do that. But who knows if he's available?"

"Stop quibbling." He overheard a voice in the background, and after a little pause she said, "Kristensen wants me to say hello from him, too."

Hm. Is that so. Well, it's no use being so obstinate. He said, "I'll try to get a hold of Petersen, and then I'll call you if he can do it."

She started saying a bunch of things about how he shouldn't be so difficult. If Petersen was busy, the world was full of taxi drivers just sitting there, waiting for a call. And besides, he couldn't call her back, because no one answered the phone after hours. There was a brief pause, then her tone changed. "Is there something wrong? Is something bothering you?"

He mumbled something about how he had been numbed and maybe he wasn't feeling completely himself, and that he had actually been looking forward to just relaxing. "You'd probably have a better time without me," he said. Inger said something he couldn't hear, so he repeated, "You'd probably have a better time without me, the three of you." He listened, but she didn't respond. Then he asked, "Kristensen's wife is coming too, isn't she?" She started to say two or three things at once, but then she interrupted herself with a hesitant, "No." She didn't say anything else, nothing about whether he was single or divorced, or if there were any other reasons that a Mrs. Kristensen wouldn't be joining them.

He didn't know what else to say. There was a long silence between them. Then she said quickly, "We'll come and pick you up. Be ready in forty-five minutes. Your new shirts are ironed and hanging in the closet."

She didn't wait for an answer, she just put down the phone there in the office, or wherever she was.

He stood there a second with his end of the disconnected line in his hand. Then he put the phone down. *She had said, "we."*

Walking into the bathroom, he thought, *How much of this can I take?* Luckily he had already showered, but he still had to shave. Second time that day.

He looked at his watch. It was six-fifteen—again.

KARL

When she came out to the parking lot, she saw Karen Højgaard standing there with her car hood wide open, tinkering with the engine. Karen hadn't been working at the packing-house for very long, and they had barely exchanged a few words now and then, when they happened to pass one another in the lot or in the cafeteria.

She walked up to her. "What's the problem?" she said.

Karen looked up. There was a smear of oil on her cheek and over her top lip. "What a mess," she said. "I thought it was a line that got disconnected." With visible irritation she yanked on something down deep in the engine compartment. "It won't turn over," she said. "I turn the key and nothing happens. The starter is totally dead."

She was going to make a suggestion, but Karen beat her to it. "It's not the charge," she said. "There's plenty of power. And today of all days," she sighed. "It's my father-in-law's birthday, and we're going over there to eat. He'll be impossible if we get there late."

Karen tried a few more things, and was in the front seat a couple of times, turning the key with frustration. "Women don't understand machinery—that's what they say." She smiled a bit crookedly. "These things are too tiny. I'm much better with combine harvesters." She gave the little Fiat a not very friendly slap, and slammed down the hood. "I'll have to call for a tow." She made a sound, which seemed to mean that, if she had been a man and not a good, honest farmer's wife with her origins in the evangelical, she would have cursed right then.

"You can drive with me."

Karen looked up, a bit doubtful, but still tempted. "You can leave it here till tomorrow. No one's going to steal it, and you can just drive with me. It's no inconvenience to drive by your place. I could do it in the morning, too." Karen thought for a moment. Then she said, "Thanks" and removed her bag from the Fiat and locked the door. They walked together over to the Fiesta. "Thanks," said Karen again, as she sat inside.

It was rush hour—if you can use that word about the traffic here—but in any case, it was the time of day when it was nice that the intersection at Strand Street had regulated traffic signals. When they stopped at the red light, Karen looked at her watch. "Well, okay," she said. "It's lucky you were running late too."

She didn't tell Karen that actually she was ahead of schedule; that for once she didn't have anything pressing or needing to be discussed, and that she had figured she would have dinner ready at a decent hour. Instead she asked her how it was going working outside the house. "Have you gotten used to it yet?"

Karen didn't really know. It wasn't the most exciting job, and really she would have rather gotten something at the nursing home, but that didn't work out. They didn't like the idea—that is, Christian and her father-in-law. It wasn't proper for a woman from Højgaard to be working at the nursing home. She sounded a bit bitter, but checked herself and quickly added that she was glad she got such a good job. She really needed to get out of the house. "It's worse for Christian," she said. She was about to say more, but then she blurted out, though with some hesitation: "What about Karl? Does it bother him that you're 'making your own way,' as they say?"

She laughed. Almost whole-heartedly. "With Karl? Bothered?" Then she said, in all seriousness, "It hasn't been any problem. He's totally accepted that being a housewife isn't enough these days on a property like that. And it's pretty nice that I'm using the education I got back then." She glanced at Karen. "And we can always use the money. It helps, anyway."

Karen didn't respond. Maybe she didn't even hear it. Maybe she was sitting there the whole time thinking about what she hadn't said before. Then she said, "It's just that Christian doesn't understand that I don't mind getting out of the house. It's like he takes it as a criticism, that he can't make the farm be like it was under his father, and that I'm abandoning him and pushing him aside, just because I got a job that, God knows, isn't all that exciting."

Inger gives Karen a look, as scrutinizing as she can manage, while simultaneously keeping an eye on the traffic. She would like to find an opening to pass the ancient Zephyr, inside which a just as ancient, heavy-set male with hat and cigar,—"Isn't that Marius Beck?"—is about to make its way out of town with a speed that hints at second gear. She says, "Is it really that bad?" But Karen continues, "It might be just as much due to my father-in-law. Maybe he's afraid of my father-in-law, always sitting there talking about how there used to plenty of work for a wife and a couple of girls on the property. But back then there was also a herdsman, a manager, plus a couple of farmhands. And now Christian is working with just one intern; and that's the way things are today, but he doesn't think about that. He only talks about how young people—that's us," and she gives a bitter laugh, "that young people take things lightly and have no sense of responsibility." She sits quietly a moment, then adds, "So you can see it wouldn't have been so good if we came late to his birthday, because I'm 'running around' outside the house."

She tells Karen that it's completely different at her place. It was mostly Karl who encouraged her to find a job, and even though it was because they needed the money, he also seemed conscious of the fact, in his quiet way, that it wasn't enough for her to just keep house and do a few odds and ends outside. "He supported me and encouraged me," she said. "But he's used to a different kind of life than Christian. His father was a small landholder and he didn't have a mother who was just for show."

Karen could see there was a difference. She grew up on a

farm herself, and she had expected more from being a wife on one of the large farms than reality could deliver. "The worst thing is how he gets so mad if I start to tell him something from in there." She cuts herself off. She's already said too much. She tries to smooth it out. "Not really mad, of course, but you know what I mean."

Does she? Even though she really tries, she doesn't recall ever having heard an unkind word or anything like that. Suddenly she feels thankful for Karl. She says, "I know. But it'll pass. You'll see."

They finally make it out into open countryside. It's about harvest time, and a certain mood of finality and expectation is simmering over the sun-drenched August landscape. "We're going to have a busy weekend, if the weather holds," says Inger.

Karen nods.

Inger says playfully, "You can still drive a tractor."

Down to the east lies Højgaard Farm, which is Karen and Christian's. The road leading from the highway is almost like an allée, down to the farm buildings, which, with the crenelated gables on the main house, harken back to a time when there were still people in the area called *proprietors*. When they turn down the drive, Karen automatically lifts her hand in greeting to a plump face seen in one of the windows of the dignified little in-law house, which was placed so everything on the farm could be kept an eye on from the east window.

"That was him, my father-in-law," said Karen. "Now he can relax with his newspaper, since we've arrived."

"He looks like he's in good shape."

"He'll live forever," she says. "And he still orders around this poor housekeeper and drives her to her wit's end. I never knew Christian's mother, but I often wonder how she managed." She sits quietly and then adds, "But all in all he's a good man. I didn't mean it like that."

They pull into the farmyard. It's large and surrounded by long whitewashed stables, which simply ooze emptiness. It is obvious they are only occupied by rats and mice and a few wild cats. Christian's big station wagon is parked by the utility room door.

They park behind it, and Karen gets out. She nods a thanks, hesitates a second, then says with a slightly embarrassed smile, "I let my mouth run." Then she shuts the door and hurries into the house.

The intern comes driving up on his motorcycle. His workday is over now too, and Inger follows behind him down the driveway. Meanwhile she's thinking about Højgaard, the elder Højgaard, whom middle-aged people still regard as one of the county's important figures. He was a county council member, a member of Parliament for a while, representative for the credit union; and he always took care of the most important issues in the area, whatever he felt would be irresponsible to leave to others. And the son, Christian, Karen's Christian, who was pretty much raised to take over his father's position, now goes around alone doing the work that the father had a whole crew of people to carry out, while he was out running meetings, making decisions and being important.

She can't help but think that it's fair, all things considered. Karl was only the son of a small landholder. Today he's a farmer, pretty much on the same level as the great proprietor's son. Of course Karl's daily activities are also different than what they thought they would be back when they got married, when she said goodbye to her job in town and moved out to the country, which she had otherwise only known from visiting family. They were half-cousins. That's what brought them together, despite the age difference.

It's different, but not worse. And at least Karl still has his livestock.

And wasn't he pretty happy too? Maybe he's even a bit proud of her in his own way. She drives into the well-maintained farmyard and makes the big turn into the garage. It's unlikely either of them will be using the car again today. She gathers up the few things she managed to buy on her lunch break and starts walking over to the farmhouse. Just then the barn door opens, as it often does, as if he had been standing there waiting for her, to say 'welcome home' just as she arrived. It warms her heart when she thinks about what Karen was sitting there talking about. She smiles at Karl.

He says, "You're home early today." He walks in front of her, entering first into the utility room.

Other people might interpret that as a bit cold, but not her. She knows him. Their marriage has taught her that he's not the type who says a whole lot.

The Way It Seems

The house sits at the edge of a small woods just by the fjord. It's an old house which was occupied for a couple generations by fishermen, back when there were still fish in the waters here. When Ole Knudsen, who came to be known as the one who caught the last lobster out by the jetty, had to go into a nursing home, the house went empty. If it had been a few years prior, buyers would have stood in line with their pens ready to sign a bill of sale, but now times have changed. A couple of people looked at the house, but left again.

The Fisher House, as it was called, went largely forgotten. The bit of yard that was there got overgrown, and a couple of windows and a door, either with or without external assistance, gave up holding themselves together. The roof got a kink in it. There's nothing so fragile as a house with nothing inside to breathe life into it.

Ole died eventually, and the heirs tried an advertisement again. There was no response, so they left the affair in the hands of all the real estate agents who operated in the area. None of them did all that much with it. The times had, like I said, changed; half the houses were for sale, and there were months in between the arrival of any serious buyer—as they call them in those circles. And the price was too high, too. One of the real estate agents, Berntsen, tried to get the heirs' representative— that was Ole's deceased brother's oldest son—to lower the price, and showed him pictures of numerous houses that could be bought for less. But there was no budging him. He had a responsibility to the others, he said. It seemed almost like he suspected Berntsen of trying to cheat him. But he had also been living for years over there in North Sjælland, where even now it was like the houses were built out of gold bricks.

The Fisher House stayed on the market for a couple more years.

One day in April—and it must have been in '91, because that was the same year that Anton's Henrik backed into the grocery window after borrowing—as the story goes—his father's car to drive a girl from Øsløs home, after a party at the community center. So it was April '91, and at the time there was a pretty steady stream going down the road to the Fisher House. We talked about it, and probably shook our heads, too. Were there really people who had fallen for that hovel?

It became evident pretty quickly that there were. And they must have been people with a bit of money, because both the carpenter and the mason required bank guarantees before starting work, and they got them, it turned out. Still it was peculiar, because no particular wealth was evident from the couple of strange cars we saw driving down there at the time. An old VW microbus that had had a few dents pulled out, but hadn't yet been repainted, and a Ford Escort, which definitely had seen better days, were the only ones that registered in the collective perception.

It was also peculiar that they didn't move in, not really, whoever they were. No moving truck arrived, and no one thought they were going to live with what Ole left behind. Not even the town's recycling center was interested in picking that stuff up. The carpenter didn't know anything—at least that's what he said; and people just passing by couldn't get a clear picture of what was going on there. The hedge out by the road was pretty neglected, and even if there were a place from where a person could get a look inside, well, the windows of the house weren't only rather small, but they had curtains which were closed in the evenings, which never happened in Ole's time.

Then, one day a truck arrived from Jørgen's Furniture. Not the big truck but a smaller box truck, so they did get some furniture after all. And they bought new. "Maybe they're newlyweds," guessed Marie, but they didn't look like it. She didn't look like the type who was going to build a nest; and regarding him, his age wasn't normal for newlyweds either. But maybe it could just have been that the beard and the hair were deceptive.

And what did they do? They were often away for a day or two, but there was no pattern. Could they be artists? For a while we tended towards that opinion, but we dropped it again when they shaped up the yard and cleaned up all around outside the house.

"It looks pretty good down there at Ole's."

"Yes, that's what I've heard."

"They're painting the woodwork."

"And they demolished the shed, but that's about all it was good for."

That's how the talk went when people were together, and eventually, we were all agreed that we should probably try to get to know the new owners, or at least get to know some more about them. It seemed kind of wrong to have someone living almost as neighbors, without having an idea of what they did or their names, apart from S. Carlsen, which was the only name the tradesmen knew, and which was the only name on the letters the postman delivered.

"It's disconcerting, knowing so little about people I'm serving," he said, when he had had a delivery down there. They had put up a mailbox by the road, so he never even got to go inside.

Of course it fell to Joanna to take up the assignment. Joanna was the most nosy person we had within several neighboring parishes—well, maybe in this whole part of the country, even. She kept no rumors, no information to herself. "She doesn't mean anything hurtful by it," people always said quickly to one another, after she had left. "Joanna is alright," people assured one another, when the conversation turned towards her. Only in certain instances, when someone got angry, was it necessary to add, "at heart."

To say she took up the assignment herself is not really the proper way to say it. It was in the air, that if someone was going to make things public, it would have to be her. And Joanna herself was just about to burst from curiosity anyway. She just needed the right excuse, she said. The couple of times she more or less coincidentally had passed the Fisher House, no one had been outside, the house seemed all closed up, or something or other had prevented her from just going up and knocking. She said it made her wonder, but that's how it was.

"I need some kind of excuse," she said.

We understood.

It was her eldest grandchild, Kise, who provided it for her. Kise had started high school and didn't live at home on the farm any more. She had moved into a dormitory, as they call them, in the city, so these days she wasn't seen around so often. But at the cousin's confirmation party she was there, and suddenly she started walking around with some papers collecting signatures. She said it was for something called, "Amnesty International." It sounded a bit pretentious the way she said it, but the idea was evidently that people would lend their support to prisoners of conscience, as she called them, and protest torture.

Well, sure, that couldn't do any harm, though it's hard to know what really lies behind something like that. And she did get some of them to sign, anyway.

Then Joanna said suddenly, "Give me one of those lists, little Kise, and I'll collect some names for you." Kise looked happy, and the rest of us looked surprised, until we made the connection. Then we nodded to ourselves. That Joanna!

A few days passed before Joanna went out on her mission. Evidently she was on her way out the door already Monday morning, but, "Then I couldn't remember how I was going to say it," she explained to Mikkel, and when she couldn't get Kise on the telephone until that evening, and then Joanna had to have some dental work done in town on Tuesday, it wasn't until Wednesday a little before nine that she was seen making her way down the road towards the fjord. Plenty of people saw her. It was a fine morning. After a couple of days of rain, the sun was shining through the stagnant air, and no one with a yard could resist going out in it with some tool or other in their hand. And when you stood with a tool in your hand, it was natural to allow yourself a moment to take in the surroundings. Look out over the fjord, for example, where Mors Island lay in backlight veiled by the humidity, which the sun was liberating from the earth. And you could follow Joanna with your eyes, as she strode along until she disappeared down the slope. Then you could hear the sound of a rake over from Karl's yard. A bit farther away there was someone mowing, and the blackbird, sitting up on the grocer's TV antenna, continued it's interrupted song.

Ulla said, "They say tourists are already starting to arrive on the fjord."

Søren nodded. "I was thinking about that too," he said.

When Joanna came back—and it was more quickly than expected—even the ones who were around the back could notice a sudden brief drop in the sound level. Several got the nearly simultaneous desire to take a look at their rakes, or straighten their backs. The mower over at Holger's sort of hesitated a few moments. Magna and Marie, who had been standing and chatting across the road to each other, stopped talking, while Joanna strode right by. And no one could interpret anything from her facial expression. She disappeared into her house. Søren laughed. The rest of us just wondered. Everyone stayed outside in their yards; it was a fine day, and morning coffee could wait.

It took a while, most of the day actually, before Joanna's expedition became community knowledge. The different parts of it had to be pieced together through more circuitous paths than usual, but towards evening, Joanna's trip was as clear to us as if we had done it ourselves—as if we had gone down the road ourselves, through the gate and up the paving stones; as if we had gotten a glimpse through the window ourselves, a quick moment that could have shaken up and piqued the interest of anyone; as if we ourselves had pulled ourselves together, suppressed our blushing and calmed our breathing; as if we ourselves had stood face to face with him, Carlsen, who was pretty much stark naked, only wearing some very tight underpants; as if we ourselves had fumbled taking out the list and begun to talk about prisoners of conscience and torture with a self-conscious voice; as if we ourselves had experienced having the door slammed shut, an inch from our faces. Not so strange that Joanna's retreat had been a bit embarrassing.

The event was relegated to experience and memory, but not conversation. There was just a bit of talk about the single concrete piece of news Joanna had returned with: they had gotten a boat.

"Just like so many others," said Niels.

"You got that right."

As time passed, we got used to it. We got used to the fact that there was something we didn't know. That there were some people we knew nothing about. We got used to nodding, completely naturally, when they drove past, and at one point we realized that he customarily answered our greeting with a discrete raising of his right index finger from the steering wheel. They rarely came to the grocery, and never to chat. When they did eventually show up, they bought usual things, like matches, toilet paper, minarine, and flour. Never bottles. But fresh orange juice.

We also got used to not knowing what they did for a living. We didn't know anyone from the census or the revenue office, but we knew, in any case, they were not on welfare. We also knew that their bank card was from a bank in Odense. The grocer had ascertained this, and we knew they had a postal account; there was no mistaking the yellow envelopes.

After a while we returned to the assumption that they were artists, or, that at least one of them was. Or, more specifically, some kind of author. It was the mailman, who one day had a certified letter that had to be signed for, and therefore had to go up and knock. Through the window he had seen the wife— which he had to call her since he didn't know her name—sitting at a typewriter. Joanna got Kise to look in the library, to see if that could be true, but Kise could only confirm that none of the five female writers with the last name Carlsen that showed up on the library's screen, could be the Carlsen that lived there. The librarian had helped Kise find their addresses.

"I looked under Karlsen with a 'K' as well, but there was only one; and that wasn't her either."

So we didn't get anywhere.

"Maybe she writes under a pseudonym," Kise said.

"Under what?"

"A pseudonym."

"Oh, that."

"And maybe her name isn't even Carlsen. Maybe they're not even married," said Bertha.

We others nodded in turn, as the conjectures reached us. Of course. They weren't even married.

But, it must be said, they did take care of their yard. And since, when he stacked firewood, it didn't look too shabby, it wasn't long before we accepted them as part of the community. But still there was something wrong. And we weren't completely at ease with it.

The grocer tried a few times to get a conversation going with them, when they came into the store. Preferably when there was only one of them.

"So," he said, as the month of July gleamed brightly down from the sky, "this is just the kind of weather that's good for people going on vacation." He continued by saying that he and his wife never went on vacation; the store had to stay open. But that they often thought about it, how it must be nice to have a job that didn't tie you down so much you couldn't travel, if you wanted to. He looked questioningly at the wife—we still called her that—but she just agreed with him. "Yes, it is nice to travel."

There was a little pause. Then the grocer asked, "Is that the case with your husband's work?" It got very quiet in the store. Ulla, who was putting some cans in her shopping cart, slowed her movements, and the other customers were also as quiet as possible, not to miss the response. But there wasn't any. The quiet was almost palpable. There was too much of it.

The wife had taken out her purse, and was standing there ready to pay. The grocer hadn't rung up the last items yet—he was waiting; but then he gave up. With a little laugh, as if he had just been distracted for a moment, he quickly said that the most important thing, naturally, was that one had a good job and made money through honest work. The wife agreed. The grocer punched in the last prices; she paid and left.

We agreed she was a bit peculiar.

"I always thought so," said Ulla.

We nodded in unison.

Another time, when it was Carlsen in the store, and he was just buying a few postage stamps, the grocer tried to guide the conversation towards geography. "A lot of people think that here we live on the outskirts. I always say, on the outskirts of what?" He chuckled. "But for you it must feel a bit different living here, since you came from quite a ways away, where your family still is, I guess." The grocer smiled hopefully, but Carlsen did not bite.

"We like it just fine," he said, putting the money for the stamps on the counter even before the grocer had added up the total. And he didn't even say good-bye when he left.

At the beginning of August there was a sporting event and a traveling circus, but the Carlsens didn't show up, even though the occasion drew people from all the neighboring parishes. Some young people who, later in the evening—must have been towards sunrise—wanted to swim, as young people are wont to do when the half-light is so enticing, reported later that they had seen light on at the Carlsens, and that the boat was gone.

"He had probably taken it out," was the general opinion. Maybe he was fishing—or something.

Now some people might think we have nothing else to do around here other than observe strangers and talk about them. But it's not like that. Normally we don't even notice people, and normally we don't talk about people; we only talk about things that happened. About the weather, about the future of the school, and about the club's top team which is playing in Division 5, and which every year, before the season starts, always has difficulty finding a coach.

Naturally, we are interested in one another's children and how they are doing around the country, wherever they may be. But strangers don't really interest us. While the two in the Fisher House did occupy us quite a bit, it was because they were so different. It was as if, in a way, they weren't there at all. And yet they still occupied a place in our consciousness, though a little off to the side, perhaps. And we saw some things that we had never seen before or never paid attention to before.

It was as if we had becaome more attentive, even though it was only once in a while that we realized it ourselves.

The grocer tried again. It was one day in September, and he

started talking about how now summertime was over and done. Carlsen nodded and started to really open up and said that it had been a fine summer. "But a bit too hot and dry," said the grocer, and from someplace behind the shelf with crackers and cookies they heard a mumble of agreement. It was Paul's Greta, who probably had a few too many pounds on her to be able tolerate the heat. A couple of other bystanders agreed with the grocer, too. The summer was a bit too dry. Then he asked, "So are you going to leave now for the rest of the year?"

"Maybe," said Carlsen. Then he added, "Maybe not." Then he left. We stood there watching him go, as well as we could, considering the grocer's windows had taken on the look of a supermarket. But we saw the car drive away, not in the direction of the Fisher House, but towards the highway.

The grocer started chatting about the morning's news from the Holstebro area. The county council had prepared a new hospital plan, but this time there was still no one satisfied with the result; not even people from Viborg, who it seemed would be sitting pretty. "It looks like they're going to pass a resolution that we can't get sick any more in this part of the county," said Søren. He says that every time they close a department or transfer a specialist to another area. "And over on Mors," he snickered, "you can't have children anymore." That was a new one, and we smiled in acknowledgement.

The talk about the hospital naturally slid over into talk about politics and politicians. And a bit of poking at one another. There's no doubt about how each of us votes, so there's not really any need to discuss it. But a bit of teasing has its time and place, and Karl is the target more often than not. His father was a radical, but Karl hasn't inherited that need to provoke. Still it has always been part of the political discussions around here to make Karl an accomplice to the country's miserable state.

He was just about to get riled up, but then Joanna came in and changed the subject. Politics isn't really dramatic enough for her. Before all that with the hospitals, the narcotics agent used to talk about increased abuse and the danger of AIDS, and Joanna got a lot of mileage out of that. Of course it was Kise she was worried about, out there in the city. "Around here we don't have junk like that," said the grocer, who then tried to get the political discussion going again, but the moment had passed. Joanna had planted a thoughtful stillness. One by one we straggled home.

The postman would be delivering the newspaper soon.

It was reported that the Carlsens hadn't left, but just had been on one of their usual short trips. At any rate they were back again, in a new car no less, and that was probably the reason we didn't notice it right away. Now there was a Toyota instead of the old VW microbus. It looked like it was pretty much right out of the factory and it was a regular sedan, though on the larger side. But it didn't have a hidden hitch, as they call them in the ads. How could they manage without one?

The Escort was gone too, but that had been gone for a good while, without our noticing.

We had plenty of other things to do besides keeping an eye on people and their activities. It really didn't matter all that much to us. One could even say that it was they themselves who had chosen to be outsiders.

Because it's not that we don't like strangers—not at all—or that it's hard to become part of our community. Take Johan and Birgit, for example, in the first house on the west side of the road towards the highway. If anyone is integrated, it's them. They have sheep, and she cards and spins and colors the wool, and sells knitted goods from her home and from a shop in town. And he's a teacher, and there has never been an unkind word between them and any of us. It's easy enough to approach them when they come by, and they go to the community center when there's an event there, and they sign up at the grocery for silver anniversaries and birthdays that are appropriate for them to take part in.

But of course they're not so unfamiliar to the area, and even though they might not exactly speak the dialect, there is a familiarity with the tone. But that's not why we like them. It's more that they have a sensibility. It's perfectly natural for them to be a part of our parish. They even take part in meetings at the rectory sometimes, even though they are younger than most of the people who go.

But the Carlsens, on the other hand, have chosen to be outsiders. It's as if they both want to be here and don't want to be here. And that's why we can't avoid feeling a bit put upon. But naturally that's their choice.

****

The weather has turned colder, and we don't see one another out of doors quite so much. Now it's more random meetings, and if we're outside in the yard, it's for a more active purpose, for something that we need to get over and done with.

Still, we stay pretty close. We're in the same boat, as they say, and that's what makes it so gratifying to live here. We accept one another, even though we are quite different. And we take each other into consideration.

For example, when rumors circulated about Kise. "Rumors" might not be the right word. "Reports" is better.

It was reported she was having some problems—that she had begun to go off track, as they say. That she was keeping bad company in town. That she looked a bit off when Gunnar and Helga had met her in the town center one afternoon.

It was also reported that her parents had tried to get her to move back home, but she refused. She had a course in the evenings, she said, and there was no bus at that time. She also said, "You could just buy me a car." Yes, she had changed.

Now, that's not something we talk about, and definitely not when Joanna is nearby. And you'd never know it by looking at her, which means you really can tell. She is eager to talk about anything else. It's rather sad actually, how hard she tries. We try to be on her side. We say, "It will all work out," when we get the chance.

But of course we all are worried. There are a lot of dangers threatening young people these days.

But then, there was the Fisher House. The Fisher House and the Carlsens is what this is all about. And a new car. Somewhat later in the fall. Sometimes they're there and sometimes they're not.

We abandoned the idea that she was a kind of author. It would have been obvious from the mail, and the postman—Jensen, that is—couldn't tell. And what about Mr. Carlsen?

Eventually we had to resign ourselves to the fact that the Carlsens were people who lived here whom we knew nothing about. So we couldn't have any obligations towards them either. That was something we could get used to. There were days when we didn't think about, wonder, or speculate about them. It was almost like back when the house stood empty.

And besides, there were plenty of other things to occupy our time. Wednesday afternoon events in the meetinghouse got started up. Gymnastics and handball started for those who had the age and desire for that sort of thing. And it was the end of September when the baker's Esther got married to someone or other from in town, someone she evidently had been living with, as they say, for a while. They had a house; we knew that much. But now they were going to get married, and it was a big wedding; a wedding there was more than a little to talk about afterwards. It wasn't until October things were back to normal again.

One afternoon the grocer said, "There was a man here yesterday. From the customs office."

"Was it about the VAT?"

"No, it wasn't him."

You could see the grocer had more to say, and he didn't need much prodding.

Niels said, "So it wasn't Kristensen."

Of course, Niels knew about that. He was the one who ran "Northwest Kennel and Grooming" in what used to be a small farm behind the meetinghouse, which doesn't prevent him from being around when something is being discussed somewhere else. But even though he doesn't have a lot of business, he still knows the VAT man quite well, so it was really an expert in that area who said, "So it wasn't Kristensen."

The grocer shook his head. "He didn't want much of anything," he said. "He said he just happened to be in the area and needed some matches."

"Did he say where he came from?"

"No."

The grocer lit a cheroot, and was about to offer some to the others, but decided against it. There were five or six of us there, after all. Niels and Karl sat on the bench to the right of the door.

"No, he didn't say where he came from or where he was going."

"From customs you say?"

"Yes. Customs and Tax Authority they call it now. That was what he said anyway, whoever he was."

The baker's youngest was done filling her basket and was ready to pay. It took a little while, and in the meantime we discussed how strange it was that someone would coincidentally come through a place like this. At this time of year, that is. In the summer it's different. And when it wasn't about the VAT.

The grocer finished giving change, and attention turned back to him. It was obvious he had more to say. Then the phone rang, and that took a little while. Karl stepped out; there wasn't any customer toilet in the store, like there is in the supermarket.

He came back. The grocer said, "He asked, by the way, if anyone here had noticed anything unusual. Out on the fjord, for example. Or on land."

"Something unusual?" There were a few of us who repeated that at the same time. "Something unusual?"

"I don't know what he meant," said the grocer. "Lights or something like that."

"He also said 'unusual activity,'" the grocer added.

We laughed quietly at that one.

"Unusual activity?"

"But we haven't have we?" said Niels. "I mean, we haven't seen anything."

"That's what I told him," said the grocer. "I said that everything was pretty much the way it always was. We hadn't noticed anything unusual or any unusual activity."

I think we each felt a bit self-satisfied, when we split up to go home. The kind of satisfaction you feel when things get into gear, as the truck manager says, when he has loads both coming and going.

November was an unpleasant month. There was one violent storm that downed several trees in yards and in the orchard, and there were also several regular storms. It rained for such a long stretch that it was getting hard to remember when the weather had ever been otherwise. And it was dark, darker than usual, even for November.

Otherwise it was a month marked by activities. Everything was underway. Besides gymnastics and handball and Wednesday afternoons, there were also lectures in the meetinghouse, and the dilettantes had started practicing for the winter show. There was a lot to live up to after last year's success with *The Sheriff's Little Girl*, or whatever it was called. "It's going to be totally different this year," said the teacher, who was the director. He had started calling what they were doing 'amateur theater.' We'll see how that turns out.

The two bible study groups had also started up, and the priest had begun something new, a study club, as he called it, in literature or something like that. The priest doesn't have a wife at present, but a couple of the women from the church council come early and make coffee, just like they do when there are larger meetings in the confirmation hall.

There is so much going on out here, things we try to keep track of, that several of us have had to get video recorders to keep up with it.

And once in a while we would discuss recent events, and this reinforced our belief that something was going on. It had to be. How else could we explain it? We had seen a couple of strange cars recently.

It made us uneasy. We would have been alright if it were just the Carlsens, but those others?

They were frequently away anyway, the Carlsens, which wasn't so strange. In these periods with storms it was no great shakes living out on the coast.

Afterwards it was hard for us to remember who had heard about it first or who had seen something first. Who had said something first to whom. But that's the way it goes. Suddenly everyone knows something, and no one knows exactly where the information came from. If it did come from anywhere in particular.

There was a hole in the boat. We knew that much. Plus a few windows down there were broken. We knew that, too. No one felt it necessary to cut the discussion short and go down there and see if it really were true. We knew it was.

Niels said, "That's how it goes, I guess."

We sat around the kitchen table. Joanna looked in high

spirits. She said, "They say it's completely gutted." She took out some cookies, even though they probably should have been put aside until closer to Christmas.

We sat there, munching. She was a wizard at baking; we had to give her that.

"How about a jigger in your coffee?"

"In light of the occasion, as they say."

A bottle and glasses were brought out. The bottle made the rounds.

"So, cheers all." We sipped and poured the rest in the coffee.

Then it was quiet for a little bit. Only Joanna couldn't stay calm. Every time we heard a car, she went to look. But it wasn't anyone special. Just people like the heating oil truck, the plumber, and Birgit, who probably was going to her shop in town.

"Come and sit down," said Karl.

Then the telephone rang, and that kept her busy for a while.

"Do you think they will report it?"

They might. Or maybe they won't. It depended on a lot of things.

"They will probably have to. Otherwise it would look bad."

We sat there again, each thinking their own thoughts. Lars tried to lead the conversation in another direction and he sent the bottle around again.

Then someone said, "What does it matter? None of us saw anything."

The Congratulant

Marius Beck had been big, in both connotations of the word. And he still was, in one sense, even though the oldest pair of pants that he still used once in while had gotten kind of floppy around his once-even-more-substantial rear. But he could still fill out a car seat, and one of the big American ones at that. When he sat down, he *sat*. And that meant, among other things, that he couldn't turn around. There were too many immobile kilograms involved.

This made it difficult to drive in reverse, because he never got used to using the rear-view mirror, let alone the side mirror, for that matter. When they moved into the new house in the extension of the housing development (the lots in the original development weren't large enough), after a week he had gotten the mason to demolish the back wall of the garage and extend the driveway around the house, so he could leave home without going in reverse. It helped protect the house, the landscaping, and the flagpole. But then the house ended up sitting more or less in the middle of a traffic circle. He did have the driveway pavers laid somewhat artistically, so it didn't end up looking so bad. And at the same time he was able to demonstrate that he was still an industrious and practical man.

Here it must also be said, that Marius Beck and his wife don't live on the farm anymore. It was sold—and sold out of the family. It's best not to mention it.

Their farm wasn't just one of the largest, it was the second largest within several neighboring parishes. And since the owner of the largest one stretched his interests across the region, not to mention nationally, it was Marius Beck who had been the prominent one in their community, was on the council and everything. He had been chairmen—if you can say it that way. He had been chairman several times over.

It was the chairmanships that he missed these days. His leadership and delegating of work on the farm had dwindled the last few years. It was like there wasn't enough to sink your teeth into with just one farmhand and a livestock manager. He missed those council meetings and delegate meetings—things with meaning, having responsibility.

He missed the contact with other important men, missed trading handshakes with the region's parliament representatives when they met in Karup or Kastrup, missed having the chance to contribute an intelligent and well-thought-out remark. He started to feel so alone, that sometimes he started chatting with people he met by chance on the street—even people that he, in days past, wouldn't have given the time of day: newcomers, the lower class, people like that.

He was going to be eighty soon. That would have to be planned quite carefully, if his reputation was going to be preserved and his respectability extended into a brand new decade.

Helga figured that the list of invitees was complete,. She was sitting at the kitchen table with a notepad, and there had been a long pause, almost a silence, from the adjacent dining room, where Marius lay on the sofa, planning. She counted. There were seventy names—and many of them were now single. So there probably wouldn't be more than a hundred and ten. It wasn't like it used to be, back when their generation didn't take up so much room in the local cemeteries.

"I guess I'll have to go out and buy some cards," said Helga.

He cleared his throat in there. It made the sofa creak. It was pretty old and didn't match the new dining room furniture at all, but Marius couldn't be persuaded to get rid of it when they moved from the farm. Now it creaked some more. He must be getting up.

He appeared in the door frame. "It's a shame we don't know

the editor," he said. "If it was the old one, we could have sent an invitation."

Helga remembered the old editor well. They had been with him a couple of times, back when Marius was still one of the newspaper representatives, unless it was the board he was on. It wasn't always easy to remember if it was one thing or the other that got him out of the house. Sure, she remembered the editor.

"But I guess we can't," said Marius, almost to himself, but still directed enough towards Helga that it seemed natural for her to respond, "What can't we?"

"Send an invitation to the editor," he hissed.

"I'm pretty sure he's dead," she said.

Marius made a sound that wasn't meant to be complementary. "The new one, of course."

Helga couldn't see why they would invite the new editor, when Marius didn't even know him. She said so. They were in the kitchen, where she was usually the one in charge.

In a somewhat long-winded manner, Marius explained to this member of the female species, that if the old editor were still there, and he had gotten an invitation, then the newspaper would have known well in advance that there was an upcoming birthday they ought to do something with. You know, for their own sake, they have to follow the important events going on in the area, and sometimes they need a little help.

But the new one? No, they probably couldn't. Marius sat down heavily at the table and began waiting for his coffee. Helga said, "You could always invite schoolteacher Krogsholt. You know he contributes to the paper." Marius mumbled something about "that twerp of a teacher"—he and Helga had of course always been supporters of charter schools, and he was even on the board of one, back when there was one here, and that's why they never held schoolteacher Krogsholt—the public school teacher—or the principal, in very high esteem. But the more he thought about it, the more he thought that it could still be a possibility. Krogsholt was a local, and they had been with him at countless events like golden anniversaries and the like, and he could sing with the others when the songs were handed out. And read telegrams, maybe.

Marius nodded. "Go ahead and send Krogsholt an invitation." The rest of his statement kind of got lost in the chaw with which Marius occupied himself while the coffee maker was brewing. But it wasn't necessary to hear every word to conclude that he seriously doubted Krogholt's mental faculties in this regard.

A couple of sips into cup number two, Marius said, "You'd better write them today." And after coffee, Helga made her way to the town center to buy appropriate invitations and stamps at the stationery store. Marius stayed in the car around the corner. It was a no parking zone, but if he kept the motor running, no one was going to come and say that he was breaking any laws. Some cars did get backed up, and there were also a few childish hotheads who honked their horns. Marius pretended he didn't notice. It wasn't his fault they didn't know him. In a way he enjoyed the commotion, and he welcomed Helga back without the least sarcasm. It made her wonder. From inside the store she could hear that the street traffic wasn't moving along at its normal rhythm, but still she had taken her time, looking at a couple of storefront windows. Maybe she should get something for the birthday party.

Marius said, "How about a little pick-me-up, since we're in town." And he got the vehicle moving, drove forward a couple hundred feet, then turned left into the hotel parking lot, right in front of the city bus which, luckily, had its brakes in good working order.

"You don't almost turn eighty everyday," said Marius.

The evening was getting on, when Marius said, "I think you'd better cross out Krogsholt after all." Helga looked up surprised from her writing. She was just about to ask if the new editor should get an invitation, when Marius said, "I'm going to put in an announcement." He looked at her with a mix of triumph and reproach. "I think you're getting old, Helga," he said mildly.

Old Helga, who was actually twelve years younger than her husband, and who also definitely looked it, made the expression on her face that she always did when Marius got out of control. "So you could have saved me all this," she said, meaning the pile of invitations and envelopes that she had already written. "And the stamps," she said. "When are we going to use all of these stamps?"

Marius shook his head. Patiently, he explained that of course they would send out the invitations too, because he wanted to make sure that everyone who was supposed to come would actually come. But there should be an announcement too. "Can you just write something up?"

Writing this turned out to be more difficult for Helga than one would think. You couldn't just write, "Remember my 80th birthday on September 14th," even though that was the intent.

They discussed it at length. Eventually they agreed to use the usual wording, even though Helga still complained that then they could have skipped the invitations and the stamps. Marius ignored her and told her to write something down. Helga paged through a couple of issues of the newspaper and wrote: "On the occasion of my 80th birthday on September 14th, I invite family, friends and acquaintances to celebrate at a party in the meetinghouse at 7pm. To facilitate the catering please RSVP at the grocery store."

She read the draft. Marius thought a little, then went outside to spit. He came back in. "Read it from the beginning." He listened carefully. "No," he said,"that's no good." There was a pause. Helga looked at him questioningly. "It sounds like we're fishing for guests, like just anyone can show up."

He thought long and hard. "We can send out the invitations now," he said, "and then we can put in an announcement 'to please withhold any acknowledgements.'"

Helga perused the announcement section, then took another newspaper and searched that one as well. She wrote. Then she read: "All considerations of acknowledgements on September 14 are kindly but firmly asked to be withheld." She looked up at him, and he had a suspicion that there might be a bit of teasing in her look. For appearance's sake he let some time pass. He wasn't going to let himself be provoked. Then he said, "Don't you sound a bit too standoffish? Couldn't you write it more along the lines of 'people don't need to send acknowledgements'?"

She wrote again: "Withhold acknowledgements on September 14." "Please," said Marius. "It should say, 'Please withhold.'" It was quiet in the kitchen for a while. Then Marius mumbled, "Please withhold acknowledgements on September 14." He still wasn't totally satisfied. He tried to explain. "Most people will understand, but what about the ones who might take it literally? The bank director, for example, or the new guy at the feed store. How's anyone supposed to know what they're used to, wherever they're from."

Helga was still looking in the newspaper. "Open house," she said. "How about announcing an open house from noon to 2pm. A lot of people do that nowadays."

Marius just about sneered with indignation. "Open house! It's going to be in the meetinghouse, and it's going to be decorated for the evening. How can we do an open house in these two rooms? If you write it up like that, a hundred people might show up."

Helga's skepticism remained unsaid, but was revealed unequivocally in the quick look she gave him. He hissed. The mood in the kitchen had deteriorated. They decided to sleep on it.

So it ended up being both. The seventy invitations to the party at the meetinghouse were sent out, and in the newspaper there was an announcement—across two columns—which Marius figured couldn't be missed by the bank manager, or other managers, or the editor, or the heads of the political associations and people like that. This is how it read: "On the occasion of my 80th birthday the 14th of September, congratulants will be received at our home from noon to 2pm. Helga and Marius Beck."

This wording was the result of lengthy negotiations and a difficult compromise. Helga had insisted on "open house," repeatedly mentioning that that was how it was said nowadays. Marius sneered, "Open house. Nonsense. Do you want the place flooded with random people?" He had even lowered himself to writing a draft of the announcement, and that was when the word "congratulants" was introduced to the proceedings.

Helga had to step aside. Despite everything, he was the man of the house. On the other hand, she was adamant that the announcement should include both their names.

Marius protested. He even laughed. "It sure as hell isn't you who's turning eighty," he said. But Helga documented, with the help of the majority of the recent papers, that this type of announcement included the names of both spouses at the bottom. He could see for himself. She held up the newspaper and pointed: "Sincere appreciation for everyone who came to my birthday celebration. Sonja and Peter Jensen." The wives were also included. That's the way it was done these days. "You don't want to seem old-fashioned, do you?" she asked.

Marius obviously didn't care. He continued making a couple of snide remarks about the eighty-year-old Helga, but it was no use. "I'm going to be doing all the work," she said, "so I want to be in the announcement."

The silence following her remark became quite oppressive. In the end, he gave in. "But you have to call it in yourself," he said. He got up with some difficulty and tramped outside to the yard. "Damned bitch," he mumbled. "Can't even have a spittoon in the kitchen."

Time passed, and it passed slowly. The invitations were sent, and the responses arrived. The announcement was phoned in; it was printed, and it was read. And some talk circulated about it.

"*Congratulants*," laughed Morten Andersen at the grocery store, when he barged in on a conversation about Marius's upcoming big day. "*Congratulants*," he laughed with the tone of voice that was used here in this area for making fun of proper spoken Danish. "I don't think they mean us common people, going around pretending to be *congratulants*." There was nearly audible applause from Jens Christian and Holger. Of course everyone knew that Morten had an old grudge against Marius, and that it hadn't gotten any smaller with time, even though recently they had sort of become neighbors. But still it was well said. The grocer didn't participate audibly or visibly in the fun. Of course it amounted to more than peanuts—the wine, beer, and tobacco that had been ordered for delivery—some to the meetinghouse, some to the house. And with everything else that was needed for such an occasion, it was a pretty good contribution to an otherwise declining turnover. When the discussion turned a bit more subdued—and more to the point, he discovered—he didn't refrain from saying that Marius has always been a good man for the area, and that unlike certain others, he never moved his business outside the parish. It was a statement that found its mark with a couple of the men present. Still it was the particular Morten-Andersen-ish way of saying "congratulants" that was memorable, entertaining everyone on their way home. And thereby the word was granted citizenship in the local language with a definition that would not be found fully in the unabridged Danish dictionary.

****

Not too many hours of September 14 had passed before Helga got out of bed. There was a lot to see to, even though the previous several days had been occupied with preparations, and she had had plenty of help. Kristine, who had been house help for them on the farm for so many years, was called in. And to Helga it felt almost like the old days, when some large event loomed.

Carefully she closed the bedroom door behind her. Even though Marius always slept like a rock, and he probably wouldn't wake up too easily, there was no reason to risk it. It would just make everything more difficult to have him around, complaining or making suggestions. She looked up at the clock. He shouldn't be woken up before seven, in any case.

After making the day's first pot of coffee, she sat down at the kitchen table and considered the situation. Maybe she should have the deliveryman bring an extra case of beer. There seemed to be plenty of wine—for the people who preferred that.

Then there was the flag. Marius had bought a new flag. And on top that he had called the surveyor to find out how big it should be, when used with a regular-sized flagpole. He would really carry on if she forgot to put it up. She rose and got it out of the closet. Then she put on her clogs and went out into the yard in the dark morning, and with quite a bit of trouble, she got the rope loosened and the ends tied on to the flag. Then she raised it into the night sky.

That was that. Good thing she remembered. She avoided both Marius's reproaches and the neighbors' joking remarks at seeing her fumbling in broad daylight with the flag, which was the biggest one the store had in stock. Looked like Marius had added a bit to whatever measurements the surveyor had given him.

She went back to her coffee cup and a half-eaten roll with marmalade.

And then there were the rooms. She had better dust and vacuum, so everything would be ready for Kristine's arrival, when it was time to put things out.

Marius sat as if on a throne, wearing his dark suit. His hair had been cut, he had had his beard trimmed a few days before, and now he sat there, looking regal with his freshly scrubbed, pink face beneath his white hair. Time approached noon, and he sat entertaining himself with his two sons-in-law—a couple of middle-aged rascals, one of whom was already talking about going on social security.

The mailman had been there with a couple of congratulatory letters, from members of the family who couldn't be there that afternoon because of geography or illness, plus a bottle of port from the bank. Marius was not too impressed that they sent it. He would have to delete the bank manager from the list of congratulants he had formed in his head, and regrettably, also from the list of congratulants from which he had expected special tributes. He said, "Young people think they are so busy."

A car approached. Was it slowing down? Marius paused in the middle of a sentence, listening. The car drove by, and Marius continued telling his sons-in-law what he had said during the general meeting of the slaughterhouse in '38.

Helga took one last look over the food. Herring, potato salad, little meatballs, smoked halibut, roast pork, red cabbage, liver paté, pickled beets, and five kinds of sausage from the butcher in the town center. She glanced at Marius, whose voice was becoming more and more distant as he spoke. She said—more or less referring to her sons-in-law: "You can start eating." The older one, the engineer, the one who was looking forward to social security, started to get up, but was brought to his seat again by a look from Marius. "We're in no rush," he said. He got Helga to bring him the newspaper from the day before, so he could show his sons-in-law the article. "Prominent farmer turns 80," it read, and his many activities were listed below. "But they were careless in more than a few places," said Marius. "It says I was on the board of the Cattle Association. Actually I was the vice-chairman." He paused. "It's strange that people like that never ask for help from the right sources."

Then he went quiet. Everyone sat listening. When they had the chance, they glanced out the window. A scooter went by, plus the blacksmith's van. "I still think you should start eating," said Helga. She looked appealingly at her daughters and sons-in-law. Not even the grandchildren had time to come by. They were going to wait until the evening.

The neighbor, who was Morten Andersen, was now busy with yard work at the end of the afternoon. He had heard it was a good time to start getting everything ready for winter, even though it was only the middle of September, and around noon he had launched into the hedgerow at the far end by the road, where there was a good view. He had said to his wife, "We have to see what congratulants look like."

Earlier in the day, he had seen the mailman come, carrying a package. And even earlier he had seen the young girl from the grocery store come riding her bicycle, with a beautifully wrapped bottle. "Probably *Gammel Dansk*," Morten had thought, and now as he thought about it again, he felt a slight yearning for a stiff drink. Still he stayed at his raking, cleaning up under the hedge. Something was bound to happen soon.

Nothing was happening. Then it was noon. Still nothing happened. That is, a little happened, but nothing really. The grocer's girl arrived again, this time with the grocer's wife as driver, and there were more bottles carried in. And a big box, it looked like. Morten worked his way over to the car and exchanged a few words with Ellen, who told him that people were calling like crazy for bottles they wanted delivered, with cards and everything. From the slaughterhouse, from the feed store and all kinds of places.

Morten gave it some thought. His face brightened with a strange downward smile, but Ellen just looked impressed. "And chocolate," she said. "The biggest one we had in the store. It was from the Severinsen's," she added. "They're teetotalers, you know."

The girl came out, chewing something, and sat down in the car. Ellen turned the car around and drove away. There were no other cars on the road. Morten felt so young inside; it was bubbling up in him. He'd better go in to Margreta, who was standing inside, watching from behind the houseplants. It was about time to have something to eat.

"They're sending things," he said in an expressionless voice, and no one except for Margreta would have been able to sense the undertone of pleasure. "They're sending things and not showing up."

He stopped, struck by Margreta's seriousness. He squirmed a bit. Margreta said, "He is your neighbor."

Morten shook his head. He went into the kitchen. The table was conspicuously not set, even though it was late. "Despite everything, Marius is your neighbor," she said again, remaining standing by the window, as if she had nothing else pressing. He protested a bit, but, as usual, it was no use.

Inside Marius's house, they had finally started stuffing themselves with the good food. There was no need to stand, since there were plenty of chairs. They sat around the table, and it wasn't that easy to keep the mood bright. The daughters and one of the sons-in-law tried. "The gift table sure is filling up," said the youngest daughter. Her husband said, "There's enough bottles to last for years."

Marius said nothing. Barely even "Cheers." It was painful to see him sitting there.

There were footsteps outside on the walk. They all looked up. "Someone's here," both daughters said in unison. Helga rose nervously. Marius looked at the clock. Quarter to one.

There was a knock at the door and it opened. Morten Andersen entered, newly shaven and hair slicked back, wearing his old suit from his twenty-fifth wedding anniversary. He had a large bouquet of fall asters in his hand. "I just wanted to say congratulations," he said.

Morten was escorted to the table, and they fussed over him as if he were a president, a manager, or some other high-standing individual. One of the daughters dashed over to get Margreta to come, but she declined. She wasn't dressed, and what would people think if she showed up in her street clothes? There was no way around it.

Morten lifted his shot glass. "Well then, congratulations." Marius acknowledged his toast and regained his bearing as Marius Beck.

He gestured towards the gift table. "I'm not forgotten entirely," he said. "But people are so busy these days, that they only have time to stay for a few minutes." Morten nodded sympathetically. "They don't know what they're missing," he said, taking another serving of the warm meatballs and the cold potato salad. Helga poured him another glass.

"Yeah," said Morten. "Time passes, but the good times don't come back to bite you, as they say."

The company enthusiastically agreed. Everyone was in good spirits now, and no one could claim that it was because of the libations.

"I've had a great many experiences and quite a bit of responsibility," said Marius, letting his gaze fade away to someplace in the past. Actually he had prepared a little speech about responsibility and duty, but it was for a larger group—and a somewhat differently comprised group—that he had imagined as an audience. He saved it. He would have to be content with using it that night at the meetinghouse.

They had arrived at coffee. They moved now to the sofa table and sat with their cups, sampling the cookies.

Marius was a bit tired. He would definitely take a substantial rest before the evening festivities.

The rest of the family was still engaged in conversation, showing friendliness and attention towards Morten like never before.

Marius woke from a little doze. He said, "Time for a cigar. Bring in the box, Helga."

Helga brought the silver cigar box from the desk and began offering them. The one son-in-law didn't smoke. Morten was on his way with his left hand, when his expression suddenly changed, and he stopped in the middle of the motion.

He pulled his hand back. He shook his head.

"I forgot I have my pipe," he said. From different pockets he dug out his pipe, tobacco, and matches, and he got it stopped and lit.

"And it's about time for me to head home," he said. "I hope I didn't impose. I just wanted to, as they say, offer my congratulations."

ORIGINAL DANISH TITLES
AND ORIGINAL PUBLICATION DATES

Danish author **Knud Sørensen** (b. 1928) was a certified land surveyor for 28 years, during which he became intimate with the Danish agricultural landscape. A book reviewer for 14 years, he has also written 48 books and won over 20 literary awards, including a lifelong grant from the Danish Arts Council. His books, most of which portray nuances of life in rural Denmark, include biographies, poetry, novels, short stories, essays and memoirs. He has also collaborated with numerous artists on art shows and art books. In November 2014 he received the Grand Prize of the Danish Academy, the highest award given to a Danish author for their body of work.

Michael Goldman (b.1966) besides being a widely-published translator of Danish literature, is a poet, clarinetist, gardener, father and husband. Over one hundred of Goldman's translations of poetry and prose have appeared in literary journals such as Rattle, Harvard Review, World Literature Today, and International Poetry Review. He teaches workshops and gives readings at universities and literary events. His recently translated books include works by Knud Sørensen, Marianne Koluda Hansen, Cecil Bødker, Benny Andersen, and Knud Sønderby. He lives in Florence, Massachusetts, USA. www.hammerandhorn.net

www.ingramcontent.com/pod-product-compliance
Lightning Source LLC
Chambersburg PA
CBHW050613190726